WICKED PLAYER

STACEY LYNN

Wicked Player

A Rough Riders Novel #3

Stacey Lynn

Copyright © 2019 Stacey Lynn

Content Editing: My Brother's Editor

Proofreading: Virginia Tesi Carey

Cover Design: Shanoff Designs

Cover Model Photography: Furious Fotog

Cover Model: Michael Scanlon

Wicked Player is a work of fiction. Names, characters, places, and incidents are used fictitiously or are a product of the author's imagination.

All rights reserved. No part of this work may be reprinted, reproduced, or transmitted in any form without written permission of the author, except by a reviewer who may quote brief passages for review passages only.

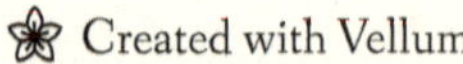 Created with Vellum

ONE

Elizabeth

I took the blindfold Tristan held in his hand. Grasping it lightly, adrenaline and desire already pulsed lightly beneath my pale skin.

It was the first time in six months I entered the halls of The Velvet Club. It had taken me awhile to get over the last night I'd spent here when I'd wanted it to become more.

"You ready for this?" Tristan asked. His light brown eyes swept over my face, down to my hands, most likely to see if I was trembling.

I was definitely trembling, but not from nerves. Anticipation sank its delicate claws into my flesh, pulling me toward the door.

Room number four. There would be a harness where I could be restrained on one wall. A bed with silken gray linens so shimmery they could have been real silver next to it. The far wall would have a blacked-out window. We'd be able to see out. If the blinds were raised, voyeurs could watch the show. That wouldn't happen though because I insisted they stay closed. As a public television figure, I had too much to lose if my identity here was ever leaked.

This was the only one I ever chose. It was also the only room where I allowed a stranger's hands, lips, and body to pleasure me. The familiarity of this room made it easier for me to give my body to a man I sometimes couldn't see.

"Anything I need to know?"

"This man needs anonymity." He dipped his head toward my hand. "That's the reason for the blindfold. Everything else, exactly what you want. Nothing extreme."

I came here, paid a huge chunk of my small salary because I knew what I liked and I learned early on that college boys were more concerned with what they got out of a girl than what they were with giving. I wasn't a selfish receiver.

I just liked a man who ensured he gave before he took for himself. Coaching frat boys who'd chugged more keg beer than their weight never interested me.

"Is he in there?"

"He wanted to give you a few minutes to get comfortable."

"Anything else I need to know?"

Tristan's face changed, softened in the way I knew he would keep his word. My anxiety calmed and I blew a soft breath out through my lips.

"He's a good man. Know all there is to know about him and I can tell you right now this guy won't hurt you." His grin turned sassy. "At least not more than you like or request. And so you know, we made changes to the room since you've been here."

"What?"

"No more cross."

I glanced at the black door, knowing exactly what was in the room, the setup down to the square inch and back to Tristan. "You didn't have to do that."

"It's your room. Your safe space. Wouldn't be safe if you had the memory of last time. Had the boys remove it today."

Perfect. I hadn't had the nerve to ask for it, but knowing it wouldn't be there helped. "Thanks, Tristan."

He stepped around me, pressed in the code for the door and opened it. "Anything for you, *ma chérie*. Alarm button is in the same place."

I didn't need the reminder. Panic buttons were always to the sides of the headboard, and one of the rules was that it had to be accessible at all times. Which meant even if restrained, my fingers would be able to brush it.

I trusted I would never need to use it again.

"Enjoy yourself," Tristan said.

I inhaled deeply. My big breath chilled my throat and expanded my lungs.

I was ready and with a smile that would bring Tristan ease, I pressed my hand to his shoulder as I passed him. "Oh, I will. Don't you worry."

He stepped away with a chuckle so sexy I almost wished he were straight. And dominant.

The door clicked closed behind him and I was there. Alone. For the first time in six months, I was back in the very room that ran me out of the club.

Like Tristan promised, everything was the same. The chair in the corner that looked perfect for a Sunday afternoon lounge with a glass of wine and a good book was more deceptive than it appeared. It curved and dipped, making sex on it absolutely delicious.

I'd been with a partner there once. The positions required more intimacy than I typically experienced. Not for lack of want, but connection.

I skipped my eyes over it to the corner where the St.

Andrew's Cross had been. In its place was a large potted plant, which explained the soft lilac scent.

Only Tristan would take away a sex toy and replace it with a pot of fresh flowers.

The scent was soothing and I glanced away as quickly as I'd seen it. The memories of last time weren't going to enter my mind. I moved to the bed and sat down at the foot of it. It was high and my toes brushed gently over the lush cream rug. This was my time. My night. This was the night I took periodically, solely for me, seeing to my own needs and I had my own routine.

As butterflies swarmed low in my stomach, I kicked off my heels and flexed my feet, brushing them over the carpet. For two years I'd done this very same thing, flexing and relaxing my hands, rolling my shoulders.

I inhaled slowly, counted to five, and blew out each breath through my lips. The lilac scent invaded, soothed me easily, and soon I was ready.

I opened my eyes and removed my clothes. Folding them methodically, I set them on top of a small dresser along with my shoes. No man I'd ever been with asked me to do this, but the process helped prepare me and get me in the right frame of mind.

For not the first time, it occurred to me how odd I was. I was controlled in every single moment of my day from pre-planned outfits to a strict cleaning schedule. Yet when it came to sex, I could only enjoy it when there was the danger and darkness, pain and pleasure. I threw myself into situations many considered reckless and yet I still knew the truth.

With one word able to fall from my lips, I held all the control. There was safety and security in the word "red." One I'd only used once.

With my clothing removed, I unclasped the white lace bra. The cool fabric scraped deliciously over my hardening nipples as it fell to my hands. It left me in only the matching thong and I re-took my seat at the edge of the bed.

The blindfold was within reach and I slid it over my eyes.

By my count, I had a minute before the door opened.

So I took the time. Breathed slowly. Rolled my shoulders. My neck. Relaxed the tension in my body.

And prepared.

TWO

Gage

"She is not just a member. She's special. Be good to her."

My brows arched at Tristan's quiet but clear warning. I'd been coming to Velvet for three years, finding it almost a year after being traded to the Rough Riders from St. Louis. He hadn't spoken to me like this after the general rule reminders when I first began.

I already thought it odd he caught me outside the door to the room I preferred. I crossed my arms over my chest. "Something I need to know?"

"The lady in there...Beth...she's been a member a long time. Left for a few months after an unsavory incident—"

"Injured?" I balked. "You didn't tell me this."

Shit. A woman who'd been injured in a club like this could be damaged. It was where trust was ultimate. If she didn't have that in the club...or me...

"*Non*, not physically. She stopped it. She also took a break but if she wasn't perfect for what you desire, I wouldn't have had her come in."

"I'm her first?" My spine prickled. This went from bad to worse. "Tristan."

"It will be well. I'm simply reminding you to be good to her. She's strong and if I had doubts, I wouldn't have called her."

This had disaster etched into the walls. "Maybe you should find someone else."

"She'll be fine."

"But now I'm not sure I'm comfortable." The very *last* thing I needed in my life was a woman claiming I beat her. It'd not only ruin my career and my reputation but my family's.

Tristan grinned. I respected the hell out of the way he and his partner Joel ran their business, but this pushed the edges of my comfort zone. That grin was a tease on his otherwise serious expression. "Trust me, you'll be comfortable. Go see her. You don't feel what she can give you after a few minutes, you can end it, and I'll explain it to her."

Uncertainty had tightened my shoulders and I dropped my arms to my sides. I shook them out to relax them. I popped my neck a couple of times.

"Okay. She's ready then?"

"And we've kept her waiting. Enjoy yourself, Bryant. I have no doubt she will. *Bonne chance.*"

The man knew I had no idea what he said when he rattled off his French. Hoping it meant something good, I kept my eyes on him as he turned and swaggered off.

He spent most nights in the security room where he'd manage the guards in charge of overseeing the main room's activities and watching for any sign of disobedience from one of the eight private rooms.

When he disappeared, her name returned to my mind.

Beth.

It wasn't real, at least I doubted it was. I'd never cared enough to ask. I'd had multiple partners at Velvet since becoming a member. Most of them were only for one night. It wasn't because I didn't want a long-term relationship. I did. I wanted the family, the wife, the children, the two dogs and cat, good home my parents raised me in. But with my lifestyle and my desires, finding that perfect woman was difficult. I'd recently begun thinking it was impossible even though the older I got, the more I wanted it.

Sex. I understood that and liked it.

How to combine the sex life I craved and my career and not worry about a scorned ex-girlfriend coming forward with accusations it'd be impossible to defend myself from? That was the kicker.

I didn't join The Velvet Club for solely privacy and sex. I came to dominate. To hear a woman's ecstatic cries as I took her to heights she'd never reached. That was my gift to them. Their gift to me was milking my cock with their tight heat while enjoying the hell out of themselves.

At Velvet, I could do that without the risk of a lawsuit thanks to the non-disclosure agreements everyone signed.

I'd kept Beth waiting long enough. I knocked on the door twice, signaling I was about to enter and turned the knob.

Let the wicked games begin.

THE ROOM WAS dark as I entered save for the soft lamp on a dresser casting a gentle glow over the whole room. I waited until my eyes adjusted to the darkness before letting the door fully close behind me. My eyes immediately went to the woman sitting on the edge of the bed.

My body arrested. My chest went tight. Everything inside me burned hot and froze to ice.

Glorious. Beautiful didn't describe the woman with long hair, silken caramel with bright blonde mixed in, reminding me of my favorite dessert. It was thick and long, wavy down to her waist.

She was in nothing but white underwear, her breasts, small but perfect, drew my gaze to her already hardened nipples. Her chest rose with every slow, controlled breath.

Good.

Fear hadn't spiked yet. With Tristan's warning still in my head, I stepped toward her. If she heard me moving, she didn't react. If she felt my presence, she didn't respond. This woman wasn't afraid unless she was well-trained, and I didn't like well-trained professional subs. I just liked a woman willing to give me whatever I asked for.

I stopped before my black dress pants brushed against her knees. "What's your name?"

I already knew it, but I needed to hear her voice to help determine if she was afraid or controlled.

"Beth. Yours?"

Her voice was husky and smooth at the same time. Rich and not too high. It didn't shake and my concerns over her fear dissipated.

"John," I semi-lied. Mine was my middle name, but no way in hell did I go by Gage Bryant within these walls. I was recognizable enough. "How long have you been coming to Velvet?"

Her toes curled into the rug at her feet. It was the only movement she'd made since I entered the room and my gaze was drawn to the curl of her toes. The bright pink polish on them as she then pressed her feet firmly into the rug. "Three years but it's been a few months."

"Since you were with a partner or at all?"

"Both," she whispered and if the room had more light, I would swear a blush fanned across her throat.

"Are you okay with being blindfolded?" She'd have to be or I'd leave but I still always asked.

She shifted then. This time at her thighs. Trim muscles showed at the tops of her legs as she did so and I couldn't hold back a grin. Was just talking to her turning her on?

I could explore that.

"Yes, I'm okay with that."

"Safe words?"

"Colors...green, yellow, and red, and before you ask..." Her lips lifted at one edge into the hint of a smile. "I will use them if I have to, but if we could get started, that'd be really nice."

Her voice softened as she spoke showing me she was turned on. The hitch in her breath, the small increase in her breathing, and the tension of her thighs made me want to ask her if she was wet. With how composed she was, I suspected I'd enjoy finding out for myself.

"It'll be more than really nice," I said, smirking though she couldn't see. "Spread your legs. I'm going to step between them and I want you to undo my belt."

Touching someone for the first time when they were blindfolded required trust we hadn't yet established. I always let the women touch me first, acclimate their hands to my body, the shape of me. Partly because it helped them loosen up.

Mostly because my dick went rock hard when trembling, nervous hands ran over me for the first time.

Soon, she'd learn I was larger than she expected. A bit of fear or wonder would creep into her voice as she realized my bulk and muscles. And then, knowing I was so much larger than her, bigger and stronger and could break her small frame without even meaning to, she'd still give herself to me.

They always did, but I really fucking liked the hint of fear in their tone and in the way they moved while they did.

She moved her knees apart, readjusted her small frame on the edge of the bed. I kicked off my shoes and stepped in between her legs. My hands went to my hips.

"You can begin whenever you're ready."

Without any hesitation, her teeth showed through her smile and her hands rose. She lacked the original tremble most did and my interest spiked. A woman blindfolded with no worry at all? It wasn't common. Tristan's warning rang in my head.

She is not just a member. She is special.

Special indeed.

Her fingers pressed against my thighs. A small shiver rolled through her at that first contact. A lightning bolt struck my spine as she pressed her small hands more firmly against me.

"You're tall," she whispered, hands roaming up to my hips. Her fingers brushed against mine at my hips and stopped. The warmth from her hand sent that lightning bolt burning hotter.

When was the last time I had such a visceral reaction to a woman? And I hadn't even touched her yet.

"Hmm," she purred. Her fingers trailed my hands, stroked the length of my fingers up to my wrists. "You seem very strong."

I was losing strength and self-control with every whispering touch.

"Yup."

"And I bet big." Her lips lifted at one corner. Brave. Sweet. Her lyrical voice seduced me even while she teased me.

I said nothing, allowing her to continue her exploration. Her hands went to my belt buckle and back down the fronts of my thighs. She brushed my quickly hardening cock like she was the one in control. And hell if it wasn't hot, watching her grin, lips parted with such fascination as her hands moved higher to my stomach.

With each passing moment, her cheeks flushed darker, her chest rose and fell with quickened breaths until she was practically panting.

I'd wager my last championship ring that she was as wet as I was hard.

She returned to my waist and finally undid my buckle.

Before I could issue another command, she asked, "May I stand?"

She'd already scooted as far forward as she could without falling off the edge of the bed.

"You may."

I didn't step back. There was little room for her to stand up straight and as she did, I took in the slight sway of her petite breasts. Trim muscles peaked across her abdomen and showed in her thighs.

Her hair swayed and swished with her movements. Long, glistening blonde tresses that would shine once wrapped around my tan fist.

Once she was standing, her hands were almost plastered to my chest we were so close. Her head tilted back as if she finally understood how tall I really was. Almost a full foot taller. Her head barely came up to my shoulders and she peered up at me.

Fucking blindfold. For the first time, I wanted to see a woman's eyes. I imagined hers were blue, perhaps a pale shade of gold that matched her hair. Either way, I knew her pupils would be dilated, proving her excitement.

I dropped my hands and fisted them at my sides, muscles bunched at my biceps as she pressed her hands there. It took all my strength not to throw her down on the bed and rip off her blindfold.

"Remove the buttons on my shirt," I demanded, my voice rough and husky. My self-control was hanging on by a thread.

Still, she interested me. Called to me. Her fingers were nimble and quick, quivering, not from fear, but anticipation. Nothing she'd shown me so far gave any indication she was nervous to be having sex with a complete, faceless stranger.

Should that bother me? Probably.

Did I give a shit? Fuck no. I was harder than I'd been in months.

She undid each button methodically, even sliding her hands down my arms to remove the ones at my wrists. And once it was draped open, pulled from my belt, my dick pressing against the zipper, demanding freedom, I grabbed her hand.

"Oh," she gasped. "Did I do something wrong?"

"No." I pressed her hand to my crotch. She'd avoided it on purpose and it was time to remind her who was really in charge. "But you've neglected something important." Her hand curled around my hard length and her breathing went erratic. "Undo the rest of my pants and free me."

THREE

Elizabeth

Touch him? John—and I doubted that was his real name if he really wanted anonymity like Tristan said—wanted me to touch him? Already I could tell how large he was. Through his trousers, which I imagined black, I could barely wrap my hand around the hardness there.

I'd been blindfolded by strangers before, but this was different. *He* was different There was something about him. His voice. The way he spoke with control. The baritone richness of his voice was a beautiful melody to my ears.

It could have been because the room was black, his voice dark and my vision blocked. But I imagined him in my head and so far, his body was even larger than anything I could comprehend.

He'd have black hair as dark as coal. Brown eyes as rich as my favorite dark chocolate bar. His lips would be full and thick, like the rest of him. Everywhere my hands had roamed, he'd felt like warm marble, his body the kind you'd see sculpted to perfection in a museum, or plastered on the cover of romance novels.

This man was no Fabio though. He'd be a warrior. A fighter of some sort.

Amazing how a lack of senses increased so much more.

Even his hand wrapped around my wrist, using both of our hands to rub the length of him was strong and hot. Searing my flesh with an indescribable *need* to do every single little thing he commanded.

"Don't get nervous now, little one," he said.

He'd not only moved closer, but he'd bent his head. His warm breath skimmed over my ear, across my cheek. I fought a delicious shiver and lost.

His chuckle, acknowledging and liking my reaction, was my reward.

"It's hard to undo your zipper when you're holding my hand," I told him. I could tease and boss with the best of them.

I craved submission. I also enjoyed submitting more when my partner had to work to earn the right to have it.

A thousand ideas flashed behind my darkened lids of how this man, this big strong man with a sexy as hell voice, could earn that from me.

He pressed my hand firmly against his cock. It was so damn thick, I yearned to feel the full weight of him in my hand. His hand let me go and I took the moment to squeeze, to test, but impatience won out and soon I was at his waist.

I undid the button.

Then his zipper.

He'd told me to free him so I didn't wait for further instruction. I pressed my hands to his hips, lingered at muscles beneath my thumbs I knew my tongue would *love* to trace at some point later. Then I was pushing down his pants, along with skin-tight boxer briefs.

He groaned as he was released and I didn't wait.

My hand went to his length. It was more impressive standing

at attention. We were so close, when I ran my hand down the full of him, the tip of his cock rubbed against my belly.

But it was his girth that made me jerk.

"Don't worry," he said, and his hand was at my shoulder, brushing my hair behind me. "I'll make sure you're ready."

"I wasn't worried." It was a lie. This guy was *huge* and I was a girl who could be easily pleased with average. I didn't judge a guy in bed based on the size of his equipment. I'd had great sex with smaller sized dicks and disappointing sex with larger men.

But this man. His confidence and the size of his body and his dick pulsing in my hand?

John could *crush* me.

"Confident and bold," he murmured. His hand was still at my shoulder, brushing along my collarbone. His hand wrapped around my throat and with his thumb, he pressed my chin up. "You have me wondering if you'll taste as spicy as you seem to be. Or will you be sweet once I get my mouth on you?"

His thumb at my chin pressed my jaw closed so I couldn't respond with words, but I could with actions. I slid my hand up and down his shaft, squeezing him firmly at the tip, teasing the drop of pre-cum. He wasn't the only one wondering what someone would taste like. My hand slid down and cupped his balls, heavy and already pulled tight. Man, he was impressive *everywhere*.

The desire to tear off the blindfold was an itch beneath the surface. What would he do? Spank me? Tie me down?

Or worse...would he leave? It wasn't the worth the risk. Not with how turned on I was.

"What do you like?" I asked, squeezing him again. My breaths were ragged. My legs trembled. He needed to tell me to lay down before they buckled.

There was a smile in his voice as he said, "So far, I like every-thing you're doing. But for now." He pressed his hand over mine again. His large hand enveloped my much smaller one as he placed mine on his shoulder. "I want you to lay down on the bed. Hands to the headboard."

Oh goodie. We were really getting started. I suppressed a smile and a sassy word that wanted to escape and sat back down. Scooting backward, I kept my face on where I assumed he was still standing. Then I heard the clink of a belt buckle telling me he was kicking his feet out of his pants. The rustle of his shirt as he removed it.

I expected him to tug at my ankles and separate my legs, bind them so we could get to the good stuff, but then his hands were on my legs.

Goose bumps trailed in his wake and I squirmed from the firm contact of his skin on mine for the first time. His hands were rough, proving he worked hard, not just behind a desk all day. He moved slowly but with intent and the bed dipped as he placed his weight on it.

Then he was over me, the warmth from his body covering my lower half, his hands at my thighs. A brush of scruff scraped across my stomach, right below my navel.

I hadn't even thought to touch his face earlier. Or his hair. His command to keep my hands at the headboard was hell. I wanted to finish my investigation.

"Stay still," he said, his lips at my stomach. He kissed me along the line of my panties from one hip to the other. I held my breath and tightened my abs. His kisses were delicious. Warm and wet, full lips like I'd imagined. The scrape of a short beard delicious as ice cream on a sweltering summer day.

"Oh God," I whimpered. My legs were taut. My ass pressed into the mattress so I didn't wiggle. "Please."

"Please what?" he asked. His tone lightened, voice gone playful. How could this *man* be playful when I was going mad? A tug of my panties brushed my hip, and then the other. He pulled them off slowly and every inch of lace sliding along my skin tortured me.

God. I'd never been so wet. My center pulsed with rabid need to have him inside of me and the knuckles of my hand ached as I forced them to stay still.

"Hurry," I whined and I couldn't find a care in the world to flinch at the neediness in my tone. "Please."

"You haven't answered me."

He'd left me. Somewhere between the panty-stripping and tummy kisses, his weight had moved off the bed. He was across the room talking and my head turned that way.

"What do you want, little one?"

Every fucking thing he wanted to give me. But boldness was key. Generalities never worked. "Your cock inside of me."

He hummed and the sound of movement along the carpet told me he was coming back. My stomach clenched in anticipation.

And then nothing happened. The room went silent. My nerves piqued.

"John?" I asked when all I heard was the thundering of my own heartbeat.

"There's so much I want to do to you I was having trouble deciding what to start with first."

Oh God. Yes. My entire body tightened with expectation.

"Roll over and crawl to the headboard. Hands at the top."

I'd never moved so fast in my life. I scampered into position and a rush of breath left me as his hand grabbed mine. A cold leather band was tightened around my wrist.

"So you don't get any ideas," he said, and that teasing tone was back. He moved around me and fastened the other. The bed dipped and my head fell. God what I wouldn't give to see this man. I could come by his words alone and a few teasing touches. My nipples ached, hardened points and he hadn't touched them yet. I should have asked. I expected his hand at my ass. Lips on my thighs. I jumped as I felt him brush against my legs and his voice came from beneath me. "Spread your legs wider and lower yourself."

"Oh God," I moaned. He was beneath me. His hands on my thighs.

Before I had time to comply, those hands pulled me down and I was on him. His mouth moved instantly and fiercely. There was no preparation, no warm-up, teasing flickers of his tongue at my slit. No, not with John. His mouth consumed me, eating me. His tongue pushed inside of me and his hands gripped me tight against him so there was no way I could move. I couldn't shift or roll my hips. I couldn't pull away. I could only succumb.

This damn man. He didn't wait to earn my submission, he took it.

I'd never been more enthralled.

A fierce fire hit me hard and fast. The beautiful kind that started at my stomach, spread outward until it pulled at my inner thighs. My muscles shook like I'd run a marathon and that heat rolled up my spine. The sounds I made were animalistic, tortured and pleasured mixed together in moans and whimpers. Words were lost to me as I abandoned any hope of decency.

Chants rolled from my lips. Nonsensical ones. Vowels formed. Consonants forgotten as my orgasm hit me. So fast. So damn fast and hard my body shook and rolled with it and even then he kept at me, sucking my clit into his mouth until it ached.

"Please," I gasped. I meant to tell him to stop. It was too much. Instead I begged for more as his hand on my hip moved, and then two fingers were shoved deep inside of me. He fucked me roughly, wildly, in a way I had never been fucked before and knew would never be again.

Shit. He was ruining me and he was only using his mouth and fingers.

"Give me one more."

"I don't know if I can." I was breathless. So close and yet fighting it. If I could see him, his chin would be drenched from me. His mouth was wet and slippery. I was wetter.

"You can." And as if to prove it, his hand slid to my back, down through my crease. His thumb put pressure at my hole, and that was all it took. Between the friction of his mouth, the delicious zing of pleasure at my backside, it took barely anything and I was doing exactly what he told me to.

The orgasm swept through my body with hurricane-force winds. I threw back my head, hair hitting my butt and right as I was coming down, he was up and behind me, his chest against my back, his hands at my wrists.

"You're fucking beautiful. Magnificent, Beth. How much more do you have in you?"

"None." I was breathless. Shaking. I needed a nap for two weeks and physical therapy to recover from everything he'd given me.

A fierce burning hit my ass and I jumped from the force of his spanking. "Now I just don't think that's true at all."

"Oh God," I whispered.

He undid the buckles at my wrists and somehow, he was tender as he rubbed where the leather had tightened around them.

"Hands okay?"

"Mm-hmm." Words were useless. I could barely nod.

"You're doing great." He was still whispering. Still being so tender and gentle. What man could be so rough and gentle?

"Let your arms down slowly, your shoulders might be stiff."

"It's not my shoulders that are stiff," I grumbled as he moved us. He laid me down and rolled me to my back.

He went straight to my thighs and parted them, kissed the

inside, close to my center. "Poor little one. I can kiss it and make it better."

I huffed a laugh. It was all I had in me. "I think you've kissed it enough."

His laugh was soft but deep, and somehow my cheeks ached from smiling. Sex with strangers was often daring. It was evocative.

Rarely was it *fun*.

The crinkle of foil grabbed my attention and despite my pleas that I was done, my knees widened for him without being told.

"See? You do need more."

"Maybe just a bit."

"It's more than a bit," he quipped back. I hadn't forgotten. But hell, I hoped I was ready for this. If he could make me sore from a good finger bang, what could he do with his dick?

I didn't have time to ask. He was above me then, his legs spreading mine open farther. His lips were at my jaw, my ear, teasing and nipping at my lobe. I turned toward him, instinctively. Not everyone liked to kiss.

He hadn't said it was a hard limit.

Tristan would have let me know.

Then his mouth landed on mine. Like before, he didn't tease, he didn't build up. He took what he wanted and slid his tongue inside, devouring the cavern of my mouth while the firm tip of him rubbed against me.

"Fuck," he groaned. He slid inside slowly, unlike his kisses and everything else, but God I needed that.

"Shit," I chanted.

"Am I hurting you?"

"No." God, it didn't hurt. It was a fullness, a weight, and it was incredible. "More."

He pulled back, and for the millionth time, I resisted the urge to remove my blindfold. When he kissed me again, he was smiling. "And you said you were done."

"You're driving me crazy." He was moving in and out, going deeper on every inward thrust but the pace was killing me.

"Trust me, I feel the same. You feel fucking amazing. So tight and wet. Burning hot. You're a fantastic fuck, little one."

"Shit," I gasped again. "Please faster."

"You'll get what I give you."

"It's just that you give such good presents."

"Fuck," he groaned, slamming deep. He collapsed on me, falling to his elbows at my sides and buried his face in the crook of my neck. "I wasn't expecting a comedy show. Goddamn, you're feisty."

His shoulders and back shook with his laughter, but then he rose, and I missed the heat of him. He was so much taller than me, my lips were at his shoulder. He'd had to bend to kiss me and fuck me. Good Lord, he was strong.

"Done playing," he said. And his tone had gone dark. "You feel too damn good. Put your hands on my wrists."

I wanted to keep them on his back, his muscles were divine and defined. With every thrust, every movement, some hard piece of him bubbled beneath my hand.

Still, I listened and adjusted until I wrapped my hands around his wrists.

He moved rapidly, thrusting his body into me, groaning while he did it. If he could finger bang me to oblivion, I'd be in another galaxy by the time we were done. He shifted and lifted my hip, went deeper, dragged himself along the rigid muscles inside of me and soon my head was tilted back, gasping for breath.

He seemed to do the same. His speed increased, his kisses stopped. His hand at my hip moved again and he leaned forward.

"Don't come yet," he groaned. "Not until I do." His hand was at my chest, moving up. He curled it around my throat and beneath the blindfold, my eyes widened.

I gasped in surprise, a small amount of fear. But he waited until my orgasm was closer. Pleasure swarmed my body and I said the only words I could make. "Please. Yes."

He grasped my throat. Just enough pressure to remind me he was there but even that little bit drove me insane. I swallowed beneath his hand and inhaled as deep as a breath as possible.

"Coming," I gasped.

"No."

"I can't..."

"You can. Hold on." Then his hand tightened further. He choked me lightly but firmly. I could breathe but it was difficult and that fear mixed with the loss of oxygen did it.

He went wild with his thrusts, pounding into me until the bed shook and creaked. It was all magnified in my ears and then he ground his pelvis against mine.

"John!" I cried out. My hand clawed at his arm. My other went to his hip. Then his hand was gone, at my breast, pulling my nipple, and it was all I needed. That sting of pain, the extra amount of air. I grabbed onto him, held on while a third and more beautiful, more painfully blissful climax careened me over the edge.

He followed immediately. Cursing and groaning while his thrusts went erratic, hard and deep and oh so damn fast I was still in the throes of my orgasm when he pounded into me and stayed there. He pulsed inside of me and took my mouth, kissing me while he grunted and released his own orgasm deep inside.

He stayed there, kissing me roughly but slower in pace. He seemed almost languid and unhurried now that he'd finished. My grip on his hip loosened.

His forehead pressed again mine, as he made small, teasing thrusts that still felt beautiful. "Did I hurt you?"

"Not even close."

"Good."

I kissed his jaw, his throat. I kissed everywhere I could reach by arching which wasn't much considering the weight on me.

Holy shit. I'd just had the most incredible sex with a man and I didn't even know what he looked like. Talk about perverse.

"I'm going to pull out. Stay where you are. I'll be right back."

"Okay," I muttered. Moving seemed awfully difficult anyway. I whimpered at the loss of him, the tender way he kissed down my belly, my thighs, to my ankles as he climbed off the bed. He was only gone for a moment, to dispose of the condom I imagined. A drawer opened and closed and I knew what that meant, but I still jumped when the warm cloth was pressed against my center. He cleaned me, wiped at my thighs and my center and then he was back in the bed, next to me, running his hand up my stomach, between my breasts, he tilted my head toward him and his lips met mine.

"You were really fantastic."

"Thank you. You too."

"I don't usually do repeats," he said and at the mention of it... what this was...something in my stomach sank. It might have been my heart. "I want to see you again. Soon."

"Okay." Did I sound cool? Too eager? I hoped for cool and nonchalant. Based on his chuckle, I doubted I did either.

"I'll set it up with Tristan then." He was whispering as if what we'd done was special. It'd been intimate and rough, but special?

To me, yes. Submitting was always gratifying. A stress relief. Hard and intense sex eased my mind and helped me relax.

But I could never remember a time where it'd felt *special*. At least, not during the first time. Which also meant this guy was dangerous.

I lifted my hand and brushed his cheek. He stilled for a

moment and relaxed as I familiarized myself with the feel of him. Strong jaw, coarse but short hair. Good cheekbones. Much like everything else about him, his face felt hard and firm, as if he didn't smile much or maybe wasn't all that happy.

He wasn't my puzzle to solve though.

"I'll make sure Tristan knows I'm up for more time with you," I said, choking down the words I really wanted to say.

Please...let me see you.

"Okay then." He kissed my nose and moved, but it felt like it took forever, almost like he didn't want to leave. "You really were great, Beth. I'm looking forward to next time."

"Me too."

"Stay here until the door closes, okay?"

What was I doing? Another round with a guy I couldn't see who would certainly keep that between us again?

This had trouble stamped in bright red all over it.

"Okay. Good night, John."

"Good night, Beth." He pressed his lips to mine one more time. He didn't use his tongue, just his mouth in a lingering sweet kiss, the kind you'd give your love at the end of a long day but needed that connection before sleep. That wasn't what this was. I had to remember that.

I didn't respond. I rolled to my side while he dressed, the clank of a buckle and the rustle of his clothes a hundred times louder than before. And then his shoes. The door opened and I imagined him looking back, perhaps biting his bottom lip before he made the decision to stay a little bit longer.

I ripped off the blindfold and sat up, hoping, wishing he was still there. Changed his mind. But the room was empty and I blinked several times to clear the haze of darkness I'd been shrouded in for so long.

"Well, Elizabeth, you sure do know how to return to Velvet with a bang. That's for sure."

FOUR

Elizabeth

"Elizabeth!"

I jumped at the sharp shout of my boss Shane's voice. He was a large man with a personality ten times larger than his waist. I'd worked at XTCP News for five years and he still scared the crap out of me every time he shouted.

Across the desk from me, Will peeked out from behind the computer monitor. His blue eyes crinkled and his shoulders were shaking from laughter. "When are you ever going to get used to that?"

"Probably never." I'd already stood from my chair. When Shane boomed, I moved. I'd busted my butt for my boss, for this moment. The moment where I learned the head anchorwoman was going on maternity leave soon. I'd approached Shane last week, essentially begging him in the most professional way possible, to allow me the anchor seat while she was out for twelve weeks.

This morning, barely awake, groggy from lack of sleep and sore muscles and my head in the clouds thinking of why those muscles were sore from Mr. Anonymous, I'd logged onto my computer, scanned my computer email, and grinned when I saw the XTCP family had a new family member.

Chase Mason Jones was born at three o'clock in the morning.

Which meant today, one of my lifelong dreams could come true.

Hope blossoming, I grabbed my tablet and stylus and hurried to Shane's door before he could boom my name again.

He had a loud voice and a huge smile, with an even bigger belly. He also wore a full salt and pepper beard he kept cropped in the summer heat and grew out in the cooler winter months. By Christmas time, he wouldn't need a fake Santa beard to play the role. He'd look exactly like Jolly Ol' Saint Nick.

He also had a wife and three kids he bitched about all the time, but in that way you knew he loved them more than he loved his beer and the Raleigh Rough Riders, our local NFL football team. And he loved his beer and football a whole heckuva lot.

I left his door opened as I entered his office. Shane was a good guy, one of the best bosses I'd ever had. The only time his office door had ever been closed was the day he received a phone call from his dad, letting him know his mother had passed away unexpectedly.

"Good morning," I said as I entered.

He pushed away from his laptop and settled his forearms on his desk. "Hey, Elizabeth. Come in and have a seat."

I was already on my way so when he was done speaking, I was able to slide right into the plush, dark gray chair across from him.

"What can I do for you today, Shane?"

My voice sounded professional. My thoughts weren't. *Please pick me. Please give me this. Please pick me.*

"As you know, Shayla is now officially on maternity with the arrival of Chase early this morning." His grin went soft, likely remembering the births of his own three kids, and before I could say anything, he continued, "Want you to know I considered your request. Thought about it. Debated back and forth."

Please pick me. Please choose me. My internal chant was losing hope by the moment.

"Okay…"

"In truth, you're a great reporter. One of the best reporters we have and I hate the idea of losing you to the desk. You're engaging. Viewers love you and you report fairly without bias while being able to inject humanity and realistic sympathy into every difficult story."

I heard it coming before he said it. Saw each letter form on his lips as they came out of his mouth.

"But I'm temporarily giving the position to Amanda."

"Amanda," I said, more of a sigh. Made sense. The beautiful and fit redhead had more experience. She'd been doing the afternoon news for seven years so of course it made sense to move her up to the evening news. "Okay." I was already nodding. "Thank you for your kind words."

That soft smile he had when he mentioned Chase being born returned, turned even friendlier.

"I said temporarily."

"Well, of course, Shayla's maternity leave is temporary."

"I'm hoping so, but to be honest, I wouldn't be surprised if she decides to leave us. Chase is her third boy. She's going to have her hands full and I can imagine, since she's mentioned wishing she could be home, that she might consider it these next few months."

Oh. *Oh.* "I hadn't heard."

He flipped his hand to the side dismissively. "Shayla's neither here nor there. I have a new assignment for you. I'm pulling you off the summer travel vacation spots for the next few weeks and putting Will on them. In two weeks, one of the Raleigh Rough

Riders is being honored and named as a major donor and planner of the new Family Center at the Children's Hospital. It opens mid-season, a busy time for our boys."

I all but rolled my eyes as he proclaimed our pro football team to be his boys. Fandom went deep in Raleigh and Shane had been waving his teal and blue flag high and proud since the team started.

"And you want me to report on the opening?"

"Yes. As Gage Bryant promotes the opening, newscasters will be essentially following him around. Fundraising events. Promotional events. He's hosting a variety of things including a bowling function. There will be luncheons, a few dinners, and tours of the new wing before it opens. I want you covering it all. Reporting everything."

Wowzers. That was a lot to put on one reporter. I'd heard about the new children's wing opening but hadn't paid much attention. Also, football was as familiar to me as Russian so other than the fact a multi-millionaire was dishing out some money, probably due to contractual obligations of volunteer time or something else written in his contract, I really hadn't given it much headspace.

"Okay. Thank you. It sounds like a great opportunity."

"It's *the* opportunity."

"Pardon?"

Shane leaned forward and lowered his voice. "This is your opportunity, Elizabeth. Nail this assignment. Put your heart and soul and your entire intelligence and everything you know about journalism into these pieces. Nail it, and I will give you the desk when it's done."

"Excuse me?" My voice went breathy. I was having trouble breathing. All my hopes returned with a rushing forcing knocking the wind from my chest. "Really?"

"Amanda doesn't want the night desk. She likes her afternoons and I'm willing to keep her there, but assuming Shayla doesn't return, I need someone ready. You're young, but ratings always jump when you're on and you're consistent and professional. I don't want to have to look outside the station if the time comes and to be honest, you were the person I considered for it, but I really want this lifestyle piece to exceed expectations." He leaned back, his palms at the edge of his desk and tilted his head. "Can you do that for me?"

"Yes." I'd turned into a bobblehead. Head shaking like a madwoman. "Yes. I can do that."

"My expectations are high, Elizabeth."

They always were. That he trusted me to do this and believed I could give him what he was looking for sent excitement buzzing to my fingertips and my toes.

"I'll do it. Thank you, Shane. Thank you for the opportunity."

"Good. Here's the schedule of events. He's kicking the events off with a press conference today after their practice." He slid a manila folder across the desk. "Inside is everything you need, including press credentials to get in. Take Jason with you. I've already talked to him."

Jason was one of the main cameramen. I'd not only worked with him frequently, but we worked well together. Plus, he was a huge football fan. Which meant he could fill me in on who this Gage guy was before the conference.

"Great." With hands shaking from excitement, I picked up the folder. "Thank you, Shane. I won't let you down. I promise."

He was turning toward his computer keyboard and grinned at me. "Never had a doubt you would, Elizabeth."

~

"THIS IS HUGE," Will said, his voice a whisper-hiss. News traveled fast and I'd barely given him a shaky smile once I left Shane's office, a quick stop at my desk before I went to squeal like a child in the women's restroom. By the time I returned, he'd already heard. "I mean it Elizabeth. This is awesome."

"It is." I rubbed my hands together. "And I'm excited and nervous and freaked. I know nothing about football or this guy. I have so many questions."

Like why him? Why was this guy dumping millions into a children's center? Goodness of his heart? Volunteer requirement? Did he have a shady background and trying to project a new image?

Will adjusted his black frames on his nose and shook his head. "Google is your friend, my dear, but I'll tell you what I know. Gage Bryant is pristine. He's a do-gooder and an incredible wide receiver. He's been to the Pro Bowl the last two years. People love him and I've never heard a hint of anything hidden in his closet the entire time he's been here."

I didn't even know how long that was. And with my knowledge of football, had no clue what a wide receiver was, although I assumed it meant he caught the ball. And Pro-Bowl? Forget about it.

"Oh God." I dumped my forehead into my hands and groaned. I knew *nothing* about football. And while I covered lifestyle pieces, they were usually fluffier. Will was making this guy sound like a local celebrity and I'd never paid attention. Had he done anything like this before? Did he volunteer frequently? I had never covered a piece for the football team before. "I have so much to learn and I have to leave in two hours for the press conference."

Will smacked the top of my desk. "Then I suppose you start doing what you do best and get to researching."

Right. Of course. I could look into any story, dig deeper. I could do this. Knowing the game of football wouldn't be that important, would it? I just had to learn who this guy was. Why the hospital? Why was he spending so much time promoting it beforehand?

This was my job, one I loved, and I could do it easily.

Lifting my head, I gave Will a thankful smile. He was one of the best encouragers we had. His wife was lucky to have him. "Thanks, Will."

"Anytime."

I did exactly what Will suggested. I pulled up Wikipedia, not the most relevant source of news but it was a starting point. I read about Gage's high school, college, and pro career learning he'd been traded to the Raleigh Rough Riders four years ago. He stayed out of the papers. His parents were mentioned, but that was it. No spouse even though he was thirty-two years old. His Instagram feed showed nothing but photos of him on the field and pics of other players. A few he'd clearly reposted and they showed him dressed in the best well-fitting suits I'd ever seen on a man.

I memorized his stats. Six-four, two hundred fifty pounds. Born in 1986. And then I stumbled on a photo spread he'd done for *Men's Health* and my jaw dropped.

Butt freaking naked. A football helmet held in front of him was the only thing covering him. And hot damn. This guy. Chiseled, strong jaw. Straight Roman nose. Piercing eyes.

He was freaking gorgeous. My heart rate kicked into fast gear. My fingertips sizzled. I had to spend weeks following *this* guy around? The very idea sent a pulse of excitement to the tops of my thighs I tried to shake away.

I couldn't get a crush on this guy. He was a source. A story. But good grief to the high heavens, he was the most beautiful if stern looking man I'd ever seen in my life.

"Holy shit," I whispered, forgetting we worked in an open office and even though I was quiet, people could hear me.

"What is it, Elizabeth?" That came from Amanda. "Oh dear. You got the Gage story?"

She was already at my back, peering over my shoulder. "Man as sexy as that shouldn't be allowed to walk free," I said.

"I know." She laughed and bumped my shoulder. "He's God's gift to women that's for sure. And yet from what I've heard, he's never had a girlfriend, at least not one he's gone public with."

"Really?" I twisted in my chair and faced her. "Never?"

She shrugged. "Not in the four years he's been here. And I'd know. Rough Riders are my team. I follow all of 'em on Twitter and Instagram. He posts a pic and gets over four thousand comments, mostly from women, but to the best of my knowledge, he's never been seen in public with a woman except his mom."

Wow. That was...that was crazy. Everything leaked.

"Hmm," I said, tapping my finger to my lips. "So I would imagine the public would want to know if he was involved, right?"

She laughed lightly. "Yeah, but watch yourself. This is a hospital piece, not a gossip column. You go digging too far and you'll blow your chance. Which by the way, I'm rooting for you." She stepped back and flipped her red hair over her shoulder. "See you later, Elizabeth. Drinks tomorrow?"

Thursday nights were our nights. The girls at the station always took off and went for an afternoon happy hour once the afternoon news was done.

I lifted my file of events. "I'll get back to you. Haven't had much time to study this yet."

"Sounds good." She waved her hand and turned her back to me, already walking away.

FIVE

Gage

"Okay. So, first, you're going to go out there and stand with the president of the hospital as well as the contracting company who's been building this addition. They'll speak first."

Karen, the hospital administration's assistant, tapped and swiped her stylus on her tablet with reckless abandon. She was speaking into a mouthpiece just as easily as she was speaking to me.

Except she didn't have to. We'd been over this for the last hour and her constant hounding was grating on my nerves.

I already knew what was going to happen. We'd talked about it last week. This morning. Two hours ago. Thirty minutes ago. With the way this woman prattled on and on, working herself into a frenetic tizzy, I was thankful we were in the hospital.

When her heart exploded, we'd have instant access to the Emergency Room.

Sensing my growing frustration as only my assistant could, Pat walked up and stepped in between Karen and me. "How about we let Gage run through his speech again, shall we? That way we can be assured he won't mess it up out there."

Karen's eyes went wide and she gaped like a fish. "Mess up?" She whipped her head toward me, panic paling her already light skin. "Mess up? You can't. We have to get this right."

I lifted my phone. My speech was on it, but I didn't have to look at the screen to know what I wanted to say. I'd grown up in hospitals like this, the outsider kid who wasn't ill but still had to practically live in them. I could rehearse my speech in my sleep at this point.

"I've got it, Karen. And I won't mess up. I promise."

Unless I couldn't get my mind off the woman from last night. I went to bed thinking of her, jacking off when I never felt the need after a night at Velvet. Then again in the morning and that wasn't because of male need, either. It was pure blonde hair and petite curves on my mind. God, she was fucking incredible. So obedient, so pliant....so damn *into* everything we did. I wanted a repeat and badly. I had already stopped myself from getting a hold of Tristan more than once. I should have been focusing on the day and the upcoming weeks. The upcoming game on Sunday. Instead, my mind was back in that room with blonde hair so sparkling white splayed out on gray sheets. Soft little whimpers, louder begs and pleas. Damn. Yeah.

Shit. Get her out of my head for three hours. That was what I needed to do. Listening to Karen droll on and on wasn't helping a damn thing. She started talking and I spaced out.

"Well, good. The local news reporters are taking their seats. We have the Raleigh stations sitting up front and the rest of the state's newscasters behind them. There's also ESPN and your old college even sent a reporter. Really, Gage, this press conference is important."

Like I didn't know. And Karen was past the point of irritating me. She was now officially pissing me the fuck off.

I'd donated millions to this project, working closely with the contractors and the hospital to get this children and family wing built from the ground up. It took two years of fundraising and lobbying my friends and any connections I had to get this thing to open up.

That I was now in a place of prosperity to be able to build something like this should have made me feel like a king. I could throw millions around and make dozens if not hundreds of people happy, even if it was on a temporary basis.

But that was the thing about happiness—it was so often temporary. Instead, all of this work, the culmination of years of planning and hard work, didn't make me feel successful.

"I need a break."

At Karen's shocked expression, I lifted a hand. "Thirty minutes. I'll be back in plenty of time."

I took the elevator to the fifth floor of the children's hospital. I had no destination in mind, just the burning need to relax and get my head in the game. In an hour, I was going to stand in a room full of reporters holding a press conference where I'd explain why this was so important to me, why I threw so much of my own money into this project—sixty-five percent of the total cost— and what the plans were for the next two weeks before the official ribbon cutting ceremony on the Sunday of our bye week. As a bonus, I'd gotten guys and friends from the local NHL and NBA teams to come on out too. It'd be hours of interacting with the kids, and every guy who volunteered had approached me because most of the men I knew playing professional sports were really fucking awesome.

Soon, I found myself outside a familiar door. My feet pulled to an abrupt stop.

I peeked in through the window and like every time I saw him, my chest tightened at the sight of Brandon. Nine years old. Leukemia. Second appearance. His cheeks were swollen and puffy from chemo. His bald head covered with a Rough Riders stocking hat. If he turned the other way, it'd have my number eighteen on the back.

He'd been in and out of this hospital ever since I was traded to the Rough Riders.

Nine fucking years old and he had spent almost half his life in a room with bright yellow walls, beeping machines, and the taste of chemo in his mouth.

A warmth pressed to my forearm and I flinched from the sudden contact.

"Sorry. I'm so sorry, Gage."

Brandon's mom Penny was there, smiling at me like she always did. That one where her lips turned up at the same time the rest of her expression pulled down. It fucking killed me every time I saw it.

It didn't take a genius to understand why I was particularly drawn to this family, this patient.

Brandon Miller was fighting to live and conquer the same disease that had killed my little brother.

"He's not looking better." I could hardly pull my eyes from his frail body, tucked and covered by at least a half-dozen blankets.

Her hand on my arm squeezed tightly. She was cold and shivery, strong as steel. I met them during his first round of chemo when I stopped for a children's visit to hand out jerseys and footballs. People thought I did it for the PR, but they were wrong.

I did it because I knew how much my brother would have loved it.

"He has moments, and if they can get the infection to go away, we'll see improvement soon."

Penny was always so hopeful. She never doubted her kid would, in fact, beat this horrible disease. Hell, she even found a way to smile after her husband left her, claiming the stress and fear was too much for him. Maybe all she had was hope to cling to. She was the most amazing woman I'd ever met outside my mom.

"I'll let him sleep, but if he wakes up, have a nurse come get me? I have a press conference to do here this afternoon." I dropped my head. "No joke, Penny. I don't care if I'm in the middle of speaking and I'll let the nurse's station know. He wakes up, I want someone to come get me."

"I will, Gage. And good luck today."

I gave her a quick hug. There was nothing between us except understanding.

"Take care."

"Always do," she said, stepping back and going toward the door.

I waited until she closed it behind her, went immediately to Brandon and tucked the blankets around him more firmly. The back of her hand pressed to his forehead and then her lips followed.

I left her to tend to her son, a new fire spreading. The reason for all of this.

I had to kick that pretty little minx out of my head for the rest of the day so I could see to what was really important.

PATRICK PEERED through the side panel and pulled back. "It's packed. The hospital's Chief Development Officer is up first, but you'll have to go out before he stands to speak."

It was like Karen had inhabited my assistant's body. I scowled at him.

A strange sensation prickled at my spine. Had to be nerves. I tried to shake it off. I rolled my shoulders and stretched my arms.

If I could have done push-ups without looking like a moron around a dozen people, I would have.

Something was happening, which was why I sent Patrick out to check. I'd hired him as my assistant two years ago when I first came up with the idea to add a family and sibling's activity center to the hospital. My goal was to create a place where patients could go play when they were healthy enough, but somewhere siblings could enjoy when they spent hours, days, sometimes weeks, living within the walls of the hospital. Always second. Always the outsider. The forgotten one simply because chemo and tests and surgeries and physical therapy and myriad appointments took precedence.

Did it make me feel like a rotten asshole for the times I hated being around my brother? Sometimes.

Most days, I just remembered how fucking cool he was before he got sick. How he could build Legos better than me and how he ran faster. He always kept his room clean where mine was a disaster. From the time he could talk, his favorite obsession was football and by the time he was six, he knew more stats than I did to this very day.

Basically, Harrison was the coolest fucking guy I ever met. I hated being in the hospital with him with nothing to do except read old, worn children's books and watch lame television.

Those days sucked.

I wanted to make those sucky days better for everyone.

But it wasn't my upcoming speech or Patrick and Karen's insanity currently making my spine itch with the need to be inside a woman. It was something else unsettling me.

I shook it off, loosened my arms like I did before a play.

"What is your problem?" Patrick asked. He stared at me like I'd just taken a shit in my pants.

Of course he would. I was never antsy.

"Nothing. It's just this weird feeling."

Like in high school when I knew the girl I crushed on was about to walk down the hall and run right into me. Those premonition moments in your life where you knew you weren't going to like what happened next.

Coupled with the fact I was still fighting against my dick going hard whenever I thought about the woman from last night, and this was a problem.

"Whatever," Patrick said and went back to peer through the panel. He turned to me and waved. "Come on. Your turn. President is out there now."

All right, asshole. You got this. Suck it up. Say your speech. Speak about the part of your life that you hate thinking of but the more you share, the more people you help.

All the mental focusing techniques I used on the field didn't work.

I walked out to loud applause, reporters settling notebooks and tablets in their lap.

And it took one second.

One fucking second.

To realize the girl I couldn't get out of my head?

She was sitting in the first fucking row.

With a press pass dangling from a lanyard around her neck. A neck I'd had my hand clamped around barely over twelve hours ago.

Holy fucking shit.

I was So. Damned. Screwed.

SIX

Elizabeth

I spent hours digging into Gage Bryant. I scoured his social media, researched his past. I copied down stats and records he'd either already set or was on his way to setting.

So far this season, he'd grabbed the record for most one hundred receiving yard for the first nine games. The previous record held it at six.

I'd studied him enough, trying to ignore how freaking handsome the man was, how genial he came across in interviews. He hosted summer football camps for underprivileged kids. He frequently gave away box seat tickets for families with sick children.

In short, the man came across as the most beautiful Saint I'd ever read about. Amanda had also been right. In the four years since he was traded to Raleigh, there was not a single photo of him anywhere with a woman other than his mom. Not at galas, not at publicity events. He was photographed with teammates and their wives or girlfriends, but he was always the single guy. Which sent a thousand questions spinning in my mind.

How was this amicable, philanthropic, gorgeous specimen of a man, still single?

It was a question I couldn't look into too much like Amanda said earlier, but that didn't stop my curiosity. He was minutes from appearing at the press conference and I was seated in the front row. Next to me, the seat was empty, but there was a label marked for Connor Hopkins. My ex. The guy who broke my heart. In the six months since he ended things, while I was still hooked to that damn cross at Velvet and left without unbinding me, I'd avoided him at every opportunity. That alone had been difficult since he worked for a competing local network.

Now I was screwed.

In order to avoid a conversation with him whenever he arrived, I busied myself with studying my notes, flipping through my tablet, reading up on the construction process on the new family and children's wing. A rustle of movement went through the gathered reporters. Murmurs increased and grew antsy. This was how a press conference always went. The bubbling excitement before a story and one as important as this was for our community had brought in several dozens of reporters.

I glanced at the makeshift stage. The Chief Development Officer, Miles McGregor, was there, fiddling with papers at the podium. Dressed in a well-cut gray suit, Miles was about as old as my parents but carried himself with an air of authority even from where I sat. Two men spoke to him, one who kept looking back behind the curtain off to the side and they walked off the stage. My eyes slid in that direction, the sway of curtains, and a spark of awareness tickled the back of my neck.

How odd. I rubbed my neck and dipped back down to my tablet. I was scrolling through local news when a shadow crossed in front of me, and a voice I knew well spoke.

"Well hello there, Lizzie."

Connor. Of course. I cringed at the ridiculous nickname. Something no one but him used.

"Connor." I didn't spare him a glance.

He took his seat, and I swore he leaned in closer so his thigh pressed against mine. I shifted and crossed my legs, moving as far away from him without bumping the reporter next to me.

"How are you? Haven't seen you out and about much recently."

He meant at Velvet where we met and we were ended. I brushed a chunk of hair behind my ear and stared at the stage. This conference could start any second now. "It's weird you've been looking for me. Doubt Mel would like it."

His girlfriend. The woman he'd started fucking the very night after he walked out on me.

It took effort, yet I resisted the urge to show any emotion. Mostly looking like I wanted to puke. How naïve I'd been to think hot sex in a private room and a few dinners meant we actually had a relationship.

It'd do me well to remember the fiasco with Connor if I saw *John* again.

"I was hoping I'd see you. I'd like to talk to you about something."

"No. Now leave me alone."

"Now, Lizzie—"

"Welcome everyone." A cheerful, feminine voice rang through the microphone, blissfully cutting off Connor's impudent retort. Like I care what he had to say. If I could have jumped the stage and hugged my current savior, I would have.

"We are here today to announce the upcoming opening of the almost fully completed Family and Siblings Event Room located on the fifth floor of our hospital. It is my honor today to introduce to you the Chief Development Officer and a man he's worked very closely with to ensure this project has been completed successfully. If you would, please do me the honor of welcoming Miles McGregor and Gage Bryant."

As the woman spoke, she turned and lifted her arm toward the side. Out walked Mr. McGregor, quickly followed by Gage Bryant. Both men smiled widely and waved one of their hands in the air.

A half-dozen men and women flanked them. I gaped at them as they sauntered to the center of the stage. I couldn't look away.

Gage Bryant's gaze scanned the crowd of reporters and then landed on me. And that tickle of awareness I felt earlier intensified to a full-blown spark, rushing down my spine.

His eyes narrowed on me and until he was standing to McGregor's left behind the podium, he didn't once look away.

Oh My God. He was sexier in person. Several inches taller and so much larger than any person on the stage. His height advantage coupled with the raised stage gave him the appearance of a giant.

The sexiest, most beautiful giant I could have ever conjured in all my youthful years when I used to dream of fairy tales and heroes.

Good freaking Lord. My lips parted as that warmth in my spine spread. My fingertips heated until I barely remembered I had to take notes.

And next to me, Connor leaned in closer, whispered in my ear. "He's not all that, but it looks like you like it. Have a crush on the superstar, Lizzie?"

I turned to him and hissed. "Stop calling me that." If I could have shot flaming darts from my eyes, Connor's black soul would be my target. "And permanently, stop talking to me. Whatever you want from me, you'll never get."

I should have turned away sooner, but I didn't. Instead, I caught the gleam in Connor's eyes. As if my disgust of him was a turn-on. God. Just my luck I had to sit next to my ex-boyfriend. Next time, I was switching seats. Screw protocol and manners.

I faced the stage, returning to finally catch Mr. McGregor had already started speaking. I mentally scribbled down another reason to despise Connor and paid attention to the reason why I was here. But even as I tried to focus on the speaker as he spoke about the hospital, the donations and the fundraising involved to get this project off the ground, it was the man at his side who continued to snag my attention.

Good Lord. Men like him shouldn't be allowed in public. I took him in discreetly, drawn to the silver tie knotted tightly beneath the collar of his black dress shirt. It sat there, snug and perfectly done at the base of his throat. His cheeks were clean shaven, his jaw square. It was impossible not to stare at him.

He was just so damn pretty.

My tongue slid out, licking my lips, and my eyes caught on his. He was looking directly at me, eyes like coal. Thick lashes. Even thicker brows pulled into two straight slashes at his forehead. One long line furrowed across.

His jaw ticked and he turned toward Mr. McGregor. I focused my attention on him as well, questions pummeling my mind. What in the hell had I done to make him look so angry? Did he not even want to be here? And why? Because the man on stage, glowering at me looked like he wanted to throttle me.

Inhaling a deep breath, I forced myself to focus. Despite his off the charts good looks, this was a job, not an afternoon hook-up meet and greet. And yet, that awareness. The way my body was responding, a warmth between my thighs, my pulse quickening. Good grief. The man from last night had ignited my libido and now I apparently wanted to jump everyone. I was being ridiculous and unprofessional.

"I will stop my excited rambling now," Miles said, earning himself a round of polite laughter. "And let the man of the hour finish explaining, most importantly, the true reason why this wing is so important. If you'll join me, please welcome the best wide receiver in the league, Raleigh's very own, Gage Bryant."

I sat motionless, hands frozen to my tablet screen while Gage stepped forward. As he moved, clasping hands with McGregor, his body moved in fluid motion, calm and smooth. Impressive for a man his size.

He reached the podium and scanned the crowd, slid to Connor next to me, and then narrowed on me. "Thank you."

He yanked his gaze away from me as if it hurt him to look at me and as he started speaking, my hands curled into fists. What was this? I'd never experienced such a strong reaction to any man and worse, I couldn't remember a man who had ever looked at me with such contempt.

I didn't have time to think about it. He was speaking and my job was to report.

"Many of you know I come from a small family in Southern Ohio. My dad is a pastor and my mom helped out at their church until she quit to volunteer at a local hospital."

My eyes were fixated on his hands. They were large, strong and tan, veined and so damn sexy. They were also curled around the edge of the podium and a man his size risked snapping the cheap wood in two if he wasn't careful. The tenseness in his body drew my focus in.

"What you don't know, is that I lived most of my young child-hood in a hospital similar to the one here today in Raleigh."

What? None of this was in the research I'd done. I scribbled down a note to double-check, but I was listening too intently to complete my thought as he continued, without preamble, bearing his soul to reporters of all people.

"My brother was eight when he died of leukemia. He'd beat it once when he was younger. Lost a year of school to the disease that ravaged his blood before we celebrated that we believed he'd been healed. When he was seven, it returned. And I know what it's like to fight the fight of childhood cancer. I know what's it like to live inside these halls, the forgotten child, the healthy kid who gets pushed to the back burner because there is a sibling who demands so much more."

Around the room, there were a few quiet gasps, a few more sniffles. My own eyes stung. Oh my God. This was horrific. My chest tightened and burned down to my stomach.

"Don't get me wrong," Gage continued. He flashed the crowd a smile, one that could incinerate a woman's panties. My very own were melting despite the professionalism I was trying to maintain. "My parents are incredible people. They didn't *try* to make me feel that way, it's just the nature of the beast when you're dealing with something so difficult."

His voice trailed off, and once again, his gaze slid across the room, bouncing from person to person. He landed on me again and when he did, that heat in my thighs began *pulsing*. Oh my God. I was turned on listening to him talk about his deceased brother. What was wrong with me?

"Over the next couple of weeks, I ask you to keep that in mind. I haven't dedicated the last several years of my life wanting and fighting and raising money and planning and sleepless nights for this new children's wing out of a sense of duty. It's out of a sense of realism. I wanted to give the kids in this hospital some-thing I never had...time to play, to be a kid, time to throw a ball around with my brother when he was too ill to leave. This addi-tion at the hospital isn't a duty to volunteer hours or because I have too much money I don't know what to do with." A small round of laughter burst and silenced quickly. "It's because I've lived this. Harrison would have loved this. I've donated my time and money not to a cause to have my name look good in the press." He flashed a smirk. "Not that you guys would do that of course." Another round of laughter. This time a little bit louder.

"I do this because this was my life and the kids that are fighting all manner of diseases and cancers and viruses that fill the halls in the building...well, they deserve something. They're not weak even when ravaged. They're not sad, even when they know the end is coming before the rest of us. These kids, the sick ones, they're the strongest humans on the planet and they deserve to have a little bit of joy and peace and fun to continue to give them strength."

He pulled to an abrupt stop and stepped back. His speech wasn't over. His jaw was open like he had more to say but his gaze went to something and I caught movement. A young woman dressed in teal scrubs hurried down the aisle.

Murmurs erupted as she grabbed all of our attention. She hurried to Gage and before she reached him, he was back, leaning into the microphone. "Excuse me. I need to go."

The woman's face look panicked.

Gage's looked destroyed. Cameras flashed as he hopped off the stage, practically hurdling the podium, and hurried back down the aisle.

He ran out the door at the back, not even saying a single word to the nurse, but whatever it happened was bad and he knew it.

I had no idea what possessed me to do it, what drove me, but I was on my feet, following as quickly as possible before I could stop myself.

I FOLLOWED him to the fifth floor, the benefit of lighted floors above elevators telling me where he'd disappeared to.

I stepped off the elevator, assaulted immediately with a painted mural showing underwater sea creatures. It was beautiful with its bright vivid colors. Humpback whale and bright coral at the bottom, bubbles coming up from sea anemone plants, the bright orange tail of a fish peeking out behind. It was incredibly well done, with dozens of fish and whale and a few sharks and stretched at least thirty-five feet. It went from floor to ceiling, the perfect bright art a kid could stare at for hours and always find something new to admire.

I shook my head and turned toward the hallway. The nurse's station was empty and thank goodness.

What story did I have to give them to get past other than, "Um, hi, I'm stalking Gage Bryant and I'm not supposed to be here, but let me through anyway?"

Right. That'd go over as well as my mom trying to get me to believe asparagus tasted just like green beans. Please.

I slowed my steps in the hallway even though my heart raced at terrifying speeds. I forced myself to look like I belonged. Rearranged the features of my face, I tried for stoic, even though my gaze bounced back and forth, into the windows at the sides of the doors to rooms. I didn't gawk. I didn't stare. Yet with each room I passed, an unknown emotion rippled through me.

These were *kids*. Of course they were. I was in a children's hospital for crying out loud. But the reality of what Gage had actually done, who he was doing it for, hadn't hit me until I passed almost a dozen rooms, filled with children too young to have to face such opposition in their little lives. And babies. Hooked to tubes and monitors, and one with so many you could barely see the tiny infant beneath the tape.

God. Help them.

I chanted the prayer in my head, my jaw aching from clenching my teeth. Gage Bryant had *lived* this. It was all so unbelievably horrible that I almost didn't notice when I found him.

His back was to me, but I'd just spent a good twenty minutes staring at his hair, his clothes, his enormous size, that my feet pulled short when I caught a glimpse of him through a narrow window.

He was seated in a chair so small it looked like it could buckle under the weight of him. His head was bowed, turned slightly to the left, his jaw moving, speaking. And on the bed, a little boy. Bald. Bright blue eyes. Sickly in color and in his bony frame.

And yet he *glowed*. His smile was so big, his age young enough to show he was still too small for all of his teeth to fit properly into his mouth. Cracked, dry lips stretched into the largest grin I'd ever seen in my life.

Why had Gage left for this? I felt like I was intruding. I shouldn't have followed him in the first place and whatever brought me there wasn't for a story. Not this kind anyway. My phone was in my pocket, but it'd stay there. No way was I taking a picture of Gage Bryant in such a private moment even if it would help the story.

"Can I help you?"

I jerked back, stunned I hadn't been paying attention and when I turned, I saw the prettiest woman, sad, such sad eyes, head tilted to the left, dried tears had ruined what little makeup she'd had on.

"I'm sorry," I said, I shook my head, feeling ten thousands kinds of crappy for whatever I was doing. "I just...Gage had been at the press conference and took off—"

I sounded like an asshole. A gossip columnist. An ambulance chaser of a lawyer doing anything for a story. And worse, it wasn't me. Shame chilled my brain. I had nothing good to say.

"You're a reporter," the woman said. She glanced in the window and back to me.

"I am. And I'm sorry. I shouldn't be here."

One shoulder of her rose and dropped slowly. "I don't know. Seems to me y'all should be meeting some of the families Gage wants to help, right?"

She spoke of Gage so personally. Then again, he was bent over the bed of who I assumed now was her son. But how long had she known him? And why did the thought it could have been for awhile *hurt*? How long had her son been sick?

"It's okay," I mumbled. "I should really go."

"I think that you, as pretty as you are, would probably make Brandon smile. Would you like to meet him?"

No way. Not with Gage there. Not with the way he'd glared at me so viciously earlier. He would not want me there. "He's not a story," I said. There was no way I was going to have her son glorified in his illness.

"Trust me," she said. "If it helps other families, other kids like him, Brandon would want to be." With that stunning response, she tossed out her hand. "I'm Penny. Brandon's mom."

"Elizabeth," I said.

"I know." She winked and her hand went to the door. "We watch a lot of news around here. Not much else is on and Brandon really loved your last story of the pregnant elephant at the zoo. He said he wouldn't have learned that much in school if he was able to be there. Trust me, he'll be thrilled to meet you."

My cheeks flamed bright hot at the compliment, and I could no longer hurry away like I should have before I even stepped off the floor. Instead, Penny had opened the door and stepped back, waving me in.

Why did it feel like I was walking a plank on a pirate ship as my feet trudged forward?

SEVEN

Gage

"You're pulling my leg," Brandon said. His frail body shook with laughter but to egg him on further, I did what he just accused me of doing except this time literally.

I reached out and yanked his ankle. "Now I am. But it's the truth. Ferrets are evil, evil little creatures."

Every time I visited Brandon I always made sure to tell him a story about an animal. Most of them were from my childhood when we lived in the house the church provided my dad and backed up to a creek. There was always some sort of animal wandering through our land. Foxes. Deer. Raccoons. Snakes and rodents.

Mom used to get so pissed off I kept coming home with toads shoved into my shirt pockets. And the day it was a baby snake in my jeans pocket I thought I'd end up sleeping on a street corner bench.

This particular story I'd told him was about my college roommate's ferrets. Hennessy loved those things like they were family.

Always carrying Tater and Tot around on his shoulders. Gross as hell.

Those things freaked me out and Hennessy had been even scarier.

"The pet store he bought them from assured him they were both girl ferrets. Turns out they were wrong."

"Ten of them, though?" His pale face scrunched up.

"Yup. Ten little babies. And they were all on my bed when I got home from practice. Covered in goo and everything."

I had to throw away all my bedding. No way was I going to just wash the sheets and comforter and sleep under sheets where a ferret had given birth. I might have been a guy and a jock, but I had some standards for cleanliness. A ferret's afterbirth crossed the line.

"That's gross." He laughed this hoarse, painful sound and we both heard the door open and turned our heads.

And what the hell?

I pushed off the chair immediately standing in front of Brandon.

She'd *followed* me? "What are you doing here?"

It was hard enough watching the other reporter look like he was flirting with her only a few feet away and I couldn't do a damn thing about it. It was even worse when I had to fight my dick going hard having Beth...Elizabeth thanks to the nametag she was wearing...so damn close to me. So far away.

And shit. She was a damn reporter. The kind who sniffed out stories and spilled secrets. And the woman I'd had bound last night, screaming out in ecstasy was now following me for the next two weeks.

It was a disaster and maybe I was staring at her, being a dick I wasn't normally, but this was bad.

Did she know who I was? Could she tell?

Her cheeks blushed and she whipped her head to Penny. "Um. Well..."

"I ran into Miss Hayes." She leaned to the side, catching Brandon's attention. "You remember her, right? From the news?"

A smack hit my back. "Move Gage. Miss Hayes? From the zoo?"

He knew her? My fucking luck. I stepped to the side and dipped my head to Brandon. "You know her?"

"Yeah...she taught me a lot about the elephants!" His dry lips cracked as he smiled and proceeded to ignore me.

"Hi Brandon," the sexy little minx said. Her cheeks were hot pink. Hands trembled at her sides. She gave me a wide berth as she stepped closer to the bed.

The mere nearness of her sent my blood boiling and not solely from anger.

This woman did it for me in a thousand different ways. My hands curled into fists. Somehow I had to resist the urge currently pummeling me to wrap my hand around her arm and yank her out to the hallway, demanding answers.

Avoiding my furious glare, one I saved for my most hated opponents on the field, she stepped lightly to the side and held out her shaking hand to Brandon. "It's so nice to meet you."

He didn't shake her hand. Brandon adjusted his pillows, sat up straighter and without warning, he flung his arms around Beth's neck, pulling her close and almost off her feet. "Hi! I think you're the greatest. We watch you *all* the time on the TV because mom always says there's nothing on but trash and news in the afternoon. And I loved when you went to the zoo."

He relaxed his hold on her and patted the bed. "Sit with me. Tell me everything about the giraffes and the elephants and the penguins, too!"

It was a miracle. He might have laughed at the ferret story, but it'd been weeks, if not months since I'd seen Brandon light up with so much enthusiasm.

Beth...Elizabeth...Miss Hayes...what in the hell should I call her? I hadn't given her enough space to sit on the bed without bumping into me and as she shifted to do as Brandon commanded with fervent glee, her eyes slid anxiously to me, nibbling her lip. "Um. Excuse me," she said, so quiet like a mouse.

Funny.

Twenty-four hours ago, I'd walked into a room with her only wearing white lace panties and a blindfold and she hadn't shown an ounce of hesitancy. Yet there she was, barely able to meet my gaze.

She had *no* idea I was the man who'd fucked her into oblivion last night.

Which worked for me.

"I'll give you two a moment," I said, my voice was gruff. Angry and relieved.

Damn it. I didn't want her to know who I was. That was the whole fucking point of the blindfold and the private membership at Velvet. So why was I relieved and pissed the hell off she was acting like she didn't actually remember me?

Talk about a blow to the ego.

I spun around and nodded to Penny. "Can I get you a coffee? Lunch?"

"I'm good, but a little walk might be nice." She grinned at Brandon. "You two going to be okay here?"

"Yeah, Mom. Miss Hayes will hang out with me, won't you?" His head whipped to hers so fast it was amazing it didn't cause vertigo. If it did, he hid it well.

She was dressed in a tight black skirt that was currently riding high on her thighs from her perch on the hospital bed. It took serious effort to pull my eyes off her legs to her face. I could have looked my fill though since she didn't notice. Her gaze was fixed on Penny, studiously avoiding me.

Huh. Did she or did she not remember? I had to find out.

"Sure, Penny. I can stay for a few minutes." Slowly, Miss Hayes's gaze moved and rose, met mine. "I'm assuming I have some time? Or will you finish the conference?"

I'd completely forgotten. As soon as the nurse hurried into the room where I was speaking, all I could think of was getting to Brandon.

Thankfully, he was still awake when I got here and now he was looking more energetic than I'd seen him in a long time. "I'll reschedule that time. Penny?"

She pressed her hand to Brandon's leg. "Have a good time. We'll be close okay though, honey?"

"I'm good, Mom," Brandon said it through a yawn and that lump in my throat grew.

Incredible how his energy levels could drop so suddenly.

"Come on," Penny said. Her hand pressed to my arm and grabbed my attention. "Let's give them a few minutes."

"We'll be back, bud, okay?"

"Sure Gage." He was already ignoring me. His eyes and attention on the pretty little blonde sitting on his bed, smiling down at him like he was the best thing since dark chocolate.

Couldn't blame her.

The kid was cool as hell.

"COME THIS WAY." Penny had her hand wrapped around my forearm and as she spoke, she pulled me to the wing almost set to open. The bright teal walls still smelled like fresh paint, but it was the Rough Riders logo that she stepped in front of.

"You're not happy I brought that reporter into the room. Why?"

I'd rather shove a toothpick into my eye than tell Penny why Miss Hayes wasn't wanted in that room. "That time was for Brandon and me. Not some reporter who followed me out of the press conference."

Penny rolled her eyes. She had that *mom* look down. It was so much like my own mom's when I was a kid and doing or saying something stupid I was fighting a smile despite still being pissed.

"Come on. You had to know you run out of there in the middle of speaking and they were going to lose their minds. That was news in the making."

She was teasing me, but it didn't sit well. I hadn't actually considered the response I'd get when I practically hurdled the podium as soon as I saw the nurse.

Mostly because I didn't know her, but she'd looked panicked, and that panic sent my blood rushing.

"Besides," Penny continued, not caring one iota I was most likely glaring at her. "Brandon loves her. Seriously, I think he has a crush on her. She's cute, right?"

She tugged on my arm playfully.

"Penny." My tone was warning. Also a bit rough. Besides, she was more than cute.

"Well, you know I'm a sucker for giving Brandon what he wants, but that's not why I invited her into the room when I caught her blushing while she peeked through the window?"

"She was what?"

"Well, she was blushing. And I have a feeling it wasn't because she was sweet on Brandon."

Blushing. *Had* she had the same visceral reaction to me I'd had to her?

I shook the thought out of my head. Thinking of the reporter led to a hard dick and I was standing two feet from a woman who was close enough to me to be my sister.

"Besides," Penny kept talking, "this is what she's here for, isn't it? I mean, I'm assuming she was at the press conference so she's covering you and the wing opening. So it makes sense she talks to one of your favorite patients."

"Brandon is not a story."

"That's where you're wrong, Gage." Her usual friendly expression vanished and in its place was the look of a mama bear. A woman who would fight and die and bleed so her son didn't have to. "Brandon is the *exact* reason for the story. Him and kids like him and their families. He is exactly why you've done all of this and people should see who you're helping. I want them to. More, he'll want to do it."

My teeth fused together and I turned to the window. It was October but unseasonably warm with no hint the weather would be cooling anytime soon. The colored leaves on the tops of the trees swayed back and forth in the breeze. I was feeling anything but gentle and calm.

Spending more time around this woman was not a good idea.

It was the absolute worst idea. But I was as much of a sucker for giving Brandon anything he wanted, too.

"Fine. Whatever Brandon wants."

She nudged me in the arm with her shoulder. I barely felt the impact and grinned down at her. "That's the spirit," she teased. "Let's get back so you can talk to her, too."

She all but dragged my hand and I allowed her to pull me back down the hallway, on the way thinking how right Penny was.

The whole freaking reason I'd wanted to create the center she'd just taken me to was for Brandon and kids like him and their families. And who better than to share his story, share what it would mean to him, than one of the bravest kids I knew?

~

"ONE MORE PICTURE." Brandon yawned. We'd been back in the room for thirty minutes and he'd been awake for almost an hour. He was fading quickly but smiling. Next to him, Elizabeth was still sitting on the bed. He was propped up on pillows and morphine to keep his pain away along with stronger antibiotics through his PIC line to kick his current infection.

"You're tired honey," Penny said, but she was still holding her phone and Elizabeth's.

Mine was firmly pocketed in my back pocket. I had enough photos of Brandon and a few other kids I'd met and bonded with, but no way was I getting it out. I didn't need the photo memory of the pesky little reporter who was distracting me more and more with every passing minute we were crammed together on Brandon's bed.

I should probably be sent to hell with the ideas I had for what I could do with her on a bed while we took picture after picture, sometimes the three of us, sometimes the two of them.

But hot damn, the woman was sexy and sweet and when Penny and I came back to the room, Brandon's cheeks had actually been pink. The first sign of healthy color he'd shown in awhile.

I figured because even though he was sick and a little kid, Brandon still had man's blood running through him and not a single man on this planet could be around Elizabeth and not get hot in at least one place.

Still, the fact I'd been hiding a hardening dick for the last thirty minutes had crossed the point of painful twenty minutes ago.

"I can come back another day," Elizabeth said. She covered Brandon's hand with hers.

"No." His eyes drooped and popped open. Hell, he'd fall asleep while talking if we didn't get out of there.

"Let's do that," I said. I'd been close to Elizabeth but seeing Brandon struggle, I moved in closer. She was right in front of me. Her shoulder to my chest. I caught a whiff of her flowery scent and squeezed my eyes closed. Good God. Just the smell of her turned me on.

"Another day, Brandon. We'll be here a lot this week and next."

He yawned again and his head fell forward. Nodding, he whispered, "Just one more. Of you two then."

His voice went raspy and I barely heard him, but as I registered his words, the woman in front of me stiffened. She shook her head and all that hair swished back and forth, brushing along the back of my hand.

Goddamn. I'd just had it wrapped around my fist and the more I was around her, two things had become clear.

She truly had no idea who I was.

But...she really fucking liked what she saw whenever she looked at me.

I could practically smell her arousal.

"Okay, Brandon," Elizabeth said. She leaned in and kissed his cheek. The pink had faded, but at her lips on his skin, he cracked a huge smile. "Only one though, and then I'll let you get some rest."

She slid off the bed, her whole back brushing my chest. I was so close, she almost stumbled back toward the bed and I wrapped my hands around her tiny waist to keep her on her feet.

"Oh." Her hands went to mine at her stomach and at that first touch of her, flesh on flesh, the same heated spark I felt last night shot right to my chest and mainlined to my dick.

"Sorry," she said and threw her hands off me.

And shit. I was a goner. "No worries," I whispered along the top of her head. "Just didn't want you falling on him." I pulled us a step back and with my hand still wrapped around her, because I was a fucking *idiot*, I gestured toward Penny.

She stood on the other side of the room, smirking.

"Take the picture, Penny." My voice was a growl.

Penny laughed, snapped a few photos on her phone and then Elizabeth's.

I dropped my hand from Elizabeth's waist and stepped back.

"I'll see y'all later. I figure by now Patrick and Karen have both lost their minds at my disappearance."

"I'll see you later," Elizabeth said. She wasn't looking at me, but at the bed where Brandon's head had fallen back. His lips were parted and his chest rose in even breaths.

Damn. The kid had fallen asleep in seconds.

"Right," I said to Elizabeth and then to Penny, "I'll check in tomorrow."

"You got it, hotshot."

I turned and hightailed it out of the room, not saying goodbye to Elizabeth.

Being around her longer could be dangerous. And stupid. It was making me think of stupid things like how I wanted that hair draped all over my body while she rode me hard and fast.

Or maybe how I wanted to see those sexy as hell eyes of her light up while she came instead of hiding behind black satin.

Yeah. Seeing Elizabeth again was going to be pure hell.

EIGHT

Elizabeth

"Come on," Amanda pleaded from her side of the four-top table. "You have to tell me what he was like. And did he smell good? These are important things girls all over the area need to know."

The woman was mad. Batshit crazy should have been her middle name. There was no way I was telling her how incredibly delicious Gage Bryant smelled, especially when he stood behind me and wrapped his strong arm around my stomach. I stumbled, not from the surprise of him touching me, but from the overwhelming arousal that shot through my body as his fingers brushed against my stomach. Even through the pink dress shirt I wore his hand still branded me like a hot iron. It had been hard enough to maintain any façade of professional composure with him in the room much less with him touching me. More than once during the photos, I caught Penny smiling, looking like she was fighting bursting into giggles. We were circling each other and had to look ridiculous.

What was more frustrating was that if I had to guess, it

appeared Gage was struggling with the same thing. But he couldn't be.

I had definitely angered him when he found out I followed him out of the press conference. That anger at some point had shifted to something else, and I didn't know if it was because he was trying his best to be cordial for Brandon's sake, or if it was something else.

It also didn't matter. He was a story and that was it. I just had to stop thinking of how attractive he was.

"There's nothing I can tell you that you don't already know. Gage is hot, he's much taller and bigger in person than I expected him to be, and under all of that he seems like a really decent guy." And when he touched me I got so turned on I couldn't help but imagine him as the man from Velvet.

And doing that had disaster written all over it. Gage Bryant was the subject of a story.

My job. That was all.

Across from me, Amanda crossed her arms and pouted. "You're no fun. And I think you're breaking about a dozen rules of the girl's club."

"What are those rules?" I asked. I took a sip of my white wine and sat back against the booth.

"The rule," she said dramatically, leaning forward, splaying out her hand along the table. "Is that it is required to spill every detail about any celebrity sighting, especially one as private as Gage Bryant. Really, it's disappointing I have to explain this to you."

"You're a nut. There's nothing to tell. I'm trying to be professional."

"Ugh." She rolled her eyes and reached for her wine, shaking her head. "You and your ethics. You're a disappointment to the profession."

I wadded up a napkin and tossed it at her face. "You're weird."

"And I'm horny as heck just thinking about you getting to spend this much time around the guy. I mean, he's an enigma. He barely updates his social media. He's rarely caught out around town. It seems like he doesn't have a personal life at all because the only time we see him is at volunteer or team events. Don't you think that's strange?"

"What, that he wants his privacy?"

"No, silly. That in the four years he's been here, there's never been a single word of him dating someone. I mean, look at Beaux Hale or Oliver Powell. They're in the news all the time with their wives, and they were before they were married. Powell could hardly step out of the hotel he always used to stay at with a woman on his arm and not have it hit the Raleigh Rich and Famous blogs."

"So you think it's strange he's a football player and he isn't a player off the field?" Amanda's logic was a curious thing.

"Well, yeah."

I waved her off. "It doesn't matter. My job isn't to uncover some hidden secret about his love life, and after meeting Brandon today and spending time with him, I really need to focus on the story." I hadn't been able to get the little boy out of my head since yesterday. It was the only reason I agreed to go out for a drink with Amanda even though I was short on time. I still needed to get dressed for a fundraising dinner in a few hours, but I figured a quick bite and a glass of wine would calm my nerves, get me relaxed so I could focus.

BECAUSE YEAH...AFTER spending an afternoon around Gage, I was totally distracted. Mostly because I wanted to know every single thing about him, relevant to the story, and most defi-nitely, not.

"See." She pointed her finger at me and twirled it in a circle. "You're so professional it's sickening."

"Can I remind you that you're the one who told me yesterday morning not to go digging too hard in the direction you're talking about?"

"Well, yeah, but you're smart. You can dig out his secrets without having to dig too hard. Men love you. You smile your sweet little innocent smile, flip your hair, and tilt your head and men are always eating out of your hands. Mostly because they see you doing that and they want to be eatin' you somewhere else."

I had taken a sip of my drink while she spoke and ended up choking. Wine burned my nose and I covered my mouth, reaching for a napkin. "You're gross," I said. Oh God, wine in the nose burned like the dickens, as my mom always said.

"I'm honest," she declared with a mischievous grin. "And remember my words next time you're talking to Gage, would ya?"

Yeah. Because thinking of him eating me somewhere other than the palm of my hand would keep me on task.

And there was no way in hell I was telling Amanda I'd been fantasizing him doing that very same thing since yesterday.

"OH GOD." My hand pressed to my stomach over my perfectly fitted and tight black dress. One shoulder and arm was completely bare. The line of fabric cut a sharp diagonal line to my other arm where that sleeve was loose and sheer. At my waist, it cinched together and was skintight over my hips and down to the floor. My ankles wobbled on my heels, even though the silver, ultra-scrappy heels were ones I'd had for years and worn dozens of times. This was, by far, the fanciest I'd ever had to dress for an event and it wasn't only that making me feel like puking.

It was because as soon as I'd left dinner with Amanda earlier, I'd gone straight home and before I got ready, I'd reached into my nightstand, grabbed my vibrator, and proceeded to take care of myself not once, but twice.

And both times I'd fantasized Gage and his dark eyes and his inky hair and his firm muscles and rigid abs above me, beneath me, holding me down, slipping me around.

During it, I'd imagined him being that guy, doing all of those delicious things, while a black strip of satin covered my eyes.

The man, John, from last night, had said he wanted to see me again, and more than once since I'd taken care of myself, I'd not only checked my phone for messages from Tristan, hoping he requested me tonight, but I'd also resisted texting Tristan and setting it up myself.

That wasn't how it worked. Not in the beginning.

My job was to sit back, anticipate his request, and in the meantime, apparently, I was also going to drive myself insane.

But God, I'd have loved to know that after I had to spend another few hours with Gage, that I could go somewhere else and have someone take that edge off, clearing my mind of all physical reactions to the mysterious football player.

THE HILLS HOTEL was the richest and most elegant hotel in Raleigh. It was a place I'd never been but had always wanted to see the inside of. As I entered the lavish lobby with its travertine tiled floor and modern artwork and sculptures hanging from the ceiling, my already wobbly legs shook more harshly. This place was so far outside my comfort zone we weren't even in the same zip code. I made my way through the security line where they checked every handbag.

"Have a lovely evening ma'am," the security guard said to me.

"Thank you."

I headed toward the elevator and as the door opened, I stepped in and off to the side. I was immediately accompanied by two couples. I didn't have to be a football fan to recognize them. I was in the elevator with Beaux Hale, quarterback of the Raleigh Rough Riders, his wife Paige, his sister Shannon, and her husband, Oliver Powell. I also didn't have to be a fan of football to have my breath stolen by the masculinity and testosterone pulsing off of them in radiant waves. Goodness. Were all football players built like they stepped out of a marble statue mold?

Conversation was quiet as the elevator doors closed behind us. I assumed part of that quietness was due to the badge pinned to a lanyard draped around my neck. The network's rainbow-colored logo along with **PRESS** stamped in the middle generally made more famous people immediately zip their lips.

I faced the doors as we rose to the fourteenth floor where tonight's festivities included a dinner and dancing in the restaurant at the top. We would eat, drink, and be merry while we slowly turned in the circulating restaurant. On any other night, it would feel like a fantasy come true. Tonight however my nerves were ragged. The drink I had earlier had well worn out its usefulness. I was no longer relaxed and prepared.

No, the very thought of spending several more hours in the room, regardless of how large and cavernous, with Gage seemed to be an impossible task. At the very least, it would test the limits of the professionalism I so boldly proclaimed to Amanda.

"Your dress is lovely."

That came from a soft and sweet feminine voice. I lifted my gaze to the gold reflective doors and caught the cute blonde, Paige Hale, smiling politely behind me and off to my side.

"Thank you." She was dressed in a buttery yellow gown. The dress dipped low between her breasts and slid gently down the curve of her hips brushing the floor. With her hair swept up with grand curls piled on her head, others flowing just past her shoulders, she looked like she could be a Disney princess. "Yours is lovely, too. It looks great with your tan."

Her friendly grin widened. "Thanks," she said. "I bought it today."

The brunette, who I knew was Shannon Powell, laughed uproariously. "You dork," she exclaimed. "You don't tell people you got a spray tan."

Paige playfully rolled her eyes and I smiled at the banter between the two friends. This was a conversation I would have with Amanda or one of my brother's wives.

"That's ridiculous. Why do I care if anyone knows I have a spray tan?"

Shannon rolled her eyes and her voice dropped an octave. "Because it's uncouth. And tonight we are supposed to be the belles of the ball." She burst into another round of laughter and this time Paige followed her.

"I think you're the dorky one," Paige replied.

"Ladies." A stern warning came from the corner. Oliver stood straight like a statue, hands shoved into the front pockets of his tuxedo pants. He wasn't looking at his wife or his sister-in-law, though. His dead serious glare was pinned on me, and when I met his through the elevator doors, they dropped to my press badge.

I looked away from him, unable to withstand the intensity. Clearly, I wasn't to be trusted listening to them.

"Yes, ladies. If we've told you once, your father and I have told you a hundred times. No bickering in public." Beaux's faux parental voice made me crack a smile.

He was standing closest to me, and as the girls fell into more laughter, I sent him a grateful smile.

He flashed me a wink. "Don't worry about the surly man in the mirror. We forgot to remove the stick from his ass."

"Beaux—"

He lifted a hand, palm out in Oliver's direction, and grinned at me. Pointing to my badge, he declared, "Off the record of course."

His tone was teasing, but a seriousness lurked behind his eyes. He might have been teasing, but he wasn't joking.

I covered my badge. "What happens on the elevator stays on the elevator. Promise."

"In that case." He flung out his arm and wrapped it around his wife's waist, yanking her to him.

Her hands slammed to his chest and she bent backward. I jumped out of the way so she didn't hit me. "Don't you dare kiss me, Beaux Hale. You'll ruin my makeup."

"Woman. What is this hell? I have to wear a tux and I don't get to make out—"

"Gross," Shannon groaned. "You're going to make me vomit." She caught my eye and grinned. "Don't mind him. He might be an adult, but he's nothing more than an overgrown ball of dweebiness and hormones."

It was all I could do to hide my smile. "No offense taken," I assured her.

SHE HELD out her hand then and pleasantly smiled. "Shannon Powell and I've seen you on the news before. You're very sweet."

"It's nice to meet you, Shannon," I said. "Elizabeth Hayes and thank you."

She dropped my hand and then slid it to the back of her

husband. "I think it's lovely that Gage has allowed reporters to follow him over the next couple weeks. He really believes in what he's creating, and I'm glad that everyone in the state will be a part of it."

"Trust me, I'm just as honored to be here tonight, and I believe the children will be when they can play in their new wing." The doors dinged as I was finished talking, and I stepped out of the elevator quickly to allow them to exit. Shannon fell in step next to me. She carried an ease about her, devoid of any pretense that she was married to one of the richest athletes in the country.

She looped her hand around my arm like we'd been friends for decades and hadn't just met. "And don't let Oliver scare you. He's distrustful of pretty much everyone."

"Woman—" he growled, walking right behind us.

She winked at me. "See? He's such a pain in the ass."

"And if you don't stop talking shit about me to a reporter, it's your ass that's going to be feeling pain later."

"Oh." She shivered and nudged her elbow into me. "That sounds delightful." She reached out with her other hand, threaded her fingers with her husband's. "Is that a promise or a threat?"

He gave her a beleaguered sigh, but his patience with his wife ended when our eyes met.

Before he could glare at me again, I pulled away from Shannon. "I'm here to follow Gage and write a story on the children's wing. I promise that's it." And because I couldn't help myself, I continued. "There will be no mentioning spankings. Now if you'll excuse me, I'm going to grab a drink and find my table."

"I'll come find you later," Shannon said. "I might not know you—but I like you."

"Same," I replied and halted my steps so they could continue.

"Enjoy your evening," Paige said to me. Beaux flashed me his sweet, All-American boy smile.

"Enjoy your tan."

She laughed sweetly and waved her hand in the air as they passed by. "Will do!"

I waited until they were in the restaurant and took a minute to calm myself.

All four of them were as down to earth as anybody I'd ever met. With the exception of Oliver, possibly nicer. And if their friendliness was any indication of how the night would go, perhaps I'd be able to enjoy myself and not be so fixated on Gage Bryant after all.

NINE

Gage

"Wow, Gage, honey. This is marvelous." My mom's hand pressed firmer on my forearm. I was escorting her into the Hills hotel restaurant and reception room where tonight's event would soon start.

"Thanks, Mom."

It didn't matter how many fancy restaurants I took my parents to or what presents I bought them, including the new Enclave SUV for her last year. I'd wanted to buy her something nicer, something more luxurious. With everything my parents had been through, and as much they'd always supported me, I always wanted her to have the best.

I also knew she'd refuse, concerned it wouldn't look good for the pastor's wife of a small, country church in Ohio to drive around in something so 'excessive,' as she called it.

I disagreed but respected her enough to get her something new and shiny but something she'd also feel comfortable driving around.

That was Sue and Graham Bryant. Simple pleasures. Gentle lives full of love and serving and gratitude.

"You done good, son," my dad said as we came to a stop.

A waiter appeared in front of us carrying a tray filled with champagne.

"No thank you," I told him. "But can you have someone bring us some sparkling waters?"

"Certainly Mr. Bryant."

"It's always so weird when they call you that instead of me," my dad said, playfully teasing me. His smile fell. "Not kidding, son. We've told you this a lot, but this, what you're doing, and what you're pouring your wealth into...well, we want you to know that you could do nothing for the rest of your life and we'll always be so darn proud of you."

"Thanks, Dad." I let go of my mom's hand in order to pull my dad to me. I grew up in a strict home, forced to not only follow the rules of the house but be a good example outside of it lest I brought any shame to my parents.

While I never necessarily got pissed about it, it was a lot of responsibility to put on a kid. And that was the crux of most of my life, because in so many ways, I was still that kid, not wanting to embarrass them.

They'd always love me, but I never wanted to bring negative attention to their purpose and calling.

Hence the membership at Velvet and why continuing anything with Elizabeth was a bad idea.

Perhaps the first bad idea I was still going to follow through with.

I walked them around the room, guiding them toward our table. We stopped and spoke with several players, their wives who embraced my mom in their arms like she was theirs, too.

It's how my parents *were*. Regardless of religious affiliation or lack thereof, people met my mom and immediately felt pulled to her. Like they'd always had her smiles and goodness and oatmeal chocolate chip cookies in their lives.

By the time I had them at our table where we'd sit with the Rough Rider's coaches and wives or girlfriends, I'd already clocked Elizabeth.

Somehow, in a room of hundreds, her presence was still a vibrant beacon.

She was off to the far side, halfway to the bar, a flute glass in her hand. Even from the distance separating us, I found her easily. It unsettled me. One night of perfect sex shouldn't have me so on edge.

I'd never before been drawn so forcefully to a woman. Sure there were women who would play the game, go digging for a guy with deep pockets and do it fluidly without the man knowing if he was even being conned, but those women had never been attractive to me.

This woman played no games and after considering her reactions to me earlier, spending way too much time after the hospital thinking about her, there was no way she recognized me from the other night.

Which meant as long as I kept my distance with her professionally, I could still see her personally.

But that meant I was forced to keep my distance, and I didn't very much like that idea, either.

She was talking to a man I didn't know, but another reporter based on the badge draped around his neck that matched hers.

Her body called to me. Wrapped deliciously in a black dress, one of her arms was completely bare. The sleeve of the other was loose and sheer but classy. A line slashed from that shoulder to just over her breast on the other side. It hung loosely on top, gathered at her trim waist and then was skin tight from what I could see, down to the floor.

She had to have on at least six-inch heels to make herself appear so much taller.

I wanted to rip them off her feet. I liked her smaller size. She was petite. She had a personality ten times larger than her height and a beauty that surpassed it all.

"She's pretty," my mom said. Her gaze was on Elizabeth.

Shit. I was doing a bang-up job of keeping my distance.

"She's a reporter covering the story."

"Hmm."

I peered at my mom. She might have been sweet and kind but biting her tongue wasn't her strong suit. "What?"

She grinned at me over the edge of her champagne flute that held sparkling water. "I didn't say anything."

I gave her a look. "That sound said enough."

"If you say so." She laughed lightly and I bent, kissed her cheek. "Don't you need to speak soon?"

"Yeah. You bring your tissues?"

"Always have them when you speak of this, honey. And I know your dad said earlier how proud we are of you, but I just want you to know, if Harrison was here, he would have grown up looking to you like his real-life hero, and he would have chosen a man worthy of that honor to look up to."

Damn her. Making me teary-eyed and emotional before I spoke was plain evil.

"Mom. If Harrison survived, don't you know I would have spent my life looking to him as the real-life hero?"

After all, that would have meant he defied death.

"Darn it." She sniffed and opened her clutch. "You weren't supposed to make me cry yet."

I kissed her cheek again and hugged her quickly. "You started it."

She slapped my back. "Such a child. Go. Make us proud."

Which meant when I walked away from my mom, my dad

taking over his job of hugging her as I passed her over, I went to the stage not thinking of Elizabeth and what I wanted to do to her at Velvet as soon as fucking possible, I went focused on the entire damn reason and purpose for the night.

My mom was a miracle worker without even realizing it.

Or, perhaps she was just that damn smart and knew exactly what she'd done.

I wouldn't put either past her.

I GAVE my welcome speech and promised the reporters I would give them a few minutes to ask the questions that I didn't get to answer yesterday due to my hasty departure. We ate dinner and once the music kicked in afterward, several of the player's wives took to the dance floor.

I was in the middle of a conversation with David Kemper and his wife Kassy, the owners of the Rough Riders. We'd spent most of the conversation talking about the season and the upcoming game, but as much as I loved football, there was only one thing on my mind for most of the night.

Like a moth to a flame, I knew exactly where Elizabeth was every minute of the evening. My sudden obsession with her should have bothered me more, but for some reason, I couldn't find the reason that would make me stay away.

"Don't you agree, Gage?"

I had no clue what David had just said. Based on the grin Kassy wore, she knew exactly where my attention had drifted. Hard not to figure out considering I was still fixed on Elizabeth.

"I think Mr. Bryant has other, more interesting things on this mind tonight, dear, than continuing to talk about this weekend's game."

Kassy winked at me.

"I can assure you, sir, we are more than prepared for the match on Sunday against Nashville." I flashed Kassy a grateful smile silently thanking her for saving my butt. Wouldn't exactly do to have the owner of my team, the man partially responsible for signing my checks and ensuring I have a job next season, to think I was blowing him off.

Kassy placed her hand on her husband's arm. "Come on honey, I'm sure Gage has other things and other people to see to this evening. Let's go bore someone else to tears with your football knowledge."

He gave his wife an unhappy look, one with much more bark than bite. Kassy threw her head back and laughed, pulling him with her as she stepped away. "Enjoy your evening, Gage. Tonight is a huge success. You should be very proud of yourself and what you've accomplished."

"Thank you, ma'am."

"Ah, and see, she has manners for everyone but her husband." David rolled his eyes but easily wrapped his arm around his wife's lower back. "And I'll end this conversation with, she's exactly right, and my wife usually is. You should be proud of what you're doing. I know I'm proud of you."

"Thank you, sir. And if you could go proclaim my awesomeness to my parents, that'd be great. I don't believe they ever tire of hearing it as well."

He tipped his head toward me, grinning widely. The Kempers knew my parents well, considering mine visited as often as they could and when they did come, they always insisted on seeing the Kempers. "That we can surely do." He turned to Kassy. "Unless my wife thinks that conversation would be boring as well."

"Oh no. I always enjoy talking about Gage's talents and awesomeness."

They walked away, leaving me shaking my head. For owners

of such a huge organization, as well as richer than rich, they were sweet and so down to earth. I figured they spent the days sitting around watching Netflix and sports, drinking American beers much like every other red-blooded American couple.

They'd both come from small towns, met in college, fell in love immediately, and were married right after college despite many objections due to their young age. Yet they'd now been married for forty years, had three grown kids and a slew of grandchildren. Every time I was in David's office, he had a new family picture with more chubby infant or toddler faces included in the framed photo.

Yeah, they were good people. And I was honored to know them, even if they thought the same of me.

I waited until they were at my parents, David cordially placing his hand on my mom's shoulder to get her attention, and then mine swung to the other side of the restaurant.

As I found Elizabeth, she was setting down another glass, still not drinking champagne. She nodded down at the couple she'd been speaking to and even from this distance, I was able to make out the words her lips were forming.

Excuse me.

She turned to leave, but it wasn't her I focused on as she did. Connor Hopkins, the asshole reporter from earlier, who'd clearly upset her based on her body language and facial expression, was standing at one end of the bar, his eyes on her ass as she left the room.

He smirked, said something to the bartender, and was quickly handed two glasses of champagne.

That smirk of his made me move to follow him. He was closer to the exit, and I was stopped multiple times by people who wanted my attention, but I brushed them all off as politely as I could.

It wasn't that Connor watched Elizabeth leave.

It wasn't even that he had champagne in his hand, even though I'd noticed she'd only had one glass of champagne all night.

No, the thing that had me fighting against forcefully shoving people out of the way to get to him, wasn't his actions, but the look in his eyes.

It was the look of a lineman right before the blitz. The one that said, "I'm going to fuck you up and there's not a damn thing you can do about it."

And any look like that in a man's eyes directed toward a woman was never a good thing.

TEN

Elizabeth

Fresh air.

It wasn't so much an urgent need to step outside after I used the restroom, but I was still hot and uncomfortable.

Good gracious. A night of even being in the room with Gage was too much for this girl to handle. Multiple times I'd caught his eyes on me. During his speech, he'd found me more than once, eyes pinning me to my seat every time he did with an intensity I'd only ever *felt* once in my life.

Not seen, because when it happened, I'd been blindfolded.

It was too much. Too distracting. I'd fought through polite necessities all through dinner, attempting to focus on the speech, all while trying to remember my questions for later, but also trying to forget the man from last night.

The sex had been incredible, and Gage was clearly the hottest man alive East of the Mississippi. Since it'd been awhile, that sex had just turned on my libido and it was now focusing on Gage.

There was no way the man who had me blindfolded and restrained last night could have been the same man.

My recently invigorated sex drive was simply confusing Gage's appeal with the rough and dark stranger.

But even as I tried to tell myself that, I wondered.

Why else would I react to him so sharply? Even when he spoke, there was a roughness that hinted at familiarity as it filtered through my ears. Being blindfolded increased other senses, which was one of the reasons I didn't mind wearing it, even around men I hadn't played with before.

But was his voice the same? It was hard to tell when he wasn't growling commands in my ear in a quiet room, but speaking through a microphone in a vast ballroom.

Still...there was something. I couldn't put my finger on it, but it was distracting me enough I hoped five minutes of peace, quiet, and cool air would help me refocus.

Connor's continued presence only made everything worse. We dated for almost a year, dinners out and evenings at Velvet. It was where we'd met. We recognized each other as reporters from rival television networks and saddled up to the bar to enjoy a drink. He'd had me in hand immediately, strapped to the cross hours after the first teasing, verbal jab thrown about which night-time news show was better.

I'd screwed that all up by falling in love with him.

God.

Why hadn't I anticipated him being around for this?

"Stupid, so freaking stupid."

"You've always been a lot of things, but stupid isn't one of them."

My eyes closed and a shiver rolled through me

Speak of the devil and he appeared. "Go away, Connor."

It was like I hadn't spoken at all. He came up next to me, close enough the light, tender scent of his cologne wafted toward me, far enough where I could reach out and touch him. Except he wasn't mine to touch anymore.

"You've been avoiding me," he said.

I'd never known him to be a sadist, not in all the time we spent together. So why was he torturing me now?

I turned away from him, gathered my courage which had somehow scattered to a puddle at my feet, before facing him.

The man I'd loved. The man who, when I told him, not only didn't return it, but had looked at me in the most pitiful way.

"I'm not avoiding you," I lied. "I simply don't think we have anything to say to each other. Not anymore."

Not now that he was engaged to another woman. A woman I'd seen him talking to a few times before we spent that last, heartbreaking night together. He assured me he'd never cheated.

I'd always believed he was a good enough man he wouldn't have done that to me. And maybe he didn't cheat physically, but emotionally?

Breakups happened. I understood. People dated, they broke up, they found someone new. It was life, as much as it sucked, and I'd tried moving on.

But why was this all happening the very week I decided to return to Velvet? The universe had a sick sense of humor and I wasn't amused.

He lifted out a glass of champagne and sipped his own while he waited for me to take it.

"No thank you. I'm here working." And I was smart enough to keep my senses about me. My mind was cloudy enough.

Connor set it on the railing close to me. I tried not to stare at him, but it was difficult. His hair was dark, not quite brown, not light enough to be blond. It had a wave to it even when he styled it. A former college baseball player, he still had the body of one, tall, muscled but not bulky. Beneath his tuxedo coat and white shirt, there'd be the hint of a six-pack. Not bulging and in your face, but just beneath the surface, appearing only when he thrust into you over and over.

Shit.

I blinked away the image and before I could repeat my request for him to leave me alone, he spoke.

"I miss you, Lizzie."

I couldn't hide my flinch. "You have Mel."

"I know. And I love Mel. But that doesn't mean I don't miss you, what we had."

He was killing me. How could he not see the pain that admission caused me? Or how inappropriate it was given the circumstances.

"Connor—"

"No, just listen. Please, Lizzie."

Damn him. He was the only one who'd ever called me that. The only guy I'd ever allowed to call me that. It had seemed too juvenile the first time he'd done it, but at the time, I'd been trussed up with rope and clamps, and he'd been torturing me with a feather of all things. God, who knew something so light, could cause so much pain to overheated skin? *"Oh little Lizzie, the things I could do with you right now and you wouldn't resist, would you?"*

I shook my head frantically. I wouldn't. I didn't just want this man inside of my body, I wanted him inside my heart.

"Stop." I lifted my hand. The memories too fresh, the first time they'd come to me in months. Damn him. I thought I was over this. Over him.

What I fool I was.

"Please stop."

He didn't stop and he didn't leave. Leave it to a Dom to do whatever they wanted regardless of the pain inflicted. He stepped closer and placed his hand on mine on the railing. It was warm but gentle.

"I do love Mel, and I know that hurts you, Lizzie. But what we have isn't what you and I had. I'm missing something and Mel knows it, and I know that what I'm missing is what you and I had."

"That doesn't make sense."

"Mel is...great." He smiled softly, the true smile of a man in love. I wanted to slap it off his face. How dare he do this to me? Here? Of all nights? "But you, Lizzie...you gave me things she won't, at Velvet." For a split second, he looked embarrassed. "She has limits you didn't, limits I need."

"Then you shouldn't have left me and fell in love with her."

I yanked my hand back, sending the glass of champagne flying. It shattered all over the cement floor and a few small pieces landed on my feet.

I stepped down and a small shard got stuck between the ball of my foot and my shoe.

"Damn it!" I shouted. I lifted my foot but trying to free it made everything worse.

His hands wrapped around my forearms. "Don't move."

I didn't listen. I couldn't. Not with him touching me so firmly in that sinfully beautiful way of his. I forgot about the pain in my foot. I struggled, stepped all over the glass, it splintering beneath my heels.

"Damn it, Lizzie," Connor growled and his arms moved to my biceps. He picked me up like I was nothing and set me to the side. Bending down, he met my eyes. "I know what I'm saying is a shock to you, but you have to get it, Lizzie and I don't want you to hurt yourself because you're upset with me. Mel is okay with this. She knows where I stand and I should have done this privately but I know you wouldn't have seen me and you haven't been to Velvet..."

Oh, how very wrong he was, but I was suddenly thinking of dissolving my membership completely.

"Get off me," I hissed and pulled like a maniac. "This is shitty. So shitty of you to do to this to me."

"I know. But I want what I want Lizzie and I think deep down, you still miss what we had, too. Just think about it. Promise me you'll think about it."

"I think you should get your hands off her."

We both froze, heads flipped toward the opened door to the balcony.

My jaw dropped at who stood there.

Gage.

Hands fisted. Shoulders tense. His jaw so hard it could cut granite as his gaze dropped to where Connor had my arms pinned at my sides, up to his face, and then over to mine.

I could only imagine what he saw. I shook my head but strands of my hair stuck to my wet cheeks.

I was flushed and hot, chest heaving.

Connor was shocked enough he loosened his grip on me, and I stepped back, shaking my arms and rubbing them.

Not because he hurt me but because I could still feel him on me and I hated I still loved it.

I was such a screwed up mess.

"Gage," Connor said. "Lizzie and I were just catching up. Beautiful night you have here. You should be really proud of yourself."

Gage didn't respond with words. He didn't need them. He crossed his arms over his chest and continued glaring at Connor. It said enough.

"It's fine," I said. I wiped my cheeks and attempted to fix my messed up hair. "I think you have the wrong idea, but everything's okay."

"And I think when a woman is struggling and shouting for a man to get his hands off her that man should listen."

Oh no. I'd been shouting? I whipped my head toward the restaurant. No one was there. Thank goodness.

"We were just talking," Connor said. He was getting pissed. And that was never good. Gage might have been bigger, but Connor was no slouch. "And maybe you should mind your own damn business."

"Press conference I promised to finish earlier will be starting soon. Perhaps you should go find your seat."

My bet was Gage was more pissed than Connor.

Why did that make me feel good? Connor wouldn't have hurt me. Not like Gage might have been assuming. He was mostly freaked about the glass I was stepping on. He hurt me with his words not his hands.

Connor glared at Gage. Nostrils flared and from my view, both of them looked ready to brawl.

"It's really fine," I said. They ignored me, continued staring each other down. I had no doubt who would win. Connor was fierce and strong.

Gage was on a whole other planet of pissed-off male.

Connor slid his eyes to me and they softened. "Please, promise me you'll think about it."

I crossed my arms over my stomach. Perhaps it'd hold in my heart he was shattering all over again. I nodded, too afraid to answer him with words. It was just to get him to go away.

His grin slipped and he nodded once. "We'll talk later then," he said. "See you inside."

I didn't watch him walk away. My gaze moved to the skyline and the lights and the darkness settling over the city. I felt it when he was gone though because Gage relaxed.

"Did he hurt you?"

"No." The pain in my foot reminded me I'd done a bang-up job hurting myself. I wobbled to a nearby chair and sat. Unstrapping my shoes, I inhaled a sharp breath when Gage was there, kneeling at my feet.

"What are you doing?"

"You have blood all over your shoe. What happened?" His big hands brushed away my smaller ones and he went to work on the clasp, undoing it with impressive efficiency.

"I dropped a glass. Stepped on it. I'll be fine."

"You need to clean up. Let me get something."

"No." I pulled my foot back. His hands fell between his spread knees where he was crouched down. And God. He was beautiful. I was a wreck, bloodied and teary-eyed and he was in front of me, practically on his knees. "I'll take care of it."

"At least let me make sure you get the glass out."

"I'd rather take care of myself." I sounded bitchy. I hated sounding bitchy. I wasn't a bitchy person, but this wasn't what I needed. "Please. Just go."

He peered at me, worry and anger mixed in his dark brown eyes and then he nodded, pressed his hands to his knees and shoved to his feet.

"Wouldn't be any better than him if you asked me to do something and I didn't listen. So I'll go, but I will send someone out here to clean the glass."

I focused on peeling off my shoe like I was performing neonatal heart surgery. "Thank you."

I didn't breathe until he stepped away, and jumped when he called my name.

"What, Gage?" My tone defeated and with the weight of the world pressed on my shoulders, it took forever to lift my head to meet his gaze.

"That guy. I heard what he said, and don't do that with him. He's a selfish dick, using two women to get his rocks off. I might not know you, but you deserve better than his scraps."

Goddamn. I was going to cry all over again.

Why did getting that confirmation from him feel so darn good?

"You don't know—"

"I know what Velvet is," he said, cutting me off. "And I know exactly what he's meaning even if I don't know the specifics, so yeah, I know exactly what I'm talking about. He loves a woman, he takes her as she is, which means he doesn't love the woman he's with any more than he cares about you. He's an asshole and not worth your time."

What was there to say to that? Nothing. He'd stolen any intellectual or witty response I could usually think of.

Instead, my jaw slack from surprise at his bluntness, I nodded once and slipped off my shoe.

"I'll see you inside. But stay away from him. I get the idea he's a man who doesn't stop until he gets what he wants."

He left, and I waited several moments after his footsteps evaporated when it hit me.

He knew what Velvet was. Which meant he knew I liked it there. And I liked something different if he was smart enough to put two and two together depending on how much he'd heard.

He didn't look at me like I was some freak or like there was something wrong with it.

Instead, he'd done what he'd done and said what he'd said for the sole purpose of taking care of me and trying to make me feel better.

Damn. Gage Bryant wasn't only hot and sexy and kind and had a big sincere heart, he was caring and could be gentle despite his size. He could probably be brutal and arrogant and stubborn, like most men, but despite the professionalism I was trying to maintain around him, I really wanted to learn a whole lot more.

ELEVEN

Gage

I walked the hall alone this time, assuring Tristan I didn't need assistance. The hallway was dark, lit with sconces on the wall probably meant to be seductive and yet I was always creeped out by them. They reminded me of haunted houses, and coupled with the ecstatic sounds filtering beneath the other private room's doors, it was easy to understand why people into the vanilla life-style would find this evil. Wrong. Demoralizing.

I thought of it often. What would happen if my love of rough, dominating sex was revealed to the public? What would it do to my reputation as a philanthropist? How embarrassed would my own family be? What would the consequences be for my own dad and his congregation?

It'd been years since I had a real relationship, not since college when I was just discovering that soft and sweet love-making with the college girls didn't get me off like it should have. Sure, I got off, but there was always something missing. A fire. A passion. The first time a girl I dated asked me to tie her up, something completely different in me sparked to life.

It was *that*. The missing piece finally found when I had a woman tied to her bed, helpless to get away from me, forced to be under my control. Memories of that night still made me go hard. The girl, Claire, had found someone different shortly after, our short fling a purely physical thing most college students embraced.

We separated with no hard feelings.

After college graduation when fame and followers and photographers became a part of my life, reporters declaring me a role model for children, my own hometown naming a street after me, the attention on me forced me to hide my proclivities.

There was too much at stake in my life: my career, my family, the organizations I supported through volunteer and donating efforts, to risk having any woman proclaim a consensual night of intense fucking was anything different. Too many women in my life had made it clear they found me hot, but was it *me* or my money?

Funny how I grew up wanting fame and fortune and a long list of football records, but that came with a price, and the cost was trust not coming easily.

Which meant the fact that little miss reporter Elizabeth Hayes, currently waiting for me in the room at the end of the hallway, could possibly be the most epically horrible decision I'd ever made.

Too bad that after three days, I still couldn't get her out of my head.

Which was why I called Tristan immediately following our win over Atlanta this afternoon. The game was hard fought, too many errors and penalties on both teams. It was ugly and vicious. The winning touchdown coming with three seconds left, a pass I caught in the end zone, thrown by our quarterback Beaux Hale. It was ridiculous how he could land the ball straight into my hands when I was double-teamed by Atlanta's best defenders.

The amount of adrenaline still heating my veins was insanity.

Which meant tonight would be even more adventurous than the other. And if Miss Hayes still enjoyed it, then I'd have to figure out what to do afterward.

I knocked once to let her know I was coming. The instructions had been the same. Blindfolded and sitting on the bed, however this time I'd requested she remains clothed.

I craved the idea of undressing her, revealing her flesh to me in incremental measures while I bathed her skin in my kisses and torture. Exactly like I'd wanted to do at the dinner.

Hot damn. I was already rock hard at the mere thought of the beauty waiting for me.

I opened the door and stepped in. Like last time, my heart stalled for a brief moment and it took me a second to remember how to breathe.

So damn beautiful. Toes painted a light pink curled into the plush white rug at her feet. Simple black dress rode high on her trim thighs. A low scooped neckline showed off her throat. Beautiful and long, tight sleeves, drew my gaze to her hands clasped elegantly in her lap.

"You're stunning," I said.

She lifted her head so if she wouldn't have been wearing a blindfold, her eyes would have met mine. A tiny hint of a frown line peeked out from above the top of the black satin coming from between her eyes.

My spine straightened as she nibbled her lip. Did she recognize my voice after hearing it in person over the last weekend?

I'd been close to her too many times. When that asshole reporter, Connor, made her uncomfortable at the dinner Friday night. She had several opportunities to link my voice with the man who made her scream. Plus, she was a reporter. She was trained to sniff out news and follow her instincts.

She seemed almost hesitant, slowing drawing out her reply. "Thank you, John."

I stepped closer, slipping out of my shoes and shucking off my gray thermal. As soon as I got her undressed, I wanted our bodies pressed together. Keeping my pants on would ensure I didn't move too quickly once they were.

My dick was already pressed against the zipper of my black dress pants, craving its release and freedom into the heat of her.

I adjusted myself as I stepped toward her. It was futile. I was too hard and rubbing myself only made things worse.

"Stand up," I said. I left enough space between us so I could take in every movement she made. She stood elegantly, like she'd spent years in ballet shoes. Her movements were lithe and smooth, a gracefulness born of years of training and all she'd done was stand the hell up.

And I didn't know that from seeing her a few times. Since she'd bombarded me in Brandon's room, I'd spent more than a reasonable amount of time watching her old news stories online. She had enthralled Brandon. He was almost as excited to see her as he'd been to see me the first few times I walked into his room.

Pretty wasn't the word for Elizabeth either. Elegant and refined. She put excitement and joy and a light I rarely saw in people into the most mundane stories. No person should get excited or find so much laughter in a news segment about a VFW's fish fry and steak night as Elizabeth did telling the story of the small town with some of the best eats in the state.

I'd now spent days fantasizing about how red her ass would look when I got my hand on it for following me.

She didn't walk in with a notebook and pen in her hand, dying to get the story. She'd appeared embarrassed at being caught and instantly, she became friends with Brandon, asking about *him* and not his illness. Not how we knew each other. Sure we took some photos at his request. The two of us. The three of us, all happily snapped by Penny who stood in the corner with tears in her eyes.

Some were happy ones.

Most were because she'd recently gotten news that the possibility of Brandon ever leaving that ugly ass hospital room was dropping by the day.

But now it was Elizabeth standing before me, and I had to get my shit together.

To spank her properly, I needed to be fully engaged.

"Turn around." Her dress was skintight and as I assumed, a zipper appeared down the back of her dress.

"What are you going to do?"

I tsk'ed twice. She knew better than to ask. "Ah, whatever I want, little one. You ready?"

"Yes. Whatever you'd like."

It was a good answer. Not only appropriate but sincere and it was all I wanted to hear. I closed the space between us and my hand went to her hair. It was long, straight tonight, and hung down her back like a sheet of gold. I wrapped my fist around it, tugged lightly so I could bend and press my lips to her jaw.

She smelled like flowers and sunshine, pure beauty and joy. For not the first time I wondered if I could reveal myself to her.

She had as much to lose as I did if our kink was made public. A woman who liked to be spanked and dominated? That wouldn't go over so well for a female public figure, even if the double standard sucked ass. She'd be ridiculed and shamed and probably lose her job. I'd bring embarrassment to my charities but would probably gain a few thousand female followers on social media.

My lips brushed against her jaw, went right to that soft, gentle flesh beneath her ear. Her breath hitched. She shivered. Even her lids fell closed as I touched her for the first time.

Goddamn. This woman.

A weekend with her in public and only one night of sex with her and already she was screwing with my head.

As I peppered her alabaster throat with kisses, covering her with my scent, I reached up and dragged her zipper down. I moved slowly to draw out the anticipation. It was as much of an exercise in self-control for me.

I wanted her naked. I wanted to sink inside of her and ride her hard and fast, pounding into her until she'd never forget me.

I wanted to imprint on her pussy so she'd never be satisfied with another man taking her like only I could do. I wanted to fuck every good memory of Connor Hopkins out of her body and her brain.

The suddenness of my territorial thoughts jolted me and my hand froze.

"Is it stuck?" she asked.

"No." I tugged the zipper down the rest of the way, forgoing the exquisite pleasure of taking my time.

Whatever my brain was thinking was definitely in line with my dick.

I'd return to common sense and rationality after I left.

With the zipper undone, I pushed her dress forward, helping her out of the long sleeves and once it drifted to the floor, I helped her step out of it, kicking it to the side.

Her bra went next and while I'd wanted her splayed out on the bed, her mass of golden hair backdrop to the gray coverings, another idea came to mind.

My hands curved over her shoulders and I carefully guided her forward until we were at the dresser at the far end of the room. The drawers held toys and implements and a few more ideas came to mind.

Another time, I decided, before I could realize what I'd already decided.

This woman would be mine. For much longer than most women were.

"We're at the dresser. Put your hands out and hold on."

She bent down and my breath left with a forceful whoosh of air as I caught sight of her tight, trim but nicely rounded ass sticking in the air.

She hadn't been wearing underwear beneath the dress. A disobedience, one I was thankful she was already in position to be punished for.

I reached out, ran the tip of my finger through the crease of her ass. "You didn't do what I said to," I said quietly.

I pressed my fingertip to her hidden opening, loving every single one of her tiny reactions to my touch. Her arms quivered and as I slid my finger farther forward to her opening, her head fell. "Ohhhh."

"Like that?" She was wet, practically dripping. I swirled my fingertip around her already swollen clit. Damn. Hot and soaking wet already.

At least I knew thinking of and anticipating fucking me was as big of a turn on for her as it was me.

Hot damn, she was perfect.

I palmed her ass, warming it and preparing her. "How many spankings do you think you should have for not listening?"

"I tried, John. I tried to listen."

"But you didn't?"

"Well, no sir. Thinking of what you were going to do to me tonight made me too wet."

My hand on her ass stilled. I stepped forward until my dick was at her backside. She was too short for me to fuck this way, but no matter. I didn't bring her here to fuck her. Just to spank her and give her at least the first of her orgasms for the night.

I'd fuck her on the bed on her knees, probably holding them up off the bed to make it easier for me.

And better for her. I didn't even have to wonder if she'd get off on it. Her rhythmic breathing was already at hyper-speed. I bet she'd come while I spanked her and got her off with my fingers, too.

Yeah. Perfect.

"Trying doesn't mean listening though, does it? If I wanted you without panties on, I would have requested it. I spent all weekend, fantasizing about pulling down your underwear, maybe gagging you with them while I fucked your ass to muffle your screams. And now you've robbed me of doing something I would have liked."

While I spoke to her, I gathered moisture from her center and pressed against her puckered hole. She was trembling. Her breathing was already erratic and as I pressed my finger to her opening, she moaned as I slid inside.

"See? You like the idea of me taking your ass don't you?"

"Yes."

I slid my finger in farther, pulled it out slowly. Before she could ask for more, my palm was at her ass, spanking her once, then twice, two more times in rapid succession.

Her small ass bounced and turned red from my hand even as she gasped, arched for me. "Yes. Thank you," she breathed.

"You're thanking me?"

"It feels good."

"Hmm." I rubbed her ass, soothed it, spent too much time trying to slow down my own racing heart.

She has limits you don't...

I hadn't meant to stand in a corner, listening to her conversation with Connor, but once I heard what they were talking about, I couldn't help myself from eavesdropping. I should have stepped in sooner and stopped so she didn't get hurt and he didn't grab her but, as soon as he'd done that, shaking her to get her to listen, a red haze clouded my vision.

He didn't get to be an asshole and put his hands on her. Not when my hands had been on her and would be again.

So yeah, I'd listened to more than I should have, but at the word *limits* my dick had gone hard and my mind wandered.

I wasn't into the ultra hard shit. I just liked being in control. But was it possible even sweet and little Elizabeth Hayes liked more than that? Tristan had assured me she'd be perfect for me, but if this was all we did, what was poor Connor missing out on with his new woman?

Poor thing. I almost felt sorry for the asshole, and more than once over the weekend I wanted to call Tristan and demand he didn't let Elizabeth see Connor.

But that could be a mistake.

After how she was once she showed up at the press conference, I figured I didn't have anything to worry about.

She'd stood in the back looking broken and sad. She'd looked like she was paying attention, but I'd bet a million bucks she didn't hear a damn word I said, but what she didn't do, was go to Connor and take him up on his offer. And when I was done, all the questions asked and the night winding down, she'd stepped out of the room and I hadn't seen her since.

For three whole days, I'd thought about her ass. Stripping her out of a sexy lace thong or underwear and wondering what color it would be and now she'd gone and ruined that.

I spanked her again, teased her clit and her ass with my finger. I worked in slowly to her tight opening. So damn tight I had to bite back a groan as I worked on stretching her.

"I'm sorry," she said. "I'll listen next time."

"I wanted to take your ass tonight," I said again, pressing two fingers into her. "I'd been thinking of this and you want it, don't you?" She was sweating and panting. She was soaking wet and her clit was swollen. I didn't need any words of hers to know she was the kind of girl who loved a good ass-fucking.

Lucky, lucky me.

"Yes. Please."

I scissored my fingers and at her next pleasured whimper, I pulled my hand out of her ass, spanked it a few more times. "Too bad. Girls who don't listen don't get what they want."

I went to the drawer next to her and slid it open. I yanked off the wrapper on a butt plug instead. Not a small one, not one as nearly as big as I was, but with her ass stuffed, she'd be mighty full and maybe slightly in pain by the time I slammed inside of her.

My dick jumped at the thought.

I unwrapped the plug, simple black and made with soft material. I lubed it up generously and readied her body for it. "I'm going to put this plug inside you. When's the last time you had something in here?"

It was more curiosity than safety. Had Connor taken her this way?

"Um."

She hesitated and I grabbed her chin, pulled her back so I could see her face. "When?"

"Two nights ago," she whispered. "I did it. Thinking of you."

Jesus. Dirty, naughty little girl. My heart almost burst it was so pleased with her admission. My teeth almost broke from clamping them together. She was utterly perfect. "Good," I said, for lack of saying anything else. "Then you'll like this."

If she'd been stretched recently, this would be easier. I'd already stretched her so I pressed the tip of the plug against her, slowly pushed it in, giving her little time to adjust.

Her sounds and moans were enough and I paused when her shoulders tensed, just for a moment so she could breathe. While I put the plug in her with one hand, my other snaked around to her front and rubbed her hot and swollen clit.

"You going to come?" I asked. I rubbed her clit gently, taking her mind off the plug.

"Yes, please."

"Not yet," I smacked her clit and she jumped. At the movement, the rest of the plug slammed inside of her so her next noise was mixed with pain and pleasure.

Beautiful.

"Stand up." I placed my hands at her waist and turned her around. Her cheeks were flushed. So was her chest. Her nipples were exquisite hardened nubs. I pinched them and loved the sound of her gasp. Tugging her lightly toward me with my fingers at her nipples, she collapsed against my chest.

I slammed my mouth to hers before she knew what to expect and she opened immediately.

God fucking damn. How was I ever going to walk away from her?

TWELVE

Elizabeth

Good God. I took his kiss as he invaded my mouth without preamble. My nipples ached, my ass was sore and tender and so full.

I was ready to come and as he continued kissing me, his hands at my jaw and my cheeks holding me to him, I rolled my hips into him, seeking friction.

I doubted I even needed it.

If he squeezed my nipples once more or tapped my clit, I would shatter and I wouldn't care about trying to pick up the pieces.

This man was magnificent. Stunning in his bossiness and commands and so damn gentle at the same time.

I'd practically jumped with glee when Tristan called me earlier. At first, I'd hesitated, worried it'd be at Connor's request but as soon as Tristan said, *"le garçon with the blindfold wants you again,"* my heart leaped to my chest.

This was dangerous, loving what he did to me so much without knowing anything about him.

I also didn't care.

After Connor, after the weekend, I didn't care who this man was as long as he fucked me harder and longer and better than Connor ever did.

It'd be enough to move on from him forever and I still hadn't forgotten Gage's words.

Man's a selfish asshole, not getting what he needs and screwing over two women. You deserve better. Make sure you get it.

It was exactly what I'd needed to hear.

"Stop," John said. His hand went to my shoulder and he pushed me off him, keeping a hand on me so I didn't stumble. "Are you trying to come before I say you can?"

"Please," I replied. I couldn't admit the truth. I wouldn't. I'd been so turned on after the phone call and the thought of being with him again, I'd had to fight against making myself masturbate before I arrived.

"I don't think you should be able to come quite yet if you didn't listen to me."

His voice had a glint of teasing. I could imagine full, thick lips cracking into a smile as he watched me writhe in front of him. So damn horny. Soaking wet.

His hand went to my shoulder and he pressed down gently. He didn't need to instruct me. I dropped to my knees, holding onto his hips and then his legs for balance as I went down.

The clink of a belt echoed in my ears. The rustle of a button and whisk of a zipper before the soft falling of his pants in front of me. He cupped the back of my head and then the tip of him was at my mouth. "Open. Take me. If you make it good enough, then maybe I'll let you come."

Oh God. I'd probably come while I blew him and then what would happen? Would it be over before we had sex?

I whimpered and wrapped my hand around him.

God. He was gorgeous. Veined and long and thick. Thank goodness for the plug. He'd ache in my ass whenever he took it.

My mouth opened and I slid my tongue over his tip getting him nice and wet. I slid my hand up and down his length, getting the feel of him, reveling in his size and his heat. The heavy weight in my hands before I took him farther in my mouth.

He wanted me to make it good for him? I'd suck his brains out through his dick if he asked.

I went to work, taking him as deep as I could, then further, moving slowly, adjusting to his size and the instant push and pull of his hips, urging me on.

His fingers dug into my hair, pulled and yanked but he allowed me some control.

"Fuck. Yes. So good, little one. Take my cock. Suck harder."

I groaned. His filthy talk hit me in heated places. He swelled in my mouth, and my hand went to his balls to feel them hard and pulled tight.

I squeezed and rolled them in my hand.

His hand at the back of my head tightened and he held me still. He thrust his cock in and out, groaning and dirty talking to me like he didn't care about me at all. The way he held me told me different.

He pulled out and his hands were at my shoulders, helping me to my feet.

"On the bed. Hands and knees."

Yes. I scrambled into position and then he was there, at my back his chest covering my small frame in a way that felt warm and protective and sexy all at once. The hair on his chest brushed over my back, his hand went to my hair, swiping it off to the side.

There was the crinkle of foil, the pause, and then he was there, sliding into me.

And between him and the plug, it hurt. My body stretched

around him and I groaned from the weight of all of him as he bottomed out inside me.

"Cheek to the bed and keep your hands by your head."

My fingers curled into the mattress as he slid out once and slammed back inside of me. His hands went to my hips, held me still while he took over.

It didn't take much. Between my blow job and the plug and the ferocity in which he was pounding in and out of me, my orgasm exploded. I dug my fingers into the bed and made sounds I'd never known I could make as my climax came so fast and hard, it felt like it had the power to break me in two.

"Oh God," I said as I came down, but he didn't let up.

His hand slid to my front, pressed against my clit, rubbed frantically while he bent over me and growled. "Again. Keep coming and clamping on my dick until I'm done with you."

I had no choice. My body operated on his command alone. I came again, another one or one long ridiculously long one, I didn't know. My body had never felt so alive before, on fire and ice cold all at once.

Then he was there, slamming in one last time, yanking me back by the hips, settling himself all the way in me. His fingertips dug into my soft flesh, aching from where he'd already spanked me and he grunted out his own release. "Fuck. Yes. Hot damn you're incredible, little one." He moved slowly, milking out his own climax, dirty talking. "So damn good. Wanna stay right here, so damn deep inside. Fuck."

I shivered beneath him, breathless. My legs hurt from being spread wide enough to take him and the knuckles on my hand hurt from my tight grip on the bedsheets.

We stayed there for a moment until he'd calmed.

He pulled out slowly, one of his large hands at the small of my back. "Let me take care of this and I'll take care of you. Stay here."

He was still so bossy, but sweet. The dichotomy of this huge man who had the strength to snap me in two but care to be gentle with me threatened to unravel me.

It's sex, Elizabeth. Just sex. Just a way to move on. Do not get attached.

I repeated the mantra. It wasn't the first time I had to tell myself this. More like the hundredth. In fact, I'd done it all weekend whenever my thoughts drifted to our last encounter.

After tonight, I needed to get a rubber band and snap my wrist whenever I got the ridiculous idea this could possibly lead to something more.

This was sex. Hell, I hadn't even seen him.

But I heard him clearly.

He'd be back for more.

Which mean when he returned, and a warm rag was pressed to my center, I was smiling.

"What's so funny?"

He didn't seem angry. "Nothing's funny. That was really nice."

"Good. I'm glad it was *really nice* for you."

So the brute could tease.

"Yeah," I sighed as he cleaned me, wiggled as he brushed against my clit, and then he moved to the plug.

I tensed at the feel of his hands on the base, but his other hand went to my back, rubbed large calming circles all over me. "I'll go slow. Relax."

I tried. I tried to relax. It should have been easy, but as he tugged it out, everything else tightened, including my sex that should have been well-satisfied. I made a sound of displeasure as it slipped from me and he was rolling me to my back.

"Still want more?" he asked.

"Yes." My hands went to my face and his warm hand gripped my wrist, tugging it to my stomach.

"No."

"Please. I want to see you."

I had to know. Know who this man was who could do all these beautifully wicked things to me and still leave me wanting more.

"No. Not yet."

Not yet. That meant it would happen. Someday.

I just had to be patient.

"Okay."

He seemed to hesitate a bit, but then he moved. The bed shifted from his weight and his mouth was *there*, taking what he wanted, hands at my thighs, stretching me wide open for him. He ate me until I was crying out for him, for more, and I came, screaming the name John, knowing it was fake, wishing I could call him by his real name. And as soon as I was done and mindless, without the care he had shown earlier, he stood.

Something soft and cool landed on my stomach. My dress. I covered my body with it, hugging it tight against me.

"You can get dressed after I leave," he said. "See you soon."

His voice had gone so cold, I shivered from it.

He dressed quickly and the door clicked behind him before my muscles were in working order.

I struggled to sit and ripped off the blindfold. The soft light from the lamp in the corner did nothing to diminish the sting in my eyes.

It wasn't from the light. It was from *him*. The man who had just completely undone me and walked away like I was nothing when he'd shown such care.

Which meant as I dressed, I wiped tears, stupid frustrating and pointless tears from my eyes.

It's just sex, Elizabeth. Don't screw up again.

The problem was, I didn't know how I'd screwed up this time.

~

I SLID into my chair at my desk and finally removed my sunglasses. Who cared that'd I'd been inside for ten minutes already. My eyes were puffy and red, from lack of sleep. I tossed and turned all night, unable to stop thinking about the weekend and the last several days. More than once I'd punch my pillow, envisioning it as Connor's face.

He'd called me a handful of times, which meant bad things. When Connor scooped a story, he was relentless. When he wanted something, he fought his heart out until it became his.

But why after six months was he fighting for me?

"Ugh," I groaned, and logged into my computer. I was only in the station for a few hours before lucky me, I had to spend more time following Gage around.

It would be so much easier to do this story if the guy was a jerk.

"Jeez. Rough weekend? I don't think I've ever heard you sound like that."

I glanced at Will over the top of our computer monitors. "Like what?"

"A wounded animal." He cringed. "And no offense, you sort of look like shit. Everything okay?"

"Everything's fine, but thanks for the pep talk." My tone was listless. Defeated. It took six months to get over Connor and find the strength to re-start a huge portion of my life and in a weekend, I was just as miserable as I'd been the night he ended things with me.

Awesome. Freaking Connor.

"Hey. What is it? Connor again?"

News reporters were a bunch of gossips. It was part of our job. Part of life. It hadn't taken long at all for word of our relationship to hit the news stations when it started and our break-up news traveled twice as fast.

"Why do you ask?"

"Because I know he's covering the hospital thing so I assume you had to see him this weekend. And there's only one other time I've seen you so miserable."

His brows arched above his glasses. Yeah yeah. Six months ago. I'd cried for weeks. Carried around a tube of hemorrhoid cream to reduce the constant puffiness around my eyes. Then I'd slept with cucumbers covering my eyes and drank more gallons of water than healthy.

He'd left me a wreck and if I was looking even mildly as bad as all of that, I was in serious trouble.

"It's not Connor." I didn't even want to say his name much less admit to him being part of the reason I had very few hours of sleep.

The other cause was a man behind a black mask, whispering dirty words into my ear while he screwed me senseless. Except in my dreams, that voice sounded a lot like Gage Bryant and when I'd ripped off the mask in my dream, it'd been Gage's face inches from mine.

So yeah, working today and following him around wasn't going to help a darn thing.

Maybe I needed to call off seeing *John* until this story was done. Another complication in my life certainly wouldn't improve anything.

"If you need to talk…"

I burst out laughing at the painful sound in Will's voice. He was a good guy, but a guy all the same. "No thanks," I assured him and smiled when relief softened his features. "If I need to bitch, I'll grab Amanda."

Or one of my sister-in-law's. They were always down for a good male-bashing session and I never minded they were bashing my brothers. Two of them were married and they'd given me so much grief when I was growing up, it was nice to know they still gave the women in their lives headaches from time to time.

"Okay. Well, if you need someone to kick his ass—"

"I'll call Blake or Jax," I assured him.

Will was a good guy but a little too sweet to kick anyone's ass. Although the offer was appreciated.

Jax would be first on my list. He was former military, operations unknown to all of us and he now ran his own security firm. He was the guy you didn't want to mess with. Hell, he was my brother and he still terrified the shit out of me. He was also the only one of my brothers who wasn't married.

Blake was an electrician. Blue collar through and through who loved his wife something fierce. They'd been high school sweethearts. He walked up to her one day when he was seventeen years old, right in the middle of the lunchroom, stared directly into Haley's green eyes and declared, "Someday, you and I are gettin' married."

He made it happen two years after they graduated high school. I was twelve when they started dating and could barely remember an important moment in my life without Haley in it. But Blake was big, a linebacker in high school with no desire to go to the next level. He was the brother who threatened all my high school boyfriends with bodily harm if they so much as laid a finger on me in an unappropriate way. If I went to him and so much as mentioned Connor's name, Connor would be in the hospital with several broken bones, minimum, and Blake would be locked behind bars.

Which was exactly why I wasn't telling any of them anything.

"Enough about me and my drama." I waved my hand in the air as if clearing the air could clear my mind, my distraction. "What'd you do this weekend?"

He ran a hand through his perfectly styled hair and made a face. "Ugh. Heather's family came into town." I'd heard stories about his in-laws. The dad wasn't so bad, but the mom? She was vicious, constantly throwing out digs and jabs at how their house wasn't clean enough, Heather's hair wasn't done right. She was overly critical and lacked acceptance. Whenever Will spoke about his in-laws, I was baffled.

How a mom could be so intentionally rude to her grown children was beyond me and anything I experienced in my own life.

"You want to talk about it?" I asked.

The look he shot me was all man.

"I'll take that as a no."

"It's a no."

"Okay then. How's the summer travel series going?"

He was visiting beaches on the North Carolina coast and traveling down through South Carolina over the course of two weeks. It meant a lot of day and overnight trips for him, and if I hadn't been giving this hospital story, I would have been pissed Shane took the travel stories from me.

"Splendid. I was in Wrightsville Beach last weekend..." He kept talking and we spent a few minutes chatting about his trip to Wilmington before his phone rang.

He answered it and I checked my emails, and when it was time, I went in search of Jason so we could head to the hospital.

THIRTEEN

Elizabeth

I was near the back of the small group following Gage down the hall. On the way to the hospital in the news van with Jason driving, I'd asked him a huge favor.

Let me hang out with him and the videographers instead of being up front. He peered at me strangely and shrugged. "Whatever. Yeah."

We planned on cutting and editing the story in the van afterward. I'd do voice-overs and I'd record my intro and closing after the tour as well. The segment was set to show as a teaser late afternoon and show in its entirety for the evening news.

I didn't exactly need to be front and center.

Small blessings would have been appreciated. Like maybe Connor ate some bad sushi and was at home suffering from food poisoning.

Unfortunately, the universe decided not to work in my favor.

There were far few reporters today, just four of us from the local stations and one from a national syndicate morning show. Apparently Gage Bryant made quite the splash on the morning shows where two women cackled and giggled while they drank wine at eight in the morning and dished about all the fun pieces of celebrity gossip.

I stayed sandwiched between Jason and another guy with a video camera hitched on his shoulder. There were far few places to hide today and if Connor dared speak to me at all I couldn't guarantee my fist wouldn't end up in his face.

Gage showed up in slightly distressed blue jeans, and a Rough Riders T-shirt, logo-stamped and placed perfectly on the curve of one of his pecs. He was menacing and so heart-stoppingly beautiful, last night's dream flashed in my eyes and made my skin flush down to my toes.

Connor arrived and gave me a smug look, swiping his gaze down the length of my body. I used to adore that possessive gleam in his eyes, but right then I was choking down the taste of vomit.

Maybe I needed to try to the rotten sushi route. Or tell my boss I didn't care much for the promotion at this time.

Anything to get me away from men who were driving me absolutely insane with too many conflicting emotions.

I had my long blonde hair styled back into a low ponytail, and a baby blue dress on that not only fit my frame to perfection but hugged every inch while covering everything to keep me professional. The heels of mine and other female reporters clicked like old-fashioned typewriter keys as we moved down the linoleum-floored hallway to the family center.

We'd come up the elevators, the same location where I followed Gage the week before, and as we passed the mouth of the hallway where I assumed Brandon still was, my gaze drifted down.

Maybe I'd stop by afterward to see him. Over the last week, being around Brandon was the only time I'd felt the least bit calm and centered. Shame that it took being around a sick nine-year-old to give perspective on what was important in life.

I repeatedly tapped my iPad to my forehead. *Forget about the weekend. Focus on the story. Don't think about Velvet for a another single second.*

Repeating it didn't help. Neither did the slight sting on my forehead from the iPad smacking it.

A hand pressed to my arm on my next whack and I jumped. "What?"

Jason's brows furrowed and his eyes narrowed. He looked at me like I was a freak.

Awesome. I was doing a bang-up job being professional.

"What's wrong with you?" he asked, taking the tablet out of my hands. "And don't break the company's shit. That's not cool."

I snatched it back from him. "Nothing's wrong. I'm distracted."

"Well, get focused 'cuz we're here."

"Wonderful."

He wasn't wrong. As we hit the mouth of the hallway, bright teal and blue double "R's" linked together lit up beneath a row of lights.

Above the team's logo, "Bryant Children and Family Center" was painted in bright teal.

Jesus. The guy had his name on a wing of a hospital. What did he think of it?

My eyes slid to Gage. He was off to the side, answering questions from the national syndicate reporter. But his arms were crossed and his gaze was laser-focused on the window across from him, like he was headed to the line of scrimmage and the game was tied in the fourth quarter. His answers were quiet, brief enough not to be rude, short enough it was clear he didn't want to elaborate. Eventually the reporter gave up and waved her hand toward the cameraman with her.

"Where do you want to start?" Jason asked me. The camera

was already on his shoulder and his face was hidden from me behind the behemoth old school looking thing.

"Let's wander," I mumbled. I flicked across the agenda on my iPad even though I'd had it memorized since last night.

Tour the wing. Ask questions. Get one-on-one time with Gage and leave when we were done.

It was laid back and relaxed, the perfect kind of interview and set up, but that didn't mean I was either of those things.

Nope. I practically felt Gage tracking me with every move we made. I gave Connor a wide berth. When he moved right, I waved Jason left. Amusement danced in Connor's eyes when he caught me avoiding him. If he thought this was a game, he was completely wrong. I didn't trust myself not to slap him and end up being the one on the six o'clock news. I could already see the headlines.

Reporter assaults ex while on assignment helping promote cancer wing of children's hospital.

Yeah. That wouldn't get me a seat at the nighttime news desk.

I zigzagged my way through the expansive area. The footage would be a bitch to edit. More than once Jason grumbled something that didn't sound polite. Already mic'ed up, I turned it on and stopped every once in awhile to give a brief, off-the-cuff statement about the hospital, where we were, a reminder when it was opening and more than one rundown on Gage's responsibilities with the project. Usually, I found passion in my work.

Not then. Every word left my throat like someone was yanking them out on a poorly connected string. And every time either Gage or Connor moved, I shied away.

Avoidance was my best policy even if I ended up looking like a fool.

We wandered to the basketball court area. Four indoor hoops about eight feet in height. They had side nets and return lanes like you'd find in an arcade and scoreboards that lit up and included a countdown.

I picked up one of the basketballs and was rolling it in my hands when Gage saddled up next to me.

His presence was unmistakable. Hair spiked at the back of my neck and traveled down my spine.

Gage grabbed another basketball and without pause or thought, launched it into the air. It swished through the net next to the one where I was lined up and rolled back to him. He spread his fingers, long and strong on an equally large palm and gripped it with ease.

"Have any questions for me? You're the only one not fighting for time today."

Are you the man from Velvet?

The question, the mere thought, made me choke so hard I covered my mouth with my hand, dropping the ball to my feet.

What was wrong with me?

He bent down and grabbed the basketball bouncing at our feet. One large hand gripped it and my breath stalled. He was crouched down, glossy black hair at the top of his head, his shoulders wide, knees spread. Time slowed as he held the ball in one hand, head tilted back. His lips pursed, eyes narrowed in a quizzical way.

He stood, every movement of it was defined as if someone had pressed the slow-motion button on the remote that was my life. When he reached his full height, he had to be closer to me.

"You okay?"

I was anything but okay. Sweat broke out on my back. Nerves lit. He was so close I had to resist stepping back out of fear, not only of his size but the brief whisper of his cologne that wafted between us.

Familiar. It took everything I had not to close my eyes, lean in and breathe him in. I *knew* that scent.

My hands tightened into balls of fists so tight at my sides my nails would leave crescent-shaped moons in my palms.

"Elizabeth?"

Oh no. I was gaping at him like a moron and it took an effort to get my mouth to move. To release my fists and reach out for the ball.

I took it from him, my every movement robotic and forced. My fingers, sweaty, hot and trembling brushed the tips of his as he held out the ball. I turned and plopped it into the net in front of me.

"I'm fine," I croaked. My hand went to my throat and rubbed it. I needed water. Air. To be far away from him before I accused him of something so improper it risked getting me fired.

"Do you have any questions for me?"

He was still standing too close. I couldn't bring myself to check the room to see if we were garnering attention.

My scalp pricked like a thousand eyes were on me anyway, even if there were only a dozen people there.

Do I know you?

That was not the question to ask.

But his voice was almost knowing...like he expected me to ask the question.

It was impossible. Wasn't it?

"Yes." I cleared my throat. Turning, I dug into my purse at my side and grabbed my water bottle. I needed to get a grip and seriously fast before I did something stupid, like shove my face into the crook of his neck to smell him. I took a long drink of water, too long, based on the way Gage's eyes crinkled at the edges. A smile played at the edges of his lips and the same time he bounced the basketball at his side.

Thump. Thump. Thump.

It matched the beat of the thunder raging through me.

"If Harrison were here," I asked, referencing his brother.

Immediately the ball stopped bounced and his back straightened. "What would be his favorite thing to do in this room?"

It was a personal question and a long shot. In my manila folder of events were strict instructions. No personal questions outside what he freely gave, and no exclusives.

His eyes closed and that hint of a smile he wore evaporated. A mask slammed down into place and until he opened his eyes, black lashes rimming his eyes opening every so slowly, I fought against apologizing. I should have, but personal curiosity stopped me.

He held up the ball in his hand. "Basketball. He'd be here as much as possible."

"Not football?" I gestured to the football game where a ball could be thrown through several different holes, each target a varying degree of points. "You told Brandon that was his favorite."

His steely eyes didn't waver from mine. There was no hint of familiarity between us anymore. It'd frozen like a block of ice as soon as he closed his eyes.

I wouldn't think about why that hurt so much.

"It was. Knew everything about the game, but more than knowing and loving something, he was a competitor." He turned and threw the ball, swished it through the net again and ignored it as it rolled back to me. "On his healthy days, he would have been here, egging me on, giving me shit about how I'd never be able to beat him. On the days he was too sick to throw, he'd sit in a wheelchair next to me, challenging me to beat my time."

My brothers had that relationship. Always pushing each other. Always trying to outdo the other. "Brothers have a special bond," I said, thinking of mine. There were times in my life when I was pretty irrelevant even if I was the third born. Older than Tanner and I by five years, Blake and Jaxon were born only eleven months apart. They were fiercely competitive in everything they did. Always trying to outplay and outlast. To say my home was like *Survivor* was putting it gently.

"You have brothers."

It wasn't a question and I nodded, grabbed the ball in front of me and shot it. It bounced off the rim, hit the backboard, swam in a circle and dropped in. It was a messy shot, but I bit my lip to keep from grinning.

"Yeah. Three of them."

"What are they like?"

My eyes slid to Gage. He was facing me, hands on his hips, head bent. Our voices were low and this conversation had jumped the track. I didn't mind we'd gone off the rails.

It fit how I'd been feeling for a week.

"Fierce. Protective. Loud." The ball rolled back to me and I picked it up and shot it again. I missed it by a mile. "Idiots. They're all idiots."

"Most guys are."

"But not you?" I grinned at him. It couldn't be helped. I wouldn't be me if I wasn't a smartass at least once during a conversation.

He tilted his chin and smirked. "I have my moments."

I tried for my most disappointed look. "Figures."

"Anything else you want to ask me?"

"I'd like an exclusive." The words popped out before I knew they were coming. Too fast for me to stop them and had I thought for a single second, I never would have said them.

His arms crossed over his chest. Scowl slammed in place. "No."

He took a step back. It felt like a mile. I'd just crossed a line. All over the agenda and rules, we were made known two things. No personal questions. No exclusives. He'd give us what he gave of his personal life and nothing else.

But I'd already crossed the line with asking about his brother.

I blamed that brain fart on going for the other. Somehow I was too comfortable around him. Perhaps it was because he'd tried to pick glass out of my foot.

"I apologize," I said. "That went too far."

"Anything else?" His jaw jutted out ferociously.

I felt like a steaming pile of dog shit. "No. I have everything I need."

He spun on his heel and left the room. I forced him to flee the entire wing and as he walked away, stalking like he needed to go hit something, all eyes in the room swung directly to me.

Including Connor's.

"I think you screwed that up, Elizabeth," Jason said.

"No shit?"

FOURTEEN

Gage

A shadow darkening the screen in front of me made me jump.

Ripping off my noise-canceling headphones, I wasn't at all shocked to see Beaux Hale, our quarterback, standing off to my side, arms crossed over his chest, eyes flicking from me to the screen.

"What?" I'd been a jerk all day at practice. Sullen and for God's sake I'd even been pouty.

Why? Because freaking Elizabeth Hayes asked for an exclusive. All reporters did, but I hadn't expected it from her, not when I'd clearly stated I didn't give them. Ever.

Too many reporters dug too deep into personal things I refused to discuss and when I said no comment, I was the one who ended up looking like a jerk.

That Elizabeth had already crossed a line in asking about Harrison already made me wary of her. But it'd felt so damn good to talk about him, too. It didn't matter he'd been gone for over twenty years. He was and always would be my brother.

"Hard day," Beaux said. He pointed at the screen where I paused it. It was a pass from last week's game. Damn ball slipped right through my fingers. I was double-teamed, but I still should have caught it. I was still pissed I missed it. Probably because before the play had started, someone had called me a pussy. Which had made me think of burying my dick in Elizabeth so I was a half-second slow jumping off the line. "You figuring your shit out?"

"Yup."

Beaux was a decent guy. One of the best. He had way too much fun in life, enjoying the ride and the high of not only his career but his new wife, Paige. They were married in the off-season and watching him get married, some guy who'd gone through way too much crap in his life, find the woman he wanted to spend the rest of it with, somewhere deep, that had splintered inside of me. Opened a yearning I'd always figured would never come.

Beaux also wasn't good at letting crap go when he had something to say. He walked around the tables in the film room and pulled up a chair next to me. Sliding on his own headphones, he left them hanging around his neck.

He didn't look at me as he linked his hands together. "Next couple weeks are going to be rough for you I would imagine."

"It's fine."

"Really?" Doubt and sarcasm rang thick in my ears. "Because if it was me, having to spend a few weeks constantly thinking of my mom and how she died and if there was anything I could have done to make her life better when she was alive, any joy I could have given her, any way I could have been less of a dick when she was truly sick." He shrugged, played it off like it was no big deal. Beneath my skin, ants started marching. Fire ants with tiny, vicious bites. "Well, that'd fuck up my game. You must be a better man that I am."

"It's not Harrison or the hospital screwing my game. And we won didn't we?"

"Yeah because Jones picked up your side."

Kolby Jones was always his second target. After I'd missed that pass, he became Hale's first target when he wasn't lobbing it to Powell in the end zone.

"Fuck off, Hale."

He drummed his hands on the table. "See...you mention fucking, and the fact it's not Harrison who has your nuts twisted, and I'm thinking it's a woman who's got you all screwed up. Man, been there."

He still hadn't even glanced at me. But what in the hell was with the pep talk from hell? I'd still had over one hundred receiving yards. So what if Kolby became his prime target in the second half. We won the damn game.

I was not talking to him about Elizabeth. I wasn't talking to anyone about her. Ever.

I grabbed my headphones, intent on sliding them back on and drowning him out when he said, "It was a great party last weekend. Paige and Shannon loved it. Had so much fun Powell and I had to carry them to the cars at the end of the night."

"Glad you enjoyed it."

"Yeah." He faced me then and his blue eyes gleamed with something I knew I wouldn't like. "But see my favorite part of the night was watching you on your knees in front of a sexy little reporter. And I think, she's a tiny thing, maybe not quite your type, but damn...if I was single, I would have been jumping all over that."

Yup. I'd called it. A fire punched my chest so fast so quick I didn't have time to school my reaction to one of disinterest. "Watch it."

Beaux threw his head back and laughed, ran a hand through

his blond hair. "Knew it. Fucking knew you had something going on with her."

"It's nothing."

Last night I left pissed after our time together when she screamed John as she came. I'd wanted it to be mine, just to see her face pinched with pleasure, exploding into ecstasy and hear my name roll from her lips with a guttural groan. I'd felt like a jerk after. Wanted to somehow make it better today even if she didn't know it'd been me that treated her like she was nothing.

But then she looked so damn cute, struck mute when I walked up. She'd flipped on her reporter hat and flashed me her professional smile and that had pissed me off more.

Not that she asked, but how in the hell could she not put it together that I was the man who had his hands all over every single inch of her body?

Did it mean anything to her?

"Yeah, I said that about Paige a time or two as well. Didn't work though."

"Seriously, Beaux. Drop it."

He didn't relent. I shouldn't have thought he would. He wasn't our quarterback and leader of our team for nothing. "Why don't you date?"

"Seriously?" I turned to him. He was exasperating as hell. "We're going to do this girlie shit? I'm trying to watch films."

"It's ten o'clock and you've been watching films for six hours."

His brows arched. Damn. Had I really been sitting in this dark room for so long? No wonder he figured there was something wrong with me.

"Don't have time to date."

"Get that. You're committed to football. Helping others. Running your charities. But I'm just wondering when you're going to stop living in the shadows of Harrison and what your parents want and finally go reaching for something for yourself."

"What the fuck?" The hell was his problem?

He lifted his hand, but I slapped it away. I didn't need his damn explanations. Crossing the line and bringing up my brother? My parents?

"Hear me out," Beaux said. He pushed off the chair and stood. I was right behind him, chest out, heart thundering, adrenaline rushing. Goddamn. I'd never wanted to punch my quarterback more.

"No."

"Listen, I get it. I do. You think I didn't want to do the same shit after my mom died? You think I didn't care about Shannon more than I did myself? I get it, Bryant. Swear to you, I fucking get it. But you're also over thirty years old and outside of football, you don't have a damn life."

I had a damn life. In the private walls and rooms of Velvet and that was as much as I needed.

"You seriously don't have any idea what you're talking about."

He shrugged. Dropped his hands. "Maybe not. Maybe I'm wrong, but I know and Powell knows and half the men on the team will tell you that if you're slaving away working only on your career, you're only living half the life you deserve. Whatever it is you want and won't reach for, whatever it is that has you looking like you're going to pummel my face, reach for it, Gage. Fucking grab a hold and take it and I swear to you, life will only get better."

He spun and headed out of the room. I was breathing like a dragon long after he'd disappeared.

Damn him. Beaux was a good guy, but I never realized how damn smart and wise he was. Still didn't mean I was admitting it.

But that didn't mean he was wrong. I'd lived my entire life, even while Harrison was sick, making sure I never brought them any disappointment, any embarrassment, working twice as hard at being three times as good as anyone else to make their lives easier.

When in the hell *was* I going to start thinking of my own wants and needs?

~

TUESDAYS WERE our off days during the season. We spent Mondays watching films of the previous games, getting screamed at whether we won or lose by Coach Pomville, and received our accolades where they were due.

For my part, I'd been lucky to miss most of the encouraging in the form of shortening when I'd had to give the tour of the hospital. That'd been why I was at the facility so late watching films on my own. Just because I missed the day didn't mean I got the day off.

Tuesday was our day off, a day where players usually spent it with their families since they missed them on the long practice days and weekends we traveled.

I didn't take a day off. I still went to work, either at charities or for the last two years, working on the construction of the new wing.

Now, with not a whole lot to do and nothing planned for the opening, I still found myself wandering down the hallways of the hospital.

I got up at five thirty, early even for me and took off to the gym where I swam for an hour, lifted for another before I realized I had to chill the hell out or I'd overdo it.

My sides were sore from a few hard tackles and while working out was important, most of our strength training occurred during the offseason.

It was the offseason that made you better during the season. The training and work you put in when no one was looking that created your biggest improvement. I learned that from my Pop Warner coach when I was ten. It was still advice I lived by and believed accurate.

But even after the grueling workout followed by a rest in the sauna, my second protein-rich meal of the day delivered courtesy of a local company who focused on meal prep delivery meals for athletes in the area, I still had too much rushing through my body.

Too much distraction thinking of Elizabeth. Too much anger thinking of Beaux's parting words. Too much guilt thinking of Harrison and what he never had. Too much of every damn thing.

Which was why I figured a stop to the children's hospital would settle me down. Nothing made you more thankful for everything you had regardless of the sacrifice it took to get there than wandering rooms and talking to children who might not ever leave the depressing looking rooms.

I took my time, hitting up as many rooms as possible. I dropped off signed footballs, a few stocking caps for the patients who were losing or would soon lose their hair from treatments. A few fleece blankets for smaller children to hug while they slept and more than a half-dozen signed jerseys for the pre-teens and teenagers who were too old for hats and blankies.

By the time I hit Brandon's room, my focus was more settled, my mind back in the right frame.

Beaux was wrong. He knew nothing of what I'd lived. He lost his mom, but he was a teenager, not the little kid who grew up being forced to wash his hands and use disinfectant every time he came in from outside or wearing a face mask to school so I didn't catch the flu or other common viruses and pass it to Harrison. He didn't know the microscope I lived under, being the small town pastor's 'surviving' child...not the son. Not the kid. The surviving one.

Like last week when I saw Brandon, I peeked inside the window, expecting to see him sleeping, his pale and sunken in cheeks looking more ashen than pink.

Instead, his mouth was wide open, throwing back a laugh and on the bed, his hands were animated. He paused, coughed into a bony fist, and then continued, excitedly telling a story.

He was doing better. Which means as I opened his door without knocking, I expected to see Penny be the object of his fascinating story.

But all I saw was that familiar haze of red in my vision.

Damn her.

Why was she suddenly taking over and invading every damn aspect of my life?

FIFTEEN

Elizabeth

Brandon's laugh was scratchy, but there was something so beautiful about it at the same time. His joy still shined through the hoarseness.

"They really tried to do that?" He threw his hands to his face and dropped it, his bony shoulders shaking.

"Yup. They also learned that Mr. Gardner was a really good shot with the shotgun."

He tossed those same hands into the air and his mouth dropped. "He shot your brothers?"

"He shot at them—"

I was immediately cut off. The door opened forcefully grabbing both my attention and Brandon's. Gage stood in the doorway and if I'd been reading wearing a red cape, he would have charged at me with horns lowered. His fury for me was unmistakable.

He let go of the handle and stepped into the room. Skewering me with a glare that froze me to my spot, he shifted his gaze to Brandon and grinned. "Hey little man, how are you doing today?"

Brandon's eyes slid from Gage to me and back again. Shrugging, he said, "I'm okay. Ms. Hayes was just telling me a story about how her brothers tried to jump on a bunch of cows and ride them like horses."

"Is that right?" He didn't glance back at me. In an instant, he managed to dismiss me. Gage pulled up the chair I had been sitting on before I became animated with my story, and sat down on it next to Brandon's side of the bed.

"How about you tell me that story," he said. He was speaking to Brandon, not me and irritation spiked. Sure, I'd only met Brandon because I followed Gage last week, but I still felt a lump in my throat when I left the hospital without saying hi to him. I'd left quickly after Gage had turned and hurried out of the room, mumbling to Jason I had all I needed. And I'd been so caught up in the story afterward, apologizing to Jason over his cursed mumblings about my strange behavior, I'd been too upset to go say hi.

But today, I'd stopped by just to see Penny and Brandon and when I arrived and Brandon was sleeping, I sent Penny down to the cafeteria.

I hadn't expected Gage to be there at all. Now, with the way he was ignoring me, shifting his back to me and giving Brandon his full attention, I almost wished I never would have come.

His actions were clear. He wanted me gone. And he wanted me gone *now*.

I wasn't a pushover. With three brothers in the house, they'd taught me at an early age how to stand up for myself. They also taught me how to learn when to walk away from a fight. The last thing I wanted to do was fight with Gage or get into any kind of argument with him with Brandon in the room. Besides, his sudden problem with me wasn't my business.

Although that didn't explain the stinging pain in my chest as he ignored me.

I stepped softly to the end of the bed and placed my hand on Brandon's blanket covered feet. "I need to get back to work anyway. Thanks for letting me hang out with you this afternoon. I'll see you soon okay, buddy?"

Brandon's grin had to have the ability to melt even the hardest of hardened hearts. His teeth were slightly yellowed, and two of them had chips in them. Most likely due to chemo damage ravaging his little body. But even with the flaws, his smile was a shining beacon able to light up Times Square on New Year's Eve. Goddamn. He was cute.

"Come see me again?" he asked in that pleading, sweet voice of his.

"I will," I promised. And I would. Even if Gage showed and made it clear he didn't want me there. Whatever his problem was wasn't my business. "I'll be back as soon as I can."

"And bring Will?"

No kid should know as many newscasters as this boy did. I flashed him a wink. "Maybe I'll bring Amanda, too."

His cheeks flushed. A pale pink hue at the apples of his cheeks. "You...well...she..."

"She's cute, I know. And she'll like you too. Later this week okay?" I'd make her stop by with me on our way out for drinks. She'd be flattered by his crush on her. He might have liked my reporting, but it was Amanda's boobs I was sure made Brandon flush like he was the healthiest pre-teen in the world.

"Thanks, Ms. Hayes."

"I told you, Brandon. My friends call me Elizabeth or Beth."

Out of the corner of my eye, Gage's shoulders went ramrod and his head turned to me. With narrowed eyes, a gleam in them shone. Something fierce. Something hot. Something that'd whipped the breath out of my lungs.

With a dangerously low voice, he rumbled, "See you soon. Beth."

I gasped. Stepped back.

His voice was gravelly. Rich and rough.

My hand went to the foot of the bed as I grappled for balance.

It was *him?*

It couldn't be. I shook my head and without looking at either of them, grabbed my purse and hurried out of the room.

Outside, I plopped against the cool wall and stared at my feet.

See you soon.

See you soon.

Beth.

Fuck.

Hands on the dresser.

Give me that ass.

My eyes squeezed shut until bright little dots shone behind closed lids.

It *was* him.

John.

And it was like he wanted me to know with that look and that growl.

Oh God.

It had happened. I was falling for the man who masked me and screwed me senseless.

And for some reason, the man seemed to hate my guts.

MY LEGS WERE STILL WOBBLING as I entered my apartment. How I managed to drive back home without swerving into a ditch was still a surprise.

How? How could that man be the same guy who spanked me and plugged me and did all the delicious things I loved and did them so exquisitely I knew I'd never find another guy who was so perfect for me?

At least sexually. Personality wise we definitely seemed to be on different wavelengths.

I locked the door behind me, kicked off my sandals, and dropped my purse on the entryway table.

"Shit," I groaned. My hands went to the back of my neck and I rubbed away the tension that had popped and flared as soon as Gage burst into that small hospital room.

They really needed to make those things bigger.

It was my day off work, and I'd planned a relaxing day. Go see Brandon, stop by the gym and then to go get my nails done. On the way home, I'd swing by the grocery store, come home and soak in a nice long bubble bath with a glass of red wine and a good book to finish out the carefree day.

Now all those plans were shot to shit. I wasn't relaxed and carefree. I was wound tighter than a stripper upside down on a stripper pole. My legs ached for no reason. My shoulders curled forward the muscles were so tense. My cupboards were bare and my wine was non-existent. And it was all because of stupid Gage Bryant and his glares and gravelly voice.

Goddamn it. How could it be him? I hadn't been mistaken, but it explained so much.

How he knew about Velvet in the first place. Why he'd looked so pissed at me at that news conference. Why he couldn't wait to get away from me afterward.

He'd screwed up my day. He'd screwed up my trip to Velvet. How could I see him again and take the blindfold and act like I didn't know it was him?

Unless...he wanted me to know.

Maybe it was driving him crazy I hadn't recognized him immediately.

"Yeah right." I snorted. "Gage doesn't seem like the guy with an easily wounded ego."

I flipped on the water to the shower and while it warmed, I wrapped my hair into a messy bun with a scrunchie. Screw the workout. A hot shower wouldn't clear my head, but at least I'd feel clean.

Afterward, I'd go to the store, stock up on the necessities: cheese and wine. And later, I'd gorge on a season of *Outlander* or *Game of Thrones*. Anything epic to take my mind off of Gage Bryant.

Easier said than done.

As soon as I stepped into the shower, and the hot water pounded against my shoulders, my back, I was assaulted with memories of him.

The way he smiled at Brandon. His story behind the reason for the center. He wasn't some damn entitled superstar doing this out of obligation. He was doing it because he wished he'd had it when he needed it. He was doing it to make a difference because it would have made a difference to him.

As my mind conjured dozens of reasons to stay away from him, my wandering, traitorous hands discovered a mind of their own.

That stupid, growly voice in my ear. The scrape of his now shaven scruff along my inner thighs. The force of his fingers against my forbidden areas.

"Damn it." My face flushed. My body warmed from nothing to do with the water.

The tops of my thighs pulsed as every memory of the two of us together in two, long but intense encounters swirled through my mind.

I couldn't stop the arousal that blossomed deep within me.

None of his growls and glares and scowls and clipped words

and impatience did a darn thing to dull the ache at the tops of my thighs.

I brushed my thumb over my nipple and shivered. They were already hard and sensitive. Aching for attention. I pinched one, ran my other hand down my stomach. Everything was lit with need. Every aching inch of my flesh was ready for him.

But would I ever see him again?

"Doesn't matter," I whispered to the shower wall. I didn't need Gage Bryant or his commands or his punishments for not listening. The memories I had of him would forever be enough to take care of me.

Which meant, as my hand drifted down to my core, already swollen and throbbing, it didn't take long to get myself off.

I came, crying out Gage's name.

"Shit." I reached for the soap and dumped way too much onto my loofah. My voice trembled as badly as my shaking legs.

I was dead wrong. The memories of Gage might have been enough to get me off, but it wasn't nearly what I needed.

My body needed him.

And now that I knew who he was, how would that ever happen again?

"THAT'S all from the Rough Riders' stadium, where dozens of children and families will be attending this Sunday's home game, right from this very own field level suite. I'm Elizabeth Hayes with XTCP. Back to you in the station, Amanda."

I grinned, fake as fake could be, and waited until Jason flipped his standard two-finger salute, letting me know we were clear.

Oh my God. A day in hell couldn't be worse than the afternoon I'd spent.

Hours. Hours upon hours watching padded and suited up mountainous men grunt and shove and tackle and run and throw.

Why had I never been a football fan before?

I'd missed too much of my life spending it in the kitchen with my mom getting manicures and learning how to braid hair. I should have been on my dad's lap, learning the ins and outs of the games so I wasn't so lost.

Today was too much. An open practice where I sat and focused, not only on the upcoming weekend where I'd be forced to watch the game from that field level suite I mentioned in my broadcast, but three hours of seeing Gage run and catch a ball, smack a player's ass, shove another to the side.

His smile was wicked but focused, his intensity a notch above everyone else, but he still maintained a playfulness that made watching him love the game he played for a living and multi-million dollar contracts and endorsements, so damn enthralling.

My panties were wet. It couldn't be helped.

I'd rubbed one out to thoughts of Gage more times than I could count over the weekend. It was amazing my knuckles on my fingers hadn't locked up.

Good God. He brought that lusting on himself with not only the things he'd done to me at Velvet, but by the way he moved on the field.

It shouldn't have hurt that he hadn't looked my way. Nope. Not even once. He'd sauntered over to Connor and answered a few questions. He'd even grinned happily down at little miss perky syndicate reporter. But me? As soon as I went to ask a question, he rose his brows, pressed his lips together, and walked away.

Which meant even while I was doing my job the best I could, I wasn't getting enough to knock this out of the park to secure my spot for the nighttime news desk.

We hadn't heard from Shayla in the last two weeks since she

went on leave. The verdict on that job would be out for months yet until she returned or gave notice, but damn it. My career was on the line and if I didn't nail it, I'd be stuck doing news reports with giraffes trying to eat my hair for the rest of my life.

And Gage was ruining it for me.

He was ruining everything for me.

The ability to masturbate happily and be satisfied enough for sleep.

He was ruining my dreams and decent night's sleep.

And hell, he was even ruining my ability to zone out on Sundays to silly love movies on the Hallmark Channel because I knew, just knew, I was now going to be tempted to turn on sports channels. And wasn't that a swift kick to the boobs?

I'd successfully managed to ignore sports all my life even with a house filled with ultra-over-the-top testosterone driven males and two weeks of knowing Gage Bryant and having his hands on me twice, I'd become a fool.

I kicked at the turf, grumbling under my breath.

My phone buzzed in my pocket and I dug it out, grinning as I read the texts from Amanda.

"Great job today! Damn those men are pretty. Drinks tonight?"

My thumbs flew across the small keyboard. **Oh yes. LOTS of drink.**

Uh oh...trouble with the hunk of meat?

I'd tell her all I could later but now wasn't the time.

A pair of black dress shoes stopped in front of me. How much worse could this day get?

"What do you want Connor?" I asked.

I didn't have to look at him to know who it was. He was the only guy in the place wearing dress shoes. The players had on cleats. The cameramen were wearing running shoes.

I typed back my quick reply. **Men suck. Talk later. Be to the station in 45.**

She sent me a "thumbs up" emoji and I stepped toward where Jason was still taking care of his equipment.

"You know what I want," Connor said.

His voice had gone soft and thready. I knew exactly what that meant.

I stopped, barely able to conceal my eye roll. He'd like it too much.

"No."

He stepped in front of me and lifted his hands.

"Seriously?" I arched both brows. Was he joking? "Do not block me with your body thinking intimidating me will get me to change my mind. My answer is no. It will stay no."

"You haven't heard what I had to say." He was smart enough to step to the side. Too bad for me he didn't walk away.

I flicked my hand in the air. "It's irrelevant."

"I'm breaking up with her."

That stopped me. How dare he. How dare he! This week of all weeks. Today of all days. This lifetime of all lifetimes. I couldn't stop the burn heating the backs of my eyes and whatever look I gave him made him flinch.

"You're kidding me. Tell me you are not doing this to me right now, right here. We are at *work*."

"I know. But tell me you don't remember how good we were. I was confused. The reason things aren't working with Mel is because I miss you, Lizzie. I don't know what happened. I wanted you then. I cared about you. I just...I got scared when you said what you did and Mel was there..."

"Don't finish that." My chin wobbled. Hot cheese on toast this man who broke my heart was not going to make me cry in front of hundreds of people. No one was paying us a lick of attention. We were reporters. Working on a story. We could have been collaborating on a story, but the only collaborating going on was my brain convincing my foot not to slam into his nuts.

It was a battle I was losing.

"Please," Connor said. He stepped closer to me. Still professional. Still not touching. The man must have seen my look and prized his balls to come any closer. "Tonight. One night, Lizzie. I'll give you whatever you ask for. Whatever you need. You don't want it, I'll never talk to you again. Promise. I know I hurt you. I'm asking for the chance to make up for it. Give me a second chance."

I swiped at my cheeks. Damn him. Why couldn't this have happened five months ago? Why couldn't he have shown up at my door with flowers and chocolates and a bottle of wine and talked to me about this?

It wasn't fair, but it didn't mean he didn't still have the power to twist my heart.

I looked up and froze. My lips parted.

Across the indoor field, Gage was staring at me. Arms crossed, helmet at his feet. He'd already ripped off his practice jersey and his pads were visible along with the blocks of muscle on his abdomen.

Even from far away I could see smoke pluming from his ears.

Well, screw him, too.

I placed my hand on Connor's arm, grinned at Gage, and beamed that same, fake grin at Connor. "I'll be there at nine."

SIXTEEN

Gage

Idiots. They all are.

Most guys are.

But not you?

I have my moments.

I was most definitely having one of my most idiotic moments ever, in the history I could remember since I tried to use a fish aquarium to climb onto the top of a shed. My foot broke right through the glass, slicing all up and down my lower leg.

Thirty stitches later and the rest of my football at the ripe old age of twelve ruined, and I was right back to being as big of a moron as that ridiculous thrill-seeking kid.

I mean, how else was I going to see Jenny Walker's boobs if I didn't climb onto my shed to peer into her window?

That was how I felt, watching Elizabeth press her hand to Connor's arm and smile at him. It was fake, but he was too self-absorbed to see it. I didn't even want to question how I knew it was fake, but I gave credit to Brandon. I'd seen her smile with him.

Whatever she gave to Connor wasn't anything close, but that didn't mean shit.

She touched him.

She smiled at him and nodded and she'd agreed to something he suggested and I already knew the only thing he wanted from her.

Coupled with the smile she flashed me, I knew exactly what he offered her.

"Fuck." I kicked my helmet on the ground and bent and snatched it up before it rolled too far.

Practice had been hell.

My week had been hell.

Ignoring Elizabeth after essentially outing myself in Brandon's room because I was so overwhelmed with her presence and how she seemed to fit *so damn perfectly* into my life had been hell.

I didn't relish acting like a jerk. It didn't come natural to me and yet, I'd been a complete jerk to Elizabeth and even when I tried to stop myself, it still happened.

What voodoo magic had she bewitched me with to make me so damn twisted up over her? We'd had two sessions together. It wasn't the sex.

Although...it was damn good sex. But it wasn't that.

It was her going to Brandon for no damn reason other than to say hi. It was the way she talked about her brothers. It was how she asked about mine.

It was how she could defend herself, and it was her comebacks and her obedience.

It was her gasps and her teasing.

It was her confidence she'd bare herself to a man she couldn't see and even that wouldn't prevent her from being free to let go of control.

She was perfect for me, and every time I turned around, I was doing the exact same thing Beaux had accused me of. I was falling for a woman and for whatever reason—because even I knew all my excuses were lame—I was too damn scared to reach for her.

I stalked into the locker room and tossed my helmet to the bottom of my locker. I was undressed quickly, tugging and snapping off buckles, yanking off my shoulder pads and shoving down my pants. I grabbed a towel and wrapped it around my waist, headed toward the showers.

I'd get cleaned up.

I'd figure my shit out, and then I'd figure out what to do with little Miss Hayes who had slithered into my brain and refused to leave.

"Good practice today," Powell said to me, passing me back from the showers.

I slammed my fist into his. "You too, old man."

He turned and lifted his arms in the air. He wore nothing but a towel and the well-known cocky Powell smirk. "You only wish you could look this good when you're as old as I am."

"Damn straight." I flung the towel I had wrapped around my neck and flipped it at him, smacking him right in his six-pack I knew women all over fawned over.

Seriously. More than one woman came up and asked for my autograph, only to then asked if Powell was as sexy in person as he was on television. Like I'd know how to answer that.

He gripped his stomach and pointed a finger in my direction. "Watch it. I'm still young enough to kick your ass."

"Yeah, yeah."

I shoved the towel back to my shoulder and hit the showers.

Today's practice had been good, despite the reporters and the questions I had to answer afterward. I was focused. I didn't drop a pass. My time jumping off the line was on point. And I was able to do all of that knowing Elizabeth was in the stands watching.

Perhaps I performed better because she was there.

I quickly pushed her out of my mind and focused on running plays in my mind. A hard-on in the men's communal shower wasn't exactly on my planned list of activities.

Ignoring the players who were celebrating our win, I washed up as fast as possible and headed back to the locker room. In less than thirty minutes, I was dressed, duffel bag slung over one shoulder.

I still had no idea what to do about Elizabeth, no idea how to fix what I knew I'd screwed up.

But it sure as hell wouldn't stop me from trying.

And if she ever put her hands on Connor again, despite him being her ex, she'd know exactly what I thought about women who were *mine* touching another man.

∼

"TRISTAN?"

"Are you through with her?"

My grip on my steel water bottle went hard. It was after nine. I was kicking back, watching a sweet as hell Navy Seal television show. At Tristan's question, my feet slammed to the floor and I was hurrying to my room. I didn't need to clarify who or what he meant. The instant thumping in my chest at the only reason he would call told me everything.

"Did she take a room?"

His French voice grated on my impatient nerves. "I ask the questions and you didn't answer mine."

Shit. Was I done with her?

No way in hell. Not by a long shot. "No."

"Then you should get here."

She was there. That's what she agreed to with Connor earlier?

When I got her back into a private room, I'd plaster her back-side with red stripes.

After talking to her in reasonably, controlled tones.

"Private room?" I repeated.

"No. She's still in the anteroom waiting to enter."

Small favors. But the fact she was there, talking to security and signing in didn't settle anything inside.

"Would you like me to—"

"Keep her busy. I'll be there in thirty but do not let her get to a room. But prepare one for me."

"*Je te comprends.*"

I hoped that meant yes. Why he insisted on speaking French when I had no clue what it meant was beyond me. He hung up and I tossed my phone to my bed. Stepping into the closet, I didn't grab the black I usually wore to The Velvet Club. Thankfully, getting your kicks in a sex and voyeur club meant pretty much anything went. Some people wore masks to disguise their own identity. Some wore barely anything at all. The women who walked around in lingerie never grabbed my attention previously and so help me God. If that was what Elizabeth chose to wore when she roamed the gathering room searching for prey, or intent on being taken...

I refused to finish the thought.

I gripped a gray shirt and yanked it off the hanger. Dark blue jeans came next. I shucked off my sweats, tugged my clothes on, and grabbed a black mask that covered half my face on the way out of the door.

Thirty minutes later, I stalked into Velvet and took a spot along a back wall where the crowds socializing were thicker and the lights darker.

It didn't matter where I stood, though. I found her immediately. All that glimmering blonde hair, spun like gold, curled and falling down her back. It helped Tristan was talking to her at the bar. Her back was to me, I had no idea if she wore a mask or if within these walls, she didn't care who saw her.

I crossed my arms over my chest and leaned against the wall. I lifted a booted foot and bent my leg, pressing the bottom to the wall for extra support.

And then I waited. The blood rushing through my veins didn't cool.

I needed to chill.

Then, I had to figure out once and for all, what would I do with the sexy little reporter, and how wicked would she let me be?

And then after? Who in the fuck knew, but I already knew we couldn't continue like this.

Later. I'd figure that out later.

My mission then was to ensure she wouldn't go fuck another man.

SEVENTEEN

Elizabeth

I almost didn't come. It was a mistake when I slid into a black tank top and short, super short but flirty black and white striped skirt.

It was a mistake when I signed in and took the wristband... pink indicating a taken sub. I didn't need more men complicating my already headache-inducing life filled with more men and lies and secrets than I could already handle.

Yeah, I definitely shouldn't have come. I might have been ready to venture into the private room with well-vetted interested men like *John,* but the gathering room had never been my thing.

I didn't make a lot of friends when I came here before and I tended to keep myself tucked into a corner at the bar. Not to drink, thanks to the standard one alcoholic drink limit. Lucky me, the club soda with lime flowed copiously.

Not exactly what I wanted so I was prepared to face Connor, so I was taking my time enjoying a glass of white wine, taking in the room.

The Velvet club was a classy place. It wasn't a trashy sex club with oiled up stripper poles. There weren't any public shows on a stage unless it was a private night for demonstrations. Those you had to register for separately and were put on before the club opened at night. They were for anyone interested in learning more, practicing techniques or learning new ones. Tristan always took the safety of his club seriously so he put as much time into training and practicum nights as he did into the decor.

Which he nailed. Rich, dark purple lined velvet chairs and booths surrounded silver tabletops. The floors were a light gray and sparkling chandeliers with thousands of tiny, miniscule lights hung from them throughout the room. It was decadent and sensual. And none of it screamed, "take me to your sex dungeon and flog me."

Thankfully. The first time I stepped into Velvet for a tour, I was freaked enough. Had it been all black and red screaming, "kinky sex happens here," I might have fled. As it was, the softness of the grays and lights along with the lure of the dark velvets and purples soothed my nerves upon entrance.

Tonight, it was that first night all over again, without the soothing presence.

That was until Tristan slid up next to me. He didn't sit and his eyes glanced at me quickly before continuing to survey the rather quiet gathering. For a Thursday, it was pretty slow. It was also on the early side.

"Hello, *chérie*. This is unexpected." His hands clasped together on the bar. "All is well?"

Everything was a tangled mess of knotted extension chords inside of me.

"*Oui*," I responded. It was one of the few French words I knew. "I'm just here to observe tonight."

"*Bien sur*. Of course." Tristan's gaze roamed the room and looked over my shoulder. As it did, his expression darkened. "Be careful this evening, *s'il te plait?*"

I stared at him dumbfounded. The French and his expression confused me.

"I'll be good," I promised, unsure it was the correct response. At his nod, he touched my shoulder. "Take care, *chérie*. Enjoy your evening."

A voice from the man I wasn't looking forward to seeing spoke behind me. "I wasn't sure you'd come, but I'm glad to see you."

Turning slowly, I took the quick moment to gather my nerves and school my expression. "I didn't come for you, Connor."

His head tilted in that cocky way of his. "Oh? Then why did you?"

"I came to clear the air. I'm seeing someone else." It was a partial lie. I had no idea what Gage and I were to each other. "And even if we weren't, I'm here tonight because the other times you've approached me we've been at work."

"I know. And that was foolish. I apologize, but—"

"No buts." I shook my head. "I loved you." At the confession, Connor jerked back. "I loved you and I wasn't afraid to admit it. Your job was to take care of me, always. And you neglected to do the one thing you're supposed to. Leaving me on that cross while you high-tailed it out of that room was humiliating."

"I know I didn't handle it well. It, well it shocked me."

"You treated me like crap and for that reason alone, I'd never have anything to do with you again. But I've also learned a lot about myself in the last six months and honestly, it's that what we had wasn't love. I confused it with love, but now that I've been with someone else, I see it clearly. I don't want you. For a night. Or for anything. So I'm asking you to drop this so we can still maintain a working relationship when we have to see each other."

I stepped away from him so he couldn't reach for me. My gaze scanned the area. Was Tristan still close? I didn't see him, and I looked for one of the security men walking around. They were noticeable by their headsets, but I didn't see any of them either.

"Connor, I'm sorry." I wasn't. I was still looking for someone to help if needed. Instead, I landed on someone else.

No. I'd recognize him anywhere, even if he had a strip of black across his eyes and over his nose. His haircut, something I'd studied along with this build made him unmistakable.

That and the fact he was gliding directly toward me, lips pressed together with vivid intent.

Oh shit.

I turned to Connor. "I wish you well. But I'm not the one for you, and even if I were, I truly don't appreciate how you've handled any of this. I was at a minimum, owed respect for our previous relationship and not only are you not listening to me, you're trying to manipulate me into giving you what you want. None of it's with thought of me, or what's best for me in your mind. Take care."

I didn't mean that either, but the angry growly mountain of a man was looming closer and I was intent on escaping.

Not that I actually believed I could run from him. His long stride could eat up my shorter one in a millisecond.

I didn't look back at Connor, but I darted into the crowd. I weaved back and forth until I came to why I had really shown up at Velvet that night.

To watch. It'd always fascinated me. People who had the confidence to fully immerse themselves in such a private experience and either not be bothered by potentially hundreds of strangers watching them, or get off *because* of hundreds of strangers watching them impressed me.

I was comfortable with sex. I liked it in a wide variety of ways. But still, even if it was with a man I didn't know, I still demanded that privacy for such intimacy. But what would it be like?

I stopped in front of the lit up room. The room was on the other side of the gathering than where I knew the one I always used was, but it was so similar, almost exactly the same except this one still had the St. Andrew's Cross in the corner and not the potted plant.

But it wasn't the cross that grabbed my attention and pulled me closer. It was the woman strapped to it.

Chocolate brown hair gleamed from soft overhead lighting. It was braided, draped over one of her shoulders. Her arms were lifted high and wide, secured to the top by wrist cuffs and her feet were the same at the bottom with her ankles.

She was fixed to the cross with her back facing it, full frontal view of her body displayed and completely naked.

The man with her, from the back, reminded me so much of Gage. Large, wide shoulders. Muscles galore all over his back and shoulders. Veins popped down his arms. He held nothing in his hands, but his arms were crossed. Furrowed brows showed focused attention on the woman in front of him as he spoke to her.

Her eyes lit with joy as he spoke. Green orbs sparkled as she answered. He moved toward her and gently settled his hand at the side of her throat. She leaned in close and spoke to him.

His response was a smile that shone. This couple weren't strangers. They weren't even play partners. They were in love and the depth of that love sent an ache to my gut.

I felt Gage come up behind me. How it was him, I didn't know except I expected him. And I seemed to have a Gage Bryant beacon attached to my libido. He came for a purpose and based on the way he'd move toward me, the way he scowled at Connor and me earlier, I had no doubt he was here to stop me from doing something stupid.

Silly man. He didn't know me at all. The only thing I

planned on doing tonight was him. I wasn't raised to toss away a gift, and I certainly wasn't about to start.

He pressed his chest to my back and slid his arm to my stomach. My hand went to his immediately and curled not only around the heat of his hand but cool satin.

Disappointing. We were back to that.

I gripped both his hand and the blindfold meant for me and continued watching the couple. The man was worshipping this woman. Strong hands with long fingers brushed over her collarbone and the curve of her breast before switching to the other. She had her eyes glued to her man, lips parted in pleasure and he was barely touching her.

I want that.

"You like to watch?" the man behind me asked.

He was bent low over me, mouth near my eye. The question sent shivers down my arms straight to my fingertips on his skin. I gripped him tighter. "Sometimes. You were a jerk."

The list of the ways he'd been a jerk was quite long.

His lips pressed my throat. My shoulder not obscured from the wide straps of my tank top. "I shouldn't have left you so rudely last time. I apologize."

Oh. We were back to that. It occurred to me then.

He didn't know I knew who he was. Or if he suspected, he wasn't ready to reveal himself. Again, disappointment flared, but curiosity of where this was going spurred me on.

"I wasn't expecting to see you tonight."

"What were you expecting?" His other hand went to my hip. He held me firmly against him. His erection obvious at my lower back. "Did you come to play?"

The grit in his voice was thick. I fought against a smile. He didn't like that idea.

Good.

"I came to talk to someone. And to watch."

"Have you ever been watched?"

"No."

"Would you like to?"

"I don't know. Maybe, if it was like them."

His head turned, chin rested on my shoulder. I closed my eyes and imagined we were that couple. It was impossible. He wouldn't even let me see his face, and I doubted he'd give me his heart. Too bad he didn't know I was holding mine in my palm. His for the taking.

"Like what? You want to be on the cross?" His voice was teasing and I felt my lips stretch into a smile.

"No. Their connection. It's beautiful."

"Hmmm."

The desire to turn around, press my hands to his cheeks and inspect as much of him I could see pulsed like an itch beneath my skin. I kept my gaze on the man and the woman. He was still caressing her. Along her sides, her breasts. Every time her eyes closed and a gentle smile tugged at her lips, he pinched her nipples. She arched off the cross, seeking him, to which he'd kiss her. Not her lips. Her throat. Her shoulder. He bathed her body in his kisses everywhere except where it was obvious she desperately craved them.

Evil man. Much like the one holding me. His breath skittered across my skin in soft gentle waves. The rhythm of his heartbeat at my back was a lullaby, drawing me in.

I relaxed into him, and he held me tighter. And when the man in the room slid his hands down to his wife's core, pressed two fingers in and yanked her to him, behind me, Gage groaned.

"Will you play with me tonight?"

It was a question, not a command, the first he'd given me as if he knew this night was our last chance for anonymity.

It had to be.

"Yes."

I'd give him this, but I wanted more. I would wait. But I wouldn't wait forever.

I'd already made that mistake with Connor and learned from it.

From behind, his hands went to my head. The cool brush of satin pressed to my forehead and then darkness overtook me.

It was strange, that satin.

As soon as it touched my skin, other areas warmed and rose to life, like him cutting off my light had a direct ignition switch to my core.

His large, warm and rough palm scraped down my arm to my hand and he clasped it in his.

"I'll move slow so you don't have trouble walking."

I gripped his hand firmly and leaned into his arm. And together, we went to the back rooms.

EIGHTEEN

Elizabeth

My body was a live wire by the time we entered the room.

It was the first time we entered together, and it was significant. For the first time, I not only knew who was going to give me unforgettable bliss, but his hand was still clamped in mine.

The door clicked closed behind us, yet all I felt was the contact of our skin. Hands connected. Bodies warmed. Oh yes.

We were so doing this.

"We're not in the same room," Gage said. He moved us so I was facing him and his hand went to my shoulder. "Our usual room was taken, but I think based on what you enjoyed from watching that other couple, this one will be just fine."

A cross. There had to be.

"Is that something you want?" he asked. His hand let go of mine, and they were at my hips, sliding beneath my tank top. Hot, burning skin pressed against my sides as he pushed up my shirt.

I wanted a bed and his body covering mine. But as he touched me, removed my shirt, my arms lifted of their own accord. And then his lips were at my shoulder. The slight scruff of his jaw running along my flesh.

"You didn't answer."

"Yes. I want that."

"Good. Turn around." He guided me and then there was the rustle of clothes. His hands slid to my back, flicked the clasp of my bra. He slid down the straps of my bra and as fresh cool air hit my breasts, his mouth was there, sucking and tasting, moving from one to the other, lower, until his hands were at my waist.

I imagined him, all broad shoulder and dark-haired, dropping to his knees before me. "Lift your foot."

I listened, lifted one foot, then the other, as he removed my shoes. He reached around and unbuttoned and unzipped my skirt. The soft fabric slid down my thighs, cooling it until his hands followed, dragging down my underwear, and everything warmed.

Guiding me toward the cross, arousal slid through me.

"Face me." His hands at my hips gently guided me backward. "I want to see you as I tease you."

"Just tease me?"

"No. I promise I'll give you everything you want." His hand cupped my cheek, fingers at my jaw and then his mouth was on mine. A firm, claiming kiss that stole my breath and filled me with life all while sending me careening out of control.

I was pliant while he lifted my hands, buckled them in. Instinctively I reached for a bar along the top I knew would be there to hold. And spread my legs. Buckles and snaps. The swoosh of his clothing as he moved. The gentle aroma of his cologne wafted in the air. By the time he had me naked and restrained, I hungered for him. In a way I knew if I lost him, if we didn't get past the blindfold and pretend secrets and masks, and he walked away from me, it'd take me far longer to get over Gage than it did Connor.

"Please," I whispered. He was still at my feet. Hands at my ankles. Running long, sweeping circles up my calves to my knees.

"Patience." He kissed my legs, fingertips ran at the backs of my knees, lips brushed along my inner thighs. He moved closer to my sweet spot, teasing brushes of his fingers and lips on my skin in places that shot sparks of flames throughout my body. "All good things come to those who wait."

I'd waited long enough. And patience had never been my strong suit.

I arched into him, buckles and straps clanking as I jerked toward him.

"Ah, ah eh," Gage teased, his lips were at my hips. Kissing my hip bones. My stomach. His hands followed, thumbs swiping at my core and sending a jolt of pleasure through me. "Stay here like a good girl and take what I give you and I promise you'll have everything you need."

He slid his fingers through my center, already wet and ready for him. "Oh. Look at you. Was it watching the couple that got you this wet or was it me?"

It'd been thinking of him looking at me like that man had worshipped his woman that had started all of it. "You," I breathed, as he slid two fingers slowly into me. "It was you."

His mouth hit my ear, his fingers crooked inside of me. My pulsed race, my breathing went ragged. "Oh God," I gasped, my head fell forward. At some point, he'd shed his shirt and my forehead pressed to the hardened curve of his chest.

"I love how easily you're turned on. How wet you get for me. How much you want it all the time." He slid his fingers in and out of me, teasing me with his words and his touch and the slick skin on his chest. "I also like that with you here, I could torture and tease you for hours, but we don't have all night do we?"

We didn't? I'd take all night with him. He kissed me. Slid his tongue into my waiting mouth. He tasted like heaven and hope, promises fueled by secrets. I came while he devoured my mouth, gasping and finding the peak, leaping freely.

"You're beautiful when you come," he whispered. His lips were lifted into a grin, pressing to the corner of my cheek. "And as much as I'd like to keep you here for hours, I also want to feel you against me. Let's save this fun for another day, shall we?"

"Yes. I'd like that."

And perhaps next time, I'd be able to see his face when he made me come instead of relying solely on my imagination.

AMANDA CLINKED her glass against mine. "Talk."

"Hmm?"

I'd gotten out of calling off our drinks the other night, but now it was Thursday Happy Hour, and I had no excuse to get out of drinks with her or her persistent questions.

It was part of what made her a good reporter. It was part of why having reporters as friends totally sucked.

Plus, I wasn't going to say no. Not after the morning I spent at the hospital. They'd opened up the new wing as a soft opening for only the current patients and their families to enjoy. The official opening was set for next week on the Rough Riders' bye week. But that morning, I'd spent three hours talking to families, my heart splintering more and more throughout the day as each story made its way not only to my notebook and tablet but to my heart. I alternated between wanting to break down and cry with many of the parents, craving to wrap the kids in healing hugs, and avoiding Gage at all costs.

That alone had taken so much effort, I was exhausted.

I usually had much more fun than I was having that day.

My head was in the clouds. Amanda noticing wasn't surprising. It also didn't surprise me she called me on it. That was

Amanda. Brash and bold, beautiful with blazing red hair. Amanda was essentially every good word that started with the letter B combined into one human. And yes, bitch was a compliment when used appropriately.

But good Lord I did not want to talk about what was on my mind.

I was sleeping with Gage Bryant.

Correction: Gage Bryant was fucking me and I was falling in love with him when we hadn't acknowledged we even knew each other. If there was a picture in the dictionary of "girls who make the worst decisions of men to fall in love with," mine would be plastered in a full page spread in bright, vivid colors.

This was worse than selfish Connor thinking he could use me, toss me aside, and pick me back up again when his new toy lost her shine.

Gage had a power over me that was different than the rest. I was falling for him despite the risks. His heart with the children. His entire life story. His focus. His character.

And I hadn't even seen his face while we were fucking. How screwed up was I?

"Earth to Beth."

I blinked. Amanda was waving her hand in front of my face giving me crazy eyes.

"Okay. There's a guy I like. It's new. And it's uncertain. So no, I don't want to talk about it more but I'm just going to say what I do like is good. Really, really good."

And scary as hell.

"See? That's the spirit." She leaned closer, rested her arms on the table. "Now tell me everything."

Yeah. Amanda was sweet and fun and a really good friend. She was also vanilla as they came. Telling her how I liked my sex? Never. Gonna. Happen.

I tipped my glass to my lips. Club soda and lime. I was so

hung up on Gage even alcohol didn't sound like fun. "That's all you're getting, woman."

"Elizabeth?"

My gaze slid toward the feminine voice and my drink froze at my mouth.

"Hi!" It was Shannon. Powell's wife. Next to her, Paige Hale was grinning. She lifted her hand in a silent hello. Before I could even respond, Shannon slid next to me. "Here Paige sit across from me." She flung her arm around me and yanked me to her. My head bounced off her shoulder and I fought a wince. "How awesome to see you here! How are you?"

"Shannon. You're scaring the normal people."

"Please." She rolled her eyes at Paige and let me go. Good Lord that woman had a grip of steel. "I'm not scary. I'm playful."

Across from me, Amanda's eyes bounced like ping-pong balls and she sputtered into her drink. "You're Shannon Powell." Her head whipped to Paige. "And Beaux's wife."

"Yes." Paige grinned playfully. "I also have a name. Paige Hale."

"Oh my gosh. I'm sorry. So sorry, that was so rude of me."

I sat back and glanced at Shannon. "Excuse her. She's excitable. Shannon and Paige, this is my friend and co-worker, Amanda."

"Lovely to meet you," Shannon said.

Paige and her exchanged greetings and when they were done, Amanda raised her brows in my direction. The classic silent, *oh we're talking about this later, twerp* look all good friends know how to dish and receive.

"So what are y'all doing tonight?"

Amanda tipped her martini glass in Shannon's direction. "You're looking at it. Elizabeth and I always head out for a few drinks after work on Thursday. You?"

Paige shrugged. "Window shopping and dinner. Mind if we

join you? I figured I'd ask since Shannon didn't give y'all a choice for more company."

"It'd be wonderful," I said. They'd been really sweet in the elevator even if it was only for a few minutes.

The waiter came by, took their drink orders and while we were waiting for them to arrive, Paige turned to me. "So, Beaux said Gage is really impressed with your stories these last couple of weeks."

It took massive effort not to sputter my drink over the table. "Excuse me?"

"Yeah. Beaux told me that Gage was going on and on about you." She folded her arms on the table and leaned in. "So, how are the stories going?"

Her head tilted to the side, blonde hair falling over one shoulder.

Right. The story. The hospital. That's what she was talking about.

I was stuck on the fact he'd actually talked about me. To teammates? And he'd been watching my stories?

It was too much information, too much heat slithering up my neck to my cheeks.

"Good. It's been fun. Challenging to make sure it's about the hospital and not the athlete, but overall, I've been enjoying it."

Next to me, Shannon chuckled. "I bet you're enjoying it. Gage is freaking hot. And nice."

"Really nice," Paige cut in. "Sexy and sweet. He's really like the perfect package."

Shannon sighed. "So much less of a jerk than my guy."

I narrowed my eyes on her. "You're married to ESPN's sexiest athlete of the year. Four years running."

"Well yeah. No one can deny his hotness. But he's also bossy. Arrogant."

Paige rolled her eyes and shook her head. "Oliver's

demanding they have a baby. Shannon wants to wait. She doesn't like the fact he keeps talking to her about it."

Amanda's brows almost flew off her forehead with shock. "You don't want to have his baby? Are you nuts?"

"I do. But I practically raised Beaux. And it's only been a couple of years." She shrugged and picked at a fingernail. "I finally have a job I love and the best husband when he's not being a bossy jerk. I just want it to be us a while longer. Is that so bad?"

"No. It's not bad at all." Everyone knew Beaux's story. Raised practically by his older sister. Their mom had worked her tail off to keep a roof over their heads and she ended up passing away when Beaux was still in high school. But it was Shannon who'd always been there for him. Who could fault her for a little more time to enjoy being married before she jumped into raising a family of her own?

"It's not bad," I assured her. "I'm sure Oliver will understand. But I totally get where you're coming from."

"Thanks. Now get Paige to understand, too."

"Me?" Paige said. Her hand went to her chest. "But I want to be an Aunt."

"Then become a mom and have your own kids if you want to spoil someone."

"For your information," Paige smirked. "Beaux and I are going to start trying as soon as the season's over. So I think if you and Oliver have babies, then we can have babies together and that'd be the best thing ever."

Shannon squealed and somehow the conversation turned to excited, animated talk of babies and Aunts and Uncles and presents and all things girlie.

We shared drinks with them, ate some dinner, and by the time dinner was done, and Paige and Shannon were handing out hugs and exchanging numbers, Amanda and I had both made two new friends. It always surprised me how quickly someone could enter your life in the most random fashion, and yet it suddenly felt like you'd known them forever. With Shannon and Paige, it was easy.

We said our good-bye's, dishing out hugs and exchanging numbers and as soon as they left, Amanda turned to me with a fresh martini.

"So..." Amanda sipped her drink. When Amanda wasn't chugging, it was dangerous. I didn't have time to brace myself before she threw down the axe. "Gage talks about you?"

Yeah. Somehow, I figured that was going to come up. Although I was hoping an hour or two of laughter would have made her forget.

"I have no idea what you're talking about."

"Mmm...hmmm."

"Are you hungry? I'm hungry." And really, screw the club soda and lime. Tonight was the perfect night to get drunk.

"We just ate." Oh. Right. She gave me eyes that said she wasn't letting this go.

I gave her eyes that said I didn't know what she was talking about.

"Fine. Then I need a drink." When the waiter returned, I ordered a martini.

Later, I took an Uber home. And when I woke up Saturday with a hangover, I had no regrets.

NINETEEN

Gage

There was nothing better than Game Day.

Every time I walked onto the field, I wasn't there to do a job, I was there to play the game I'd loved since I was seven and I first strapped on a helmet, slammed into a padded dummy held by a volunteer parent coach. I still kept in touch with Coach Mayer. That very first season of youth football embedded the love of the game in my veins. Harrison had passed away a year earlier. I'd promised him I'd play and I'd be the best in the world.

I might not have been the best, but every time I stepped onto the field, I took it all in. The energy. The excitement. The crazed fans who showed up half-naked with body paint covering their torsos and faces.

Harrison would have loved every minute, and it wasn't just my job, but it was my honor to remember him. To slam my fist to my chest and raise a hand high in the air, saluting him, giving myself a second to remember my brother. Sunday was no different. The stands were only a quarter of the way filled, but it was early, and they'd be filled soon. On the field, Philadelphia was already there. I walked on, helmet in my hand, scanned the crowd. The lights. The rumble of noise. It was like being in a tunnel and on top of the world at the same time. Words were shouted above the din, and in our end zone, Hale had on noise-canceling headphones while he warmed up his arm. I'd join him next and practice running routes with just enough energy to warm up our bodies but not wear ourselves out. Powell ran ten-yard sprints. He stopped every once in awhile to slap another player on the shoulder or talk to the offensive coordinator. A handful of defensive linemen warmed up with cardio.

Reporters and cameramen were setting up and it was the reporters on the field level box behind the padded walls where my attention finally settled.

Mostly to a pretty little blonde, long waves draped over her shoulders almost concealing the teal and blue jersey she wore.

To my shock, eighteen was stamped in bright white letters right across her front.

She was wearing my number. And seeing her in it knowing my name was stamped across her shoulder blades at the back, rocked me to my feet.

I hadn't wanted Thursday to go as it had. I'd wanted to take my time with her, to slide inside of her and remove her blindfold, but there was something about the moment we shared after I took her off the cross, after I stripped out of my clothes and laid her on the bed.

I'd crawled up her body, kissing every inch of her skin, chuckling as she arched into me, rolled her hips up to meet mine.

I pinned her hands over her head, itching to remove her mask to see her eyes when she came. To finally see what she truly looked when I slid into her, but I'd stopped.

One more night with the anonymity even though she'd already given away she knew who I was. It was stupid to keep pretending. It was also immature.

But was I ready to take us public? For the first time in my professional life, I knew that moving forward with Elizabeth wouldn't just change everything.

It risked everything as well.

Seeing her in my number?

Being with her was worth it.

I headed that way. A gaggle of kids were jumping and laughing. The healthier ones on their feet while the sicker ones were sitting in wheelchairs. And I finally admitted to myself that I wasn't moving straight toward Elizabeth, the reporter, to answer more questions. It was her, laughing with the kids and showing how genuinely good she was that made me realize what I'd spent weeks trying to deny.

I started falling for the pretty little blonde as soon as I walked into that room weeks ago when she wore nothing more than a smile and white lace panties and I'd kept falling for her, when I saw how hard she worked and how much she loved the kids at the hospital.

This was a woman who had the potential to give me everything I'd always wanted.

At the wall in front of the kids, several teammates stood, signing autographs for the kids and their parents.

I headed there, forced my feet to move as I focused on settling my heart.

Her gaze, wild with excitement, head thrown back in laughter at something one of the kids at her side said to her landed on me and sobered.

A pink hue slid to the apples of her cheeks. The hint of her tongue slid across her bottom lip as her gaze went hazy.

Had I not been dressed for the game, that look would have made me drag her to the ground so I could myself to the hilt deep inside of her.

Damn.

"Hey! How are my brave favorite fans doing?" I called to the mass of kids screeching my name as I grew closer.

Kolby Jones, one of our other starting wide receivers, slapped my pads and our center, Matthews, gave me a chin lift. They signed a handful of notepads, shoved in their direction by the kids.

"Dude," Jones said. "Some of these kids want to take our jobs from us someday."

"Yeah?" I scanned the small crowd of excited faces and pointed to one of the kids in a wheelchair. Brandon was still too sick to come, but this kid looked like it was a risk for him to be there as well. "How about you? You want my job someday?"

"Nope." He grinned, all teeth and stretched lips. "I'm gonna be Quarterback. But for Dallas."

"You'll have to work hard."

He slapped his hands on the armrest. "As soon as I'm outta here I'm gonna start training."

I laughed with the kid. He looked eight or ten. I guessed he was older. That was the thing about kids being sick, they grew old souls but their bodies took longer to catch up.

He shoved his football in my direction and I took it, scribbling my name on to it. "You get out of that, you get a hold of me. I'll grab Beaux and we'll teach you everything he knows."

"Wow. Really?"

I tossed the football back into his lap and capped his pen. "Absolutely. What's your name?"

"Hunter."

"I'll see you around, Hunter. Thanks for coming today."

Closer to him, without looking, my skin prickled with awareness. If Elizabeth had looked at me like she wanted to jump my bones a few minutes ago, there was something a lot deeper in her gaze when I met hers now.

"Hey. You came."

She flipped her hands in the air. "Wouldn't have missed it."

I gestured toward her jersey. "Because you needed an excuse to buy a new jersey?"

She pinched it with her fingers and tugged it away from her stomach. "What? This old thing?"

A look passed between us. That recognition, and if I had any doubt she knew who had her blindfolded and strapped to a cross only three nights ago, it'd make me a fool to try to pretend otherwise now.

Not when I wanted her so bad and enjoyed being around her so much.

I leaned in as close as I could and still keep it professional. There were cameras and kids all over the place. "We'll talk later. Keep your phone close."

It was the last time I'd ask Tristan for anything. After we talked, I'd no longer need Tristan to schedule anything between Elizabeth and me again.

It was a statement, not a question, and I meant it as such. I wasn't giving her the option to back away.

"Okay," she said, and her eyes gleamed. Based on that, I figured I didn't need to worry, but I'd spent too many years keeping my private life private to risk taking chances, even if I was pretty certain she was definitely worth all of it.

WE GOT SLAUGHTERED BY PHILADELPHIA.

We played our hardest and got outplayed. Our butts whooped.

It was the first time I walked into the locker room knowing I'd played my best, we'd done everything we could and it hadn't been enough.

It was also the first time I didn't give a shit.

I had a whole other game play running through my mind and itched to get started on it.

By the time I showered and changed after the game, I bypassed the sports reporters. Beaux usually answered the post-game conference anyway, and the kids from the hospital had left at halftime.

Elizabeth had been there after the game, in the same field level suite, with the other reporters invited to attend with the hospital kids. A few hospital staff remained.

And Connor Hopkins had been hovering near her back, still wanting her.

Well, the fucker could keep trying, but there was no way he was getting his hands on her ever again.

After tonight, she was going to be all mine. Completely.

TWENTY

Elizabeth

"You're pretty mopey. You that upset about the loss?" I asked Blake. My brother gave me a strange look from across the table. Whatever. He'd been rude all day.

They'd ribbed me all evening once I showed up late for dinner. I was still in my Rough Riders' jersey, for some reason thinking it was a good idea to buy one with Gage's number. The team had played amazing today and still hadn't been able to pull out the win. By the time I showed up to my parents' house, all the men were acting like I was the cause of the loss. The fact they'd already lost one and had the hardest schedule in the NFL didn't seem to register with any of them.

How my mere presence at a football game could affect a win, I had no idea. Somehow, I was supposed to have Hayes' Super Fan abilities to ensure Hale didn't get sacked or our offense didn't make a ridiculous amount of false start penalties.

Men.

"No," he grunted and shoved a bite of my mom's lasagna into his mouth.

Next to him, Haley patted his hand. "He's not upset about the game. He's been like this all week."

"Oh?" my mom asked. That got her attention. Marcia Hayes had superpowers for all things, dying to fix what was broken in her children's lives. When Connor and I broke up, she randomly showed up at my apartment to bring me comfort foods because nothing cured a broken heart like a mother's home cooking.

My dad, Ron, had held up a beer and scowled and said, "Any man who doesn't see you're the most precious gift on the planet ain't worth your time, darlin'." Like Blake, he was a man of few words. A vet in the Marines, he'd worked as a firefighter ever since he was discharged. He was now one of the battalion chiefs overseeing several forestations. He worked twenty-four-hour shifts several days a week and even when he wasn't living half his life at the stations, he was always ready to roll out if a fire started. He breathed his job like it was his life and loved it only a smidgeon less than he loved his family.

And even if I was raised in a house full of boys, I'd had Dad wrapped around my finger since I could toddle into his lap and suck my thumb, resting my head against his chest.

Yeah. My parents and family rocked, even if they were a little bit overbearing, a whole lot in your business.

"There's nothing wrong, Mom," Haley said. She'd been calling my mom *mom* before Blake and she even graduated high school. That was what my mom insisted on and when Marcia Hayes declared something as fact, we learned early on to fall in line and go with it. "But Blake and I do have something to share. We were just waiting until Jaxon got here."

He was gone. Again. He was usually the only Hayes outside my dad allowed to miss Sunday's dinner due to his job having uncertain hours. But this was two months in a row which was something even he tried not to do.

"Jaxon has a job on the coast. Gone until it's taken care of."

Arched brows rose on my forehead and I turned to my dad. "Taken care of?"

He shoved a breadstick into his mouth and took a bite. "You know he can't talk about it."

As the owner of a security firm, he often couldn't talk about his work, but that sounded ominous even for me. Whatever. I learned long ago that Jaxon was the black sheep of all of us. How he could survive the Hayes family and not be loud and obnoxious but stern and serious was beyond me. He took overprotective to a whole other level and more than one of my friends or boyfriends when I was younger was terrified of him at first sight.

To me he was just an overgrown snuggly bear. If that bear was ready to rip out your heart with his claws at any moment if you crossed him.

"News?" my mom asked. "Tell us. It's good news, right? Like the best kind of news I've been wanting to hear since y'all said '*I do*' years ago?"

"Yeah, Mom," Blake said. His jaw jutted out.

"Really?" I squealed.

"Yes!" Haley nudged him with her elbow and her gaze whipped through the rest of us. "We're having a baby!"

"Oh!" My mom jumped from her chair so quick it toppled to the floor. She rushed Haley and threw her arms around her. "Congratulations! This is the best news!" She shook Haley back and forth, grinning at my dad. "Isn't this the best, Ron? We're going to be grandparents!"

My dad grunted something that sounded like he was happy. I was stuck on Blake's sullen expression.

"Why don't you seem happy about it?"

"Because," Haley said. "He's terrified something bad's going to happen. He won't let me lift a finger. Won't let me leave the house. Practically had a coronary when I was carrying a basket of laundry the other day."

"Right." I nodded. My brothers were notoriously overprotective. "Because women are dainty little creatures who haven't been birthing babies since the beginning of time."

"Yes." She patted my mom's arms still wrapped around her. "That's pretty much it."

"I'd take advantage of it," Heather said. She pushed back from her chair and I followed her. We both pulled Haley to her feet and gave her a hug.

"This is exciting news! I'm so happy for you," I told Haley.

She hugged me back equally fiercely. "Thank you. We're excited. Aren't we Blake?"

"Yup."

I shoved his head. "Don't be a grouch. You're going to be a dad."

"Yeah, and if it's a girl, I'm royally fucked."

He grabbed his beer and took a healthy swallow. I slapped him on the back of the head and turned back to Haley.

"Tell us everything!" I gushed.

I spent the next several hours surrounded by family. We talked about the game. They gushed over my reports I was doing on the hospital and Gage. I feigned professionalism every time his name was mentioned so I wouldn't blush, but the entire time, I had my phone waiting in my back pocket.

And when my phone finally buzzed, it was nearly impossible to not grab it immediately.

I waited a whole two minutes before I checked it.

Smiled when I saw the message from Tristan.

Eight pm. Room four. You know the drill.

TWENTY-ONE

Gage

It was different tonight. Different than I'd ever experienced and I hadn't seen her yet. Tonight, I was already in the room. I stood in the corner, arms crossed over my navy blue T-shirt. I had a harsh bruise on my side from a tough tackle courtesy of Philadelphia's cornerback. I'd spent time once I got home soaking in an ice bath even after my shower and the game. Then I'd showered again, popped some pain pills. The time couldn't go by fast enough and stretched on forever.

So I wasn't all that excited about the fact she was running late. Or that it'd taken so damn long for her to confirm the meeting in the first place.

But damn. My hands were already hot. Palms ready to slap them against her petite, heart-shaped ass.

If only she'd get there. I checked my phone again.

Ten minutes. Was it possible she wasn't going to show at all?

Before I could linger on that thought too long, the doorknob turned. The light behind her from the hall left a gentle glow over her features.

She'd changed since the game. No longer dressed in blue jeans with rips at the thighs and knees and a skintight jersey bearing my name, she sauntered into the room with a pale pink dress, curving over the slope of her breasts. Thin straps I could break with a quick yank. It fit her chest, an extra piece of fabric belted around her waist and the pleats billowed out from her hips, the skirt creating a fullness that fell to just above her knees.

She was beautiful, gliding in on matching pink heels, stilettos that looked deadly and yet she didn't wobble despite the fact she was blindfolded.

The door closed behind her, a lamp in the other corner of the room the only glow. I waited until she stepped forward, had her hand on the dresser to steady herself and helped guide her toward the bed.

"You're not alone," I said. I propped the heel of one boot against the wall and as she walked in, I dropped it.

"You're here?" Her fingers clasped together in front of her and she turned toward the corner where I stood. "Blindfolded again?"

"For now."

I pushed off the wall and stepped to her. "Take three steps back so your calves touch the bed, but don't sit." I stopped her when her back was to the bed. Easier for me to place her on it. Her waist was so small my hands could practically wrap all the way around her. When she'd been blindfolded, I'd taken her in a variety of positions, and yet none the way I wanted now. Her straddling my hips, arms bound behind her, wrapped in my hand. Her small tits bouncing as she rode me. As she *used* me for her own pleasure. All that hair flying. Her chin tilted up. I'd imagined it a dozen times, fantasized about how small she'd appear while she claimed what was hers even while I still had command of her body.

One corner of her lips tipped up. "Are you going to touch me?"

Yes. I'd get there. Soon, as long as this conversation went the way it needed to go. "We have to talk."

"Well." She smiled, pretty pink lips stretched happily. "That's something new and kinky."

This woman. How I wanted to bend her over my knee and spank her until she came from the friction of her clit pressed against my jeans.

Patience.

I dropped the preamble. To get through this, we had to rip it off.

Crossing my arms over my chest, I succinctly said, "You know who I am."

Her hand went to her blindfold.

"I didn't say you could remove it."

Her hand fell back down. She tangled her fingers together and twisted the fingers on her other hand. It was the first time I'd seen her nervous.

"You know who I am," she said, instead of answering the question. "You've known for longer."

I detected a whisper of annoyance as she spoke and pushed it out of my mind.

"Yup." There was no point in denying it.

"Please, Gage—"

"Don't." I stepped forward, cutting her off. My jeans were at her knees and then pushing in between them. I bent over, taking her to the mattress and pinned her in with my hands just above her shoulders. "Don't say my name. I can leave right now, and you can never prove this was me in here with you."

She licked her lips and that frown line of hers dipped between her eyes, above the black satin. "I don't understand."

God she smelled good. Inches from her, it was near impossible not to strip her down, lay her bare, have her straddle me on the lounge chair where I could hit the end of her with my dick.

"You've met my mom and dad. You know what they do. This gets out, what I like, what I do...how do you think they would take that? How do you think their congregation would handle it? And the children's hospital? With me as their poster boy, what would the ramifications be if it came to light I enjoyed beating women?"

She jolted as if I'd slapped her. "Wow." Her hands went to her cheek and she brushed back her hair into a ponytail, let it fall. She looked away from me, mouth dropped. "Wow. And I thought..." she didn't finish the thought. Instead, her head whipped back to me, blonde hair trailing in the air behind her. If I removed the blindfold, I imagined arrows darting from her pretty blue eyes. "I would never do that."

"And before you remove that blindfold, I needed to hear it. I'm not trying to be a dick, Elizabeth."

"You're failing." Her arms crossed over her chest. That sweet little grin of hers formed a perfect scowl.

"And in a second, you'll have a decision to make. We can forget I'm a dick and get to the good stuff. Maybe." I stepped closer. My hand went to her waist and slid up her side to below her breasts. "It all depends on the choice you make."

"Oh? I get to make choices now in how these nights go?"

"Once. And not the whole night. Just whether it really begins or ends."

"Ends?"

"Your choice. But you have to know the cost."

"Okay..."

I ran a finger down her arm. Back up. To the fragile little strap. I tugged on it, pulled it over her shoulder and kissed her collarbone. "We can have one more night, Elizabeth. Exactly how the others have gone, maybe even better. And if you choose that option, that's it." The scent of her reeled me in. Sweet and flowery. God. She was tempting.

"And my other choice?" Her voice was a mere breath. Melodic even through the roughness. At the base of her throat, her pulse thrummed.

"Option two," I whispered, my lips at her ear. "If we remove the blindfold, we be *us*, but before you make that decision you make it knowing it means that when we're done here, you and I will walk out, hand in hand, and I'll be taking you back to your place for round two."

She exhaled harshly, parted lips ripping warm breath against my cheek. My lips were moving at her jaw, teasing, tempting. Her hands gripped my shirt at my hips. "Is that what you want?"

I'd given this a lot of thought. "I always thought I had to put a lot on hold to play football, to live for Harrison, to be the son my parents needed. And sometimes it got to me, trying to be the perfect guy. So I thought I had to keep these relationships private, knowing if a woman and I didn't work out, I couldn't risk this part of me getting out. But maybe I wasn't putting anything off. Maybe I was waiting for the woman I could trust with all of it."

Soft, warm fingertips trailed up my shirt. Walked up the buttons of my shirt and rested on my chest. "And that's me?"

"I think that I want to figure that out and it's the first time I've been willing to take that risk which, I'm really not trying to be a dick, but it says a lot about you, and what I'm beginning to feel for you."

"Gage..."

My name trailed off her lips and her hands went to my neck. She rolled to her toes, reaching up as she pressed her palms to the cut of my jaw. I met her halfway, bending down and sealed my lips to hers.

"Tell me that's a yes."

"Of course it's a yes." Before she changed her mind, before I could, I lifted the blindfold and flung it off. Her eyes blinked several times, adjusted to the darkness in the room.

And then full, beautiful lips spread into a smile.

Right before I slammed mine against her and kissed her.

TWENTY-TWO

Elizabeth

His kiss was a brand. Hot hands on my body, mine on his face. My eyes drifted closed despite my overwhelming desire to see every feature on his face, up close, pressing against me for the first time.

I melted into him, thankful for the high heels I wore to barely come close to matching his height. But the aid of the shoes placed me at the exact height to have his erection press against me.

"God," I gasped, against his mouth. His hands tangled in my hair, held me to him as he devoured me, swept his tongue inside. Heat from him rolled off, warming my skin straight to my soul.

We were connected. I'd spent two weeks around the man, doing nothing but thinking of him and his hands and his body and his work and his heart and even then, I barely knew him, I was falling for him.

He pulled on my hair, and the sudden jolt of pain made me whimper into his mouth. "How hard do you want it tonight?"

I didn't. I wanted soft and slow and to take my time running my hands along every inch of his skin.

Still, I replied, "Whatever you have, I'll take it." And man. I would do that for him, and it wasn't just the overwhelming pulse of need thrumming through me.

As if he understood, he pulled back, licking his lip. His look was panty-melting. Thank God I wasn't wearing any.

"We'll do hard later. So your screams can echo off the walls of your bedroom."

Breathless, I made a sound, too lost for words and replies and then he was undoing my zipper, slipping my dress down my body. Every scrape of fabric against my skin, every press of his lips against me, spurred me on. And then I was lifted, hands on my waist, placing me on the bed. His hands went to my knees, spread me, and then like I'd so often imagined, Gage dropped to his knees in front of me.

"Yes." His lips were on me. Tasting me, tongue flicking, driving me mindless as I clung to his hair.

I tugged, the first time I'd had true freedom to grab hold of him, and I lifted my head to watch every single moment. Our eyes met, and oh God, just the desire gleaming in his eyes, the intensity in his furrowed brow as his tongue slid through my folds, followed by his fingers.

My hips arched, thrust to him, needing to get closer. He gathered my wetness, slid to the back.

For a moment, my eyes rolled back to my head. His finger pressed against my ass, slid in. I gasped and arched into him. Oh God. The pleasure. The overwhelming mix of sensation had my thighs pulse, that familiar bundle of fire igniting, stretching, expanding until I gripped the sheets with all of my might.

"Oh God!" I cried out, head thrashing as my orgasm hit me so quick, so intensely, it rippled and rolled through my body in an almost excruciating measure.

He continued devouring me, fucking my ass, sucking my clit until the longest orgasm of my life rolled to another, slowly drawing out every sensation. I committed this moment to memory, the moment my eyes met his as he pulled back, pressed his lips to my inner thigh, wickedness in his eyes, and yet sated at the same time.

Goodness. It *pleased* him to do that to me.

I wanted to make him the most pleased man on the planet for as long as he wanted to be mine.

"We're not done," he proclaimed, standing, ripping off his T-shirt, shucking off his jeans. He was naked. And finally, I saw him in all of his glory. And there was a lot of gloriousness to take in.

"I might be," I said on a breath. I wiped my hair off my forehead. Nothing could hinder this moment, not even a strand of hair to block my vision.

"You're not. There are things I want to do to you we haven't tried yet."

Oh goody. He crawled over me, body braced above mine and my hands roamed his stomach. The blocks of muscle at his abs, the thick ridge delineating them. The hair that ran over his pecs, down the center of his stomach, straight down to his thick and heavy dick.

God. I'd known he was big. I'd felt the stretch around him, but seeing him, standing straight and proud as he bent low and kissed me, swept his tongue into my mouth and shared the taste of me. Good Lord.

It was a good thing I'd been blindfolded for our first few encounters, otherwise, I might have lost my mind from the vision of him naked.

Before I could come up with a snappy comeback, or any words, he rolled us. My thighs went to his hips. His hand went to his cock where he stroked it, holding me at my lower back.

"Ride me."

I covered his hand with mine. "You're giving me control?" I didn't think he had it in him.

I barely got the question out before he had my hands pinned behind my back with one of his. His hand gripped my wrists together and he lifted his thighs. "The illusion of it."

The pressure of his thighs forced me forward until I was up and on my knees, over him, rubbing the tip of his cock against my soaking wet center.

I pressed myself against him as he wrapped his hand around his thickness, and good gracious. The sight of him holding himself for me made my mouth drool. I wanted that dick in my mouth. In my hands. I wanted to take my time and savor the rigid feel of him.

"Condom," I gasped, freezing right as I was there, his head at my opening.

His head pressed back to the bed, eyes closed in pain. "Get tested before the season, and we have to keep them up to date for here."

His eyes opened then, narrowed on me, trusting me with something so important...giving me a vulnerability it was clear he didn't give to many.

If anyone. The thought of it made my heart leap.

We were both clean. Tests were required frequently at Velvet.

"I'm on the pill."

"You okay with taking all of me?"

A tremor rolled through me at the mere thought. All of him? I wanted nothing more. Still, that he was willing to give that to me sent a strange burning sensation to the backs of my eyes.

"Yes." I nodded. Probably bobbed like a bobblehead. "I want that."

He yanked me down at the same time he pushed up his hips, and he was there, sliding into me. He was so big it was painful from the mere force of it and I cried out in the beautiful mixture of too much and not enough that eclipsed every thought in my brain.

"Oh." My head fell, gaze to our connection. Our bodies pressed together. The tightness of my stomach matched to the steel of his abs.

"Fucking hell," he groaned. His face was a mix I knew matched mine. "Fucking hell that feels good. So damn good."

"I've never..."

His eyes snapped open. Hips thrust up. "Me either. Feels fucking incredible. Now move before this ends way too damn soon." I wasn't given the option. His hips slammed up, forcing me down onto his shaft. With his hands caging mine, I didn't have to do a thing.

We found our rhythm, rocking slowly. My body rubbed against him, the end of him deep inside of me, stretching me.

"Oh God," I moaned. Hair stuck to my cheeks. My lips were parted. And below me, Gage was focused purely on me, my body. His forehead lined, such intensity stamped on his features, I rode him, needing to see him unravel for the very first time.

And it wasn't long, wasn't long at all before his hips bucked wildly, slamming me down on him at the same time.

We came together, and it took all my strength not to collapse to his chest while he road out the rest of his climax, eyes on me the entire time.

It wasn't just the best sex I'd had, it was the most intense, not because of what he could do to my body and the pleasure he could wring from it, but because I knew for the first time, my heart was fully invested.

"I'll follow you to your place. Where's your car?"

His chest was beautiful. All rippled and thick. My gaze fell and stalled at the thick black hair below his belly button.

"Elizabeth?"

"Hmm?"

"Car?"

"What?"

His thumb and finger pinched my chin, tilted my head. Laughter danced all over his expression, twisting his lips up. "Can you focus?"

"I was focusing."

"On all the wrong things." He kissed me hard and fast, slid his hand to the back of my neck and before I knew it, I was on my back and he was hovering over me. When he pulled back, I was just as distracted as I'd been before. "Where's your car?"

"Out back."

"Okay. We'll get to mine and I'll drive you to it."

He was full of plans. Had been planning on coming back to my place since I first entered the room. "Why my place?"

He kissed me again, nibbled on my lips. I'd almost forgotten my question when he stopped and slipped his tongue over my bottom lip. "Because I have to get up early tomorrow to go watch film and workout and you go to work later. This way you can sleep in. I have a feeling you'll need it."

Well. When he put it like that. "Then let's go."

We dressed slowly and with his hand clamped around mine, he led me through Velvet. It wasn't until we were outside and the fresh, chilly air smacked me in the face I could make out the tightness in his expression.

It took a lot out of him to walk through the club with me. What he said earlier made sense. It made complete sense even if I'd been shocked and angry when he first mentioned what it could do to his reputation if someone found out.

It's why I joined Velvet in the first place. Yet he had status on a whole different level than a reporter in Raleigh. His platform garnered national attention. So while he'd been rude, I could let that go.

As long as he didn't let it happen again.

We reached his car and he opened the door to his large white SUV. "You're nervous," I said as I climbed into my seat, the plush leather immediately hugging me.

He looked to the doors of the club and back to me. "It's not you."

And the worry in his eyes. God, I understood him maybe more than he gave me credit for. "I get it, Gage. Really. Thank you for trusting me with this part of you."

"I can tell you one part specifically that wants your trust." He leaned into the doorway and kissed me.

"Later. Soon."

"Damn straight, little one." He closed the door, and I shivered from that nickname.

It was so sweet. So perfect.

I buckled up even though we were in the parking lot. Habit and all that, and when we drove around and reached my Explorer, I was planning on hopping out when Gage stopped me.

"Hold up." He hopped out of his side and met me at the door. "You have your keys?"

I held them up in my hand. "A smart woman always does in a dark parking lot."

"Good." He walked me to my car and right as I went to beep the locks, he turned me. I was up against the side of my own vehicle, his body against mine, his hands at my cheeks. His mouth pressed against mine and I opened for him. He kissed me like he'd never taste me again, like he'd gotten a hint of his favorite new treat and needed to order a dozen more.

I kissed him back with equal fervor. My hands at his chest. His arms. I inspected his upper body with in-depth precision. Eventually, my hand landed on his stomach and I pushed him back.

"Wait until we get to my place."

His grin went wicked, oh so beautifully wicked and sexy and

so beautiful I memorized it, tucked it into my memory bank so I'd always have it with me.

"I'll follow you."

He opened my door and waited until I had the car on and seat belt fastened before he shut the door and returned to his SUV.

MY APARTMENT WAS a fifteen-minute drive from Velvet. A newer complex with three stories of apartments. The buildings had walkways in between each individual one but were U-shaped and the shared space in the middle of the courtyard had a large pool, hot tub and a massive outdoor kitchen area. It even had an on-site event planner where there were weekly activities like yoga in the fitness center, Wednesday wine nights, and football game Sundays on the large outdoor screen television.

So far, I'd partaken of few events except for the occasional wine night, but it was a great way to meet neighbors.

It was a great place. Not exactly ritzy but definitely not low-end. It catered to single professionals, and I'd just moved in a year ago.

I'd never been embarrassed to bring anyone to my place, but as we pulled in to the parking lot, the lights of Gage's Lincoln Navigator following me close the whole time even though he'd put my address into his GPS in case we got separated, nerves lit in my fingertips and traveled to my gut.

This was a guy whose last five-year contract had been over seventy million dollars. Which essentially meant he made more money during one football season than I'd ever see in my lifetime. His clothes were high-end where mine were Target and T.J. Maxx. Heck, even the dress I'd bought to wear to the fundraising gala last week had been rented at a fraction of the cost it would have cost to buy anything.

His SUV alone probably cost more than my annual salary.

And I was bringing him to what had to be a humble abode, probably barely nicer than his college apartment.

The differences in our lives hadn't registered until I slowed down, pointed at the visitor parking spots of which there were plenty and pulled in to my assigned spot only five spots down.

By the time I climbed out of my five-year-old Explorer, I was tempted to run to my apartment, lock the door behind me, and pretend the last two weeks had never happened. Too bad he was so much bigger than me, and most likely way faster, and he could catch me easily or else I might have tried.

He met me in the middle of the parking lot, arms loose at his sides, his strides easily eating the space between us. Good gracious, the man was all that and a bag of chips. Frightening in his size and his intensity, and yet his very presence made me feel protected and safe at the same time.

"Hey." *Hey?* Might as well slap myself silly and call it a night.

His answering grin made my knees weak. "You get nervous on the way here?"

How did he read me so well? I flipped my keys around my thumb and shrugged. "Maybe?"

"Figured you would. That's the other reason we're here. My house is farther away and I was worried you'd back out halfway there."

My nose scrunched and his answer was to laugh again. "I'm not sure it's great you think you've already got me figured out."

"Not much to figure out." He reached for me, took the keys out of my hand, tossed them into his other one and threaded his fingers through my hand. "You want me. I predict you'd get nervous bringing any man to your apartment and at some point on the drive, you realized your home is much smaller than mine and you're wondering what that says about you. Or me."

Wow. He was really good. And also, I was holding hands with Gage Bryant. Taking him to my house. My bedroom.

How had the world gotten so insanely awesome and wildly twisted?

"That pretty much covers it," I mumbled, tucking hair behind my ear and watching my feet as we headed toward the building.

"What floor are you on?"

"I'm in number 212."

The stairs to all apartments were outside. So I allowed him to read the signs, head the right direction.

"This is a nice place," he said. He was scanning the area. It was well-lit and the owners and management company did a great job of keeping the bushes trimmed along the first floor. Each apartment had a small, barely big enough to be called a patio or porch, but nonetheless, people tried to decorate them for the holidays. Outside my front door was a five-foot chunk of barn wood I'd painted and stenciled at a ladies' wine and craft night with Amanda last fall. It was white, the letters spelling out *Welcome* in all caps in a bright teal color.

"Rough Riders' colors," Gage said, pointing at the sign as we reached my porch. "Nice choice."

Idle chit-chat. Friendly conversation. How did we get to this crazy place?

"Hey." He tugged on my hand and pulled me to him. His thumb was at my chin, tipping my head back. His eyes danced between mine and dropped to my mouth. "You remember my dad was a pastor growing up? Swear to God, Elizabeth, you got nothing to be embarrassed about with how you live. I grew up on clothes from second-hand stores and garage sales and ate more grilled cheese sandwiches than I have dollars today. I'm just a guy, who really wants to get to know you." That smile of his turned predatory as he continued. "And I also want to get you into your bed, make you scream so loud your yells echo all over this building so everyone knows you're taken."

Well, if I hadn't been nervous before I certainly was now.

"That okay with you?"

"Ummm." It sounded fantastic. It also terrified me and had me shaking in my heels. I mean...the whole building? It was pretty big.

He kissed my lips and pulled back, slipping the key easily into the lock. With his hand on my lower back, he guided me inside my own apartment.

I flipped on lights, kicked off my heels and then we stood there. Gage's gaze surveying my apartment like whatever I had and however, I decorated was important to him.

Me wondering if regardless of what he'd said, which had meant a lot, did he find it lacking.

"You've made a home."

I tried to envision what he was seeing as if it was the first time. Forty-inch TV on a simple TV stand. Barn doors that that slid closed to hide my cable streaming box. Two tan couches that didn't look special, but were good quality, large and comfortable. A dark purple chair angled in the small space with an ottoman so you could put your feet up and relax. Bookshelves on the other side of the TV stand, mostly stacking with picture frames and the few books I owned and loved.

The kitchen table was round and had four chairs. I'd actually bought it at a garage sale and refinished it, stained and painted it to match the TV stand. There wasn't artwork on the wall, but a few signs with inspirational quotes.

It looked sparse but clean, not overly decorated but said I tried.

But was it a home? I loved it.

"Thanks." I headed toward the kitchen and pulled out the

filtered water pitcher I kept filled. "Would you like some water? Or something else to drink? I don't have much but white wine."

"Water's good."

I grabbed an extra glass for him, not surprised he made himself at home by dropping his own keys on my kitchen counter, kicked off his shoes and slid into one of two stools at the small bar.

"You mentioned your parents outside. Are y'all close?"

He grinned as I asked the question and took his glass from me. "Yeah. Love 'em to death. They're good people."

"Seemed they raised a good son, too. I know we've really only been around each other for work, but you have to know I really admire you for what you've done with the hospital."

If I wasn't mistaken, a slight pink hue stained his cheeks before he scrubbed his hand down his face and sighed. "Life isn't always easy, you know? And I have more money than I know what to do with even being smart with it. I figure it's my job to give back to more than just people who like football."

"Like I said." I tipped the glass in his direction. "A good guy."

"And your brothers? The idiots? Your parents? Are you close with them?"

"Yeah. Just saw them for dinner tonight. My ma still makes us all gather once a month for a family meal. One of my brother's and his wife announced tonight they're pregnant so that was exciting."

"What are they like? Your brothers?" As he asked, he stood from the stool and nodded toward the couch.

It took me a minute to follow him. With the way he was acting earlier, I figured we'd show up and go straight to the bedroom.

Guess he wasn't kidding when he said he wanted to know me, and if he wanted to know me, he'd learn about me through my family.

So I told him all I could about Blake and Tanner, mentioning

Jaxon in passing. His current job and past in the military made it difficult to discuss him in depth. I told him about Heather and Hayley and my mom's bossy disposition and my dad's lovingly grumpy one. We ended up talking for hours, well after midnight, and when I finally yawned, he took me to bed.

And when I screamed, hours later, I didn't care if the entire complex did hear me.

TWENTY-THREE

Gage

She was so damn pretty. Her hair, wild and tangled covered most of her bare back. She'd fallen asleep last night almost as soon as I climbed into her small bed and wrapped her in my arms after cleaning us both up. I'd laid there and slid my fingers through her hair long after she was sleeping.

This woman. She undid me in ways I didn't expect and it wasn't solely the sex, although knowing she liked what I craved was a definite necessity.

She laid on her side, still facing the side where I'd slept. One hand under her cheek, the other pressed to the pillow I'd used like she was searching for me even though I wasn't on it anymore. A sweet pink coated her fingernails. Brighter than the dress she wore last night. It still didn't eclipse the look of ecstasy when I made her come. At Velvet, on her home turf, both were places she was comfortable which was why I wanted our first time out of the club to be here.

But as soon as I could get my hands on her again, it was my room that would be shaking from her cries.

I had an hour to get to practice. The sun was barely up, pink lighting up the edges of the treetops, and for the first time in my career, crawling into bed and fucking off a day had never been so appealing. If there was any chance I could talk her into doing the same, I might have tried.

Too bad I knew exactly what she had on her plate for the day. This week was chockful of events. Kicking off today with an evening of bowling at a local bowling alley. The team would be there, fans who paid way too damn much for a ticket just to bowl with the team, and tonight, the parents of current patients were our special guests.

I still had to check in with Penny to see if she was coming. I hadn't heard how Brandon was doing over the weekend and when it came to him, no news was better-than-expected news.

I tapped out a reminder on my phone to give Penny a call later.

Sliding the phone into my pocket, I sat down on the bed and kissed the back of Elizabeth's hand. I grinned as I kept kissing her. She smelled like me and sex and still that sweet hint of flowery perfume I now knew was body lotion based on her bathroom counter. Her arm flinched when I kissed her elbow and by the time I was at her shoulder, lazy blue eyes, still glassy from sleep and lack of sleep peered at me.

"I gotta get going." I brushed my hand through her hair. Damn. It was so fucking soft. Felt so good and by the way she always closed her eyes and gave me a sleepy smile when I did, she liked it too. "I'll see you later, though, right?"

She rolled to her back. The sheet was down by her waist. There wasn't a hint of nerves as she sprawled out naked, almost completely exposed to me. I inspected her body with meticulous fashion, memorizing every dip, every little freckle. Two small ones were right at the edge of her breast and I kissed her there, then her nipple.

"You're a horrible tease," she whispered, voice husky and sleepy.

I couldn't stop touching her.

"You're tempting. What do you expect me to do when you're showing off your hot little body?"

She laughed softly and she pressed her hand to the back of my head. Her slim fingers brushed over my scalp to the back of my neck and as I continued kissing her breast, her hips started rolling.

I grinned at her, tongue sliding around her nipple. "Need something else?"

"Always when you're around."

Her hand moved in that direction and holy shit that was hot. I batted away the sheet, watched her slide two fingers through her slit.

Which just gave me a great idea for what we'd do next time. She'd get me off. Then I'd watch her get herself off.

But this morning, pleasuring her was my job, one I took seriously. I brushed my hand down her stomach, readjusted my position on the bed so I had a better view.

Her knees bent and thighs opened wide. Her fingers glistened with her juices and as she rolled them around her clit, showing me exactly how she liked to take care of herself, I grabbed her fingers in my hand.

Sucking them into my mouth, my eyes closed. A rumble grew in my chest. Heaven. She tasted like heaven and still a hint of me. Which was fucking hotter than I would have thought.

"Gage," she gasped. "I was really close."

I sucked her fingers again and replaced hers with mine. "This is mine," I said, running my fingers around her swollen and throbbing clit like she'd done. "You get to use it when I say."

"And when you're not around?"

"You wait for me."

"And if you're out of town?" Her face scrunched with displeasure.

Little minx. I slapped her clit and she gasped. Eyes closed from the sting of it but by the quivering breath, she also really liked it.

"Then I'll FaceTime you and you can show me. In fact," I bent down and kissed her as her movements went jerky. It took nothing to get this girl off, or I just knew exactly what she wanted. "I think we'll do that next time. I'll sit there, stroking my dick, and you'll spread your legs. You'll want my dick in you. You'll ache for it, Beth. And even then, all you'll have are your tiny fingers."

"It's not the same," she gasped. Her head thrashed side to side. Hips arched and pressed against me. I shoved two fingers into her, found that perfect rigid area inside, and rolled her clit with my thumb.

She went off like a rocket and I kissed her through it and when she was done trembling and I pulled back, kissing her nose one time and then her cheek.

"I really have to get going, but I'm really pissed about it."

She laughed softly, rolled and wrapped her arms around my shoulders. I pulled her so she was sitting next to me, leaning against me. "Thanks for trusting me."

She meant at Velvet and me allowing the blindfold to come off.

"Thank you for earning that. Not many do."

"I'll make sure it's worth it."

Cheeky thing. "You already have. Later? You'll be at the bowling alley."

She pulled back and scooped her hair into her hand, holding it in one fist at her shoulder. Grinning and no longer looking sleepy but well-fucked, she grinned. "I'll be the girl in the ugly shoes with her very own pink glitter ball."

"You have your own ball? You didn't mention this last night."

We'd talked about her brothers. Sports. What she did outside high school or after work for fun. Bowling hadn't been brought up.

She slid her feet to the floor and put her hands on her hips. With a jaunty wink and zero embarrassment as she stood naked and exposed in front of me, she said, "I can't have you learning all my secrets quite yet. Where's the fun in that?"

Little did she know, I was looking forward to the journey of delving into all of them.

~

SHE WASN'T FUCKING KIDDING about the bowling ball. Or the shoes.

I was throwing a fifteen-pound bowling ball down the wood lane for the hundredth time of the night barely managing to conceal my hard dick and swollen balls.

Good God. This woman knew exactly what she was doing when she showed up at the bowling alley earlier. Her shoes, black and bright pink, striped with white were the most ridiculous shoes I'd ever seen. But she had her own bowling shoes.

Her shirt was a classic bowling shirt with a black collar and hot pink fitted tight to her body. I swore the thing was two sizes too small for her. It made her look tinier than she already was but at the same time, somehow did amazing things to her breasts.

Her hair was pulled back into a ponytail that swished and swayed to the rhythm of her hips.

When she entered the alley, she'd flashed me a wink and a low wave, immediately moving over to the other reporters.

We hadn't talked about Connor last night. Hell, I hadn't even brought up what she'd been doing at Velvet. Why he approached her there. His motivation was obvious. I'd heard enough at the gala, but it went against my instinct to keep my eyes off her too long. Especially when it became obvious every time Connor moved closer, she moved away.

She did it smoothly and impressively. She'd catch him in her peripheral vision, say something with a laugh to whoever she was talking to, and then she'd skirt right on to the next person. And most of those people she spoke to were parents.

Cameramen were there, following the actions on the sidelines along with photographers for all the local stations. It wasn't the time to cause a scene even though every time she caught my eyes on her and her head dipped, acknowledging me, the urge to say fuck it and cause a scene screamed at me.

More than once she offered a comforting squeeze to a parent's arm. A light and quick hug to a mom on the verge of tears. There were well over a hundred people there tonight. Fans, parents, and players.

We'd been put on teams, intermixed with all and while we did this event every year, this year was my favorite one yet.

Not only because it was packed, but finally, I had a woman with me who I'd be fucking honored to have on my arm in public. She was younger than me, so young I hadn't even bothered to ask her age but I knew she'd only been working at KSTP (station name?) for five years. If she started working there right out of college that was at max twenty-six.

At thirty-two, we weren't so far apart our ages would raise eyebrows, but she was still young enough where her grace impressed me.

A slap on the back jolted me. Oliver's grin told me he'd totally caught me checking her out.

"Shannon likes her," he said.

"What?" She hadn't mentioned meeting Shannon at all. And it was just like Powell to not even mention her name. Clearly, I wasn't hiding my fascination. "What are you talking about?"

"The reporter you're looking at like you want to throw her into the storage closet and stay there for hours."

Whatever. Powell was a cocky prick. He was still one of the best tight ends in the league, but we all knew he'd be retiring soon. I wasn't that many years behind him either which meant the rush and love of the game would soon be in our rearview.

And I hated thinking about the fact there were rumblings this year of it being Powell's last season.

I grabbed my bottled water from the table and took a hefty gulp. "Don't know what you're talking about, Powell."

"Play it that way, but I'm just sayin' Shannon likes her. Thinks she's good people and even when you were talking about Miss Hayes the other day something clicked I thought you should know."

I was still stuck on the fact his wife had met Elizabeth enough times to know anything about her, but the depth of his tone made me pay attention. "What is it?"

"You know her brother. And I'm saying, tread carefully with her. You fuck with her, screw her over in any way and he can ruin you."

"What the fuck are you talking about?" I caught Elizabeth's gaze and her eyes widened. Damn. I scrubbed my hand down my face. I was strung tight and glaring at her. I shook my head once and dragged it back to Powell.

"Jaxon Hayes?" Powell's brows rose. "He's the dude who helped out Beaux and Paige when he had that stalker fan. Guy's dark as shit. Runs his own security firm. Any of that ring a bell?"

Last night she spent most of the night talking about Blake and Tanner. She'd mentioned Jaxon in passing, said he worked a lot but the conversation had turned to her sister-in-law's and it hadn't registered.

"No shit?"

"Pretty sure. Don't even know if Paige put it together when they all had dinner the other night."

Dinner? Elizabeth had dinner with Shannon and Paige, wives of two of my closest friends on the team and hadn't thought to mention that to me?

"Gage! Your turn!" The shout came at me through a tunnel.

"We'll talk later," Powell said. From the scoring table, Kolby Jones was giving me an expectant look. Powell lowered his voice to a low rumble. "Don't know your gig. Not with women and it ain't my business but I know you don't play the field and I know you haven't had a public girlfriend in all your time in the league. I'm just warning you to tread carefully. Jaxon isn't someone you want to mess with."

"Right," I gritted out my response.

Then I went to the ball return, grabbed mine and slammed it down the lane. The smack of the ball hitting all ten pins didn't calm me down.

As soon as I was done with my turn, not registering the slaps to my shoulders, the one parent who squeezed my arm a little too playfully, I grabbed my phone out of my pocket and typed out a quick text.

We need to talk.

She'd mentioned me not learning all her secrets yet, but just how many was she hiding?

TWENTY-FOUR

Elizabeth

Something shifted. I felt it in the air and the heat of Gage's glare as soon as Oliver started talking to him. It sent me reeling, him staring at me like he suddenly wanted to rip my head off.

It threw me off my game and on my next turn I didn't even manage to pull off a spare. Normally I would have been disappointed. Not quite the showing I wanted to put on, not only to show off for Gage but because I'd been reigning Amateur Bowling Champion three years in a row in my teens. It'd all started as fun family trips to the bowling alley when we were kids and turned out, I had a knack for throwing the ball straight down the lane. I was twelve in my first local competition and ended up coming in third place, beating out teenagers who'd been competing for years. I had never been particularly good at sports. Not team ones anyway. I didn't have the coordination or size for volleyball or basketball. And even with soccer, my legs were shorter than most. I got tossed around the field and outrun in sprints regardless of how quick my legs carried me. But bowling had clicked somehow and I'd always enjoyed it.

I'd been having fun all night, despite Connor's attempt to get my attention. If he thought I owed him anything after his attempts at Velvet last night, he was dead wrong. I'd said all I needed to say to him and now I wanted him to stay exactly where he belonged.

In my past.

The parents I spoke to were incredibly sweet. The fans who had paid to attend were wide-eyed and awestruck at the players who were there. All of them had such wonderful things to say, and all the parents who attended were more than willing to tell me their children's stories. I supposed nothing helped them open up more than drinks flowing. This was a night to forget their stress while at the same time honoring everything going on in their life. I had enough stories on the voice memo app on my phone to give me several days worth of work. It'd also been one of the most fulfilling moments of my career, talking to some of the moms and even the dads as tears formed in their eyes. Yet all of them were so hopeful. So thankful Gage was giving their families a place where their hospitalized kids could have a glimpse at a regular childhood.

Before that glare from Gage, I'd had a hard time not running to him and throwing my arms around him, telling him how much I adored him in front of the crowd. Did he even know how inspiring he was?

That desire was yanked back and fizzled as soon as he turned his back on me.

My phone buzzed in my pocket and I glanced over my shoulder. Gage was there, standing at the scoring machine for his team three lanes down. His brows were arched, daring me. Mad. He also had his phone in his hand and lifted it before sliding it into his back pocket.

I turned from the team I was bowling with and stepped toward the stand of bowling balls for a brief moment of privacy.

My breath caught as I pulled out my phone and swiped the screen.

We need to talk.

Nothing good ever came from those words. My chest heaved and ached at the abruptness of his text.

What could he possibly mean by that? I'd seen him talking to Oliver. Was he mad I hadn't told him about Shannon? I hadn't exactly had time with the blindfold and all the hot sex.

A shadow fell over me and then the voice from the man I'd been avoiding all night was too close for comfort. "Been wanting to talk to you all night."

Good grief. Just what I didn't need right now.

"I have nothing to say to you." I turned to walk away from Connor when his cold voice stopped me.

"Don't have to talk. Just have to look at something I want to show you."

Stupid. So stupid. I had no idea what made me look at the phone in Connor's hand he shoved in front of my face but when I did, my knees locked so I didn't fall over.

The screen wasn't even grainy from the darkness in the club. How he'd taken such a clear photo was beyond me. But there was no mistaking the girl in the photo.

Me. Staring at the room where a man naked from the waist up had his back to a woman. My lips parted.

And behind me? Gage. He'd been wearing that mask that covered most of his face, but it wouldn't take an idiot to figure out it really was him.

I reached for Connor's phone, but he pulled it out of my reach and swiped another photo. More of them, with Gage's hand beneath my breast in a room full of dozens as we watched the scene.

Oh. Fucking. Shit.

"What's your point?" I snapped at him. "You share those and Tristan will rip your membership away."

"My point is I'm concerned. This is Gage Bryant, Lizzie."

God. I hated that fucking name. "You know nothing about him."

He was pissed at me about something, but that didn't mean I wasn't ready to defend him. To the death of everything else if I had to.

"I know he doesn't see women more than a handful of times before he ditches them. I know that not a single woman he's ever been with at Velvet has meant a damn thing to him. He's no good for you."

"And you are?" My gaze did a quick scan of the room. No one was paying us attention and we were separated enough we couldn't be overheard, but that'd soon change if I didn't get my shit under control.

Oh God. Was this what had Gage so pissed off?

"Have you shown those pictures to anyone?"

Connor tucked his phone into his pocket and smiled. I'd never wanted to slap his pretty smile before, but my palm itched at my sides to do it. "Not yet. But I don't think your boss would like this. Shane's a pretty stand-up guy, but even he wouldn't allow some sex deviant on the nightly news and you're being considered for that promotion, right?"

"You..." I stumbled back. My God. How had I ever thought I loved this man? "You would try to ruin my career because I won't sleep with you again? And you say Gage isn't good for me?"

"I'm saying if this gets out, your career is ruined anyway. I'm just looking out for you."

"Bullshit." I was sweating. My hands shook. My chin trembled. From anger. Fear. Worry that everything he was saying was true.

Oh God. All I'd ever wanted in my life was to be on the nightly news, behind the desk during the prime time slot. And Connor wasn't altogether wrong and for some reason, I hadn't considered any of the risks involved with Gage, or the potential for photos leaking like Connor took.

My eyes landed on Gage. His back was to me but like he felt me gaping at him, he turned.

The blood drained from my face at the fury in his eyes. He took it in and in that split second his fury changed to confusion. Eyes slid to Connor next to me.

My entire body turned to ice.

I shook my head as Gage's brows arched. He stepped toward me and I put up my hand.

I needed some fucking fresh air before I passed out.

"Go to hell, Connor," I mumbled. "And delete the damn photos immediately."

He called my name as I skirted around the stand of bowling balls. I dodged cheap plastic chairs, piles of shoes strewn about. The rattle of pins falling and bells dinging for strikes drummed in my ears like I was in a tunnel.

I hurried outside, ignored the burst of cooler, wet air outside and hugged my stomach.

It wasn't until I was around the corner that I slumped against the brick wall and dropped my head.

Oh God. I was going to pass out. I couldn't slow my racing heart.

Connor wasn't altogether wrong. If anyone ever found I got my kicks by going to a kinky sex club, my reputation could be ruined. Being with Gage would put a spotlight on me and make me much more recognizable than I already was, which wasn't much at all. But if I were on the prime time news slot? That'd change.

Throw in Gage Bryant? It could change everything.

Gravel crunched and he was there. I wasn't even surprised he followed me. I was less surprised I knew him by his long strides and presence alone. Gage had that effect on me from the very beginning. That very first night at Velvet.

Somehow I recognized him from the very beginning before I ever saw his face. Like his soul called to mine.

God. I was losing my mind.

What a ridiculous thought.

"What'd he say to you? And while we're on the subject of Connor, why don't you tell me why every time I see him with you, you're pissed and hurt and he won't get a clue."

Freaking Connor. I'd allowed him to ruin my life for far too long.

My hands were on my knees and I pushed up. Every sharp edge and crack of brick scraped at my back as I stood. My shoulders ached from stress. My knuckles stung. My eyes were still watering as the chilly fall air whipped around us.

"He has pictures of us on his phone."

Gage stepped toward me, stopping far enough away so I couldn't even reach for him. Not that I had any intention of it with the stern and distrustful look on his face. "At Velvet?"

"In the social room when we were watching that couple and then the other night when we were leaving. I don't know how many." I re-did my ponytail and wrapped it up into a messy bun to keep strands from whipping me in the face.

Gage's hands went to his hips and his head dipped. His jaw jutted forward as he lifted it. "How do you know Shannon?"

"What?"

"Shannon. How do you know her? And Paige while we're on it."

He tossed questions at me like accusations. I shook my head to clear it. "I don't understand."

"See, I'm trying to figure out, how every time you're around

Connor it always sends you running off, but maybe that was the plan and now I'm seeing things aren't adding up. You and Connor. Your history at Velvet and yet acting like you had no idea who I was at the first press conference. The fact you haven't said anything to me about knowing Shannon or Paige, even though your brother was the guy who helped them last fall when Beaux had a crazed stalker fan. And then there's your request for the exclusive even though in the contract it's stated one wouldn't be given. So what I'm trying to figure out is what your real story is?"

I stepped back to get away from him. My head hit the brick, but even the sting from cement on my skull was minor in comparison to Gage's accusations and implications. But I knew one thing.

I was just as dumb and idiotic with him as I'd been with Connor because apparently, fantastic mind-blowing sex didn't equal love. Trusting someone was futile.

And men? I gave my heart to all the wrong ones.

I skirted off to the side to put space between us. I was shaking my head. My whole body trembled.

A good cry and a package of Oreos was going to be how I spent the rest of my evening.

"Wow." I finally managed to say. "I don't know if you're just that paranoid or are just that big of a dick, but either way, I have nothing to say to you."

"Why? Can't explain any of it?"

Had he slapped me he couldn't have hurt me more.

And whatever. I had nothing to lose, but I was really fucking tired of men thinking they could walk all over me. "First of all, I met Shannon, Paige, and both their husbands in the elevator on the way to your gala. They talked and laughed. I promised I'd keep my mouth shut about anything because I was there to do a job. Second." I paused, inhaled, and lifted two fingers in the air as I punctuated the word. "My brother's work is private and I don't know shit about what he does and yeah, I knew what he did after it became public because he told me what he could, but again...that was personal and family shit he came to me with. And third, we've been straight with each other for less than a fucking day, Gage. One day. I don't owe you shit but the fact you'd even think I'd be trying to pull one over on you simply because my job reports *news* is a slap in the face.

"Last night, with you on my couch, and in my bed, I had all I needed from you because I thought I had *you*. I'm just glad to know you aren't even close to the man I'd built up in my head and thought you were." I stepped away, lifting my hands and then dropping them to my thighs. Walking backward, I glared into his narrowed dark eyes. "You can take your blindfolds and your kink and your accusations, and you can shove it all up your ass. I'm done with you and all of this bullshit. I have a job to do, a promotion to earn, and Connor in there is probably right...being with you, that could ruin all of it. So I'm out. Have a nice life."

I spun and hurried back into the bowling alley before I burst into tears.

Two minutes. Just two minutes. Change your shoes. Grab your purse. Get in your car and get home. Then you can lose it.

It took a dozen tries to unknot the bowling shoes and I kicked them into my bag, grabbed the bowling ball from the ball return. I grabbed Jason's attention and waved him over. The night had at some point dissolved into a night of fun. Cameras had been put away. Reporters no longer had their phones or tablets out. Parents bowled next to players and everyone laughed.

Not me. It was chaos in my ears, overtaking my senses.

I stood, purse and bags draped over my arm and met Jason halfway. "I'm heading out," I said. I'd met him at the bowling alley while he'd driven with equipment from the station. "Can we get together tomorrow morning to splice all of the stuff from tonight."

"Yeah. But you don't look good. Need me to take you home?"

"No. But thank you." He was young and sweet. We also lived on opposite sides of the city.

"Okay. Text me tomorrow and I'll meet you at work whenever."

I did a quick mental scroll of my day tomorrow and my heart dropped to my feet. Tuesday. The Rough Riders' day off and they were all coming to visit the kids again. It wasn't necessary but gave me an excuse to check on Brandon.

Damn it.

"Early," I told Jason. "And I know that sucks, but I have to get to the hospital at ten. Can we meet at seven?"

"You're killing me. But yeah. I can swing it."

"Thanks." I squeezed his biceps and ducked my head and got the hell out of there.

Hurrying to my car, I kept my head down, keys out and ready.

I hadn't seen Gage come back in and another confrontation wasn't on my to-do list.

Tears were already forming as I replayed it in my mind. Good God. What was it with me having completely horrible judgment when it came to guys? It'd been a day! One day when we even knew who were fucking face to face and I get handed that bullshit?

No freaking way.

I tossed my bowling bag into the back of my Explorer and settled in my chair. Turned the keys. Started the engine and right as the lights lit up, shining right at that alley, I saw him.

Gage. Ankles crossed. Arms cross. Shoulder against the wall. And his eyes? I didn't have to see them to know he was focused on me.

Well, I hope you feel like shit, asshole, because you just screwed over a really good thing.

I pulled out of the parking lot and didn't look back, despite how much it killed.

And when I got home? The Oreos and red wine I opened tasted like heartbreak and misery.

TWENTY-FIVE

Gage

With you on my couch, and in my bed, I had all I needed from you because I thought I had you.

We've been straight with each other for less than a fucking day, Gage. One day. I don't owe you shit.

She was right. All of it. Every pain-filled word she hurdled back at me made me feel shittier by the minute.

It wasn't right. It was wrong before I said anything. Somehow, I'd known it. That quiet voice telling me to calm the hell down. And I might have been able to withstand had she not mentioned pictures.

The little fuckwad had photos of us? It was the exact fear that had kept me from getting close to women at Velvet.

And I hadn't known she was up for a promotion at work.

Why? *One day.* We'd had one conversation about family before. We hadn't had the *time* to talk. But it felt like I'd known her my whole life. It felt like we'd known each other for weeks or months, knew each other inside out. That was how strong our connection was.

Or had been before you skewered it with your asshole bullshit.

But damn it.

"She was right. And you're a piece of shit." I splashed cold water on my face. My sleep had been crap and I gave up hours before I needed to wake up.

I'd make it better. I had to. Already she was more important to me than anyone I'd ever met outside my parents.

Which wouldn't explain at all why I'd jump to the absolute wrong conclusions.

It'd have to wait. All of it. I was late to get to the hospital and my phone had been silent since last night. To top it all off, Penny hadn't returned my call or shown up at the hospital which meant my first stop was to see him.

I finished getting ready. My idiocy and making amends with Elizabeth would have to wait.

At least until I came up with a game plan, but there was no way I was letting her walk away from me again. Her doing it last night was bad enough, but I'd fix it.

I was fucking Gage Bryant. Winner of awards and owner of records. I could do and win anything I put my mind to. She just deserved something more than a throwaway "I'm sorry."

"YOU'RE QUIET TODAY," Powell said next to me. "Have anything to do with the girl who ran out of the Super Bowl last night on the edge of tears?"

She'd been crying? "Shut up, Powell."

"You screwed it up that bad? That must be a record."

I barely resisted the urge to punch the grin off his face.

"Oh fuck off, Powell. How many times did you screw things up with Shannon?" Beaux rolled his eyes and turned to me.

"Seriously. It was a lot. I wanted to kick his ass more times than not."

"You wanted to kick my ass because you didn't like that I was trying to make you a better ball player."

"That's because you can't fix perfection—"

"Ladies," I called out and shoved the palms of my hands into their faces. Riding with the guys from the practice field to the hospital was only one of the minor bad decisions I'd made in the last twenty-four hours. "Just because you live with women doesn't mean you have to become them. I'll handle my shit with Elizabeth."

"But will you fix it?" Beaux asked. Danny Rudolph was driving. I figured his presence would keep the other two quiet. I should have known better.

A locker room had more gossip than a beauty salon. Not that I'd been in one of those in my lifetime. But the ladies in my small town always knew what was going on and my mama always said it was Mrs. Perkins, owner of Betty's House of Beauty who knew all the good stuff.

"Because you were such a fixer when it came to Paige?" Powell asked, shoulders now shaking with laughter.

"Fuck off. Wasn't my fault her friend hitched a train to crazy town, but yeah, I did step in and fix it. I took care of her shit even when she hated me for it and I'd do the same all over again. Except better." His voice dropped and it was a punch to my chest. Paige had ended up in the hospital after her so-called friend essentially kidnapped her. It was Elizabeth's brother, Jaxon who was supposed to protect her. Somehow, he'd let his guard down and while Paige ended up with a few scrapes and bruises, the crazed stalker had ended up dead.

Beaux didn't talk about it much, but it was obvious why things moved so quickly after that with him and Paige. She essentially moved in with him immediately, not willing to waste another second apart.

Which meant as soon as I figured out *how* to fix things with Elizabeth, I was doing the same damn thing. I might have only had one night with her, but waking up without her this morning made everything worse.

"I was a dick," I admitted. My palms scrubbed down my jeans. She'd be there today and I still didn't know how to react. What to say. How to behave. I was a thirteen-year-old boy with a crush on his eighth grade English teacher all over again, sporting a hard on at the thought of her, a mumbling clueless fool when I looked at her.

"Was a dick to Jenny when we dated," Danny piped up from the front seat. "Know what helped?"

"What?" And good Lord. How had this car ride ended up being a therapy session?

"Orgasms. Lots of them."

"I think giving her those before I got to know her caused part of this."

He snorted and continued. "Chocolates and flowers."

That I could do.

"And falling to your knees and apologizing, a lot of begging. A lot of groveling. That helped."

"Probably the most," Powell agreed. He turned to me and smirked. "What can I say? A man on his knees knocks a woman down every single time."

Now that? That made complete sense.

SHE LOOKED like she slept less than I had and that was essentially saying she looked like shit. She also refused to look me in the eyes. Her hair was in that messy bun she'd wrapped it in last night. And the flashback almost made me drop to my knees then and there.

But it was her eyes, dark-rimmed circles beneath them, swollen and bloodshot that hurt worse.

Shit. I hadn't just hurt her. It was worse than that and that made my hands curl into fists and tense at my sides to avoid grabbing her and slamming my mouth to hers right in the middle of the waiting room on the fifth floor.

Instead, I gave her space. I was there to see the kids. I hitched the duffel bags filled with hats and footballs and a host of other items including ridiculous foam fingers over my shoulder.

"That didn't go so well," Danny muttered as my gaze bounced off Elizabeth and down the hall. "I think you might need more than chocolate."

"Shut up," I grumbled.

He slapped his arm to my shoulder and shoved me forward. "Anyone can fix things, it's you. You're the best guy there is Gage Bryant."

"If that were true I wouldn't have been such an asshole to her."

"Eh. You've got a dick. Sort of comes with the territory."

Idiots. All of them. Elizabeth had told me that. Right there in the center where Danny and I were headed. Which meant if she could think that about her brothers and love them, perhaps I'd be able to show her I was worth it, too.

"True that," I replied.

We entered the first room, a seventh-grade football player who'd recently made local news for getting a spinal cord injury during one of his own games. He'd regained feeling in his arms but hadn't yet in his legs.

I blew out a breath. Today was for the kids not the problems of my own making.

It took effort, but I plastered on a smile and shoved Beaux

and Powell out of the way. "Hey man, Gage Bryant. How's it goin'?"

His dark brown eyes skipped and jumped as he took us all in. "Wow. I can't believe y'all are really here."

His hands went to his bed like he was trying to push himself up and frustration etched his features. I reached around Beaux and grabbed the remote on the side of his bed. Then I hit the button, lifting him up so he was sitting. I said nothing, acted like I'd done or noticed nothing. He might have still been a kid, but he was a competitor which meant he didn't want to seem weak, especially not around us.

"You're Javier, right?" I asked and grabbed his hand. His grip was weak so I was careful. "What position did you play?"

"Cornerback." He looked down at his legs and back to me, frustration gone, determination replaced and in that split second, he earned the respect from all of us. "And I *will* play again."

Powell held out his closed fist. "Damn straight you will."

WE WORKED our way down the hall stopping in every room where parents had given prior permission. I hadn't seen Elizabeth since the waiting room when we stepped off the elevator and that was hours ago. Jason was following us with his camera and in fact, it was mostly just the cameraman staying close. They gave us privacy in some rooms, respected the choice of some parents to stay in the hall, and when we entered the room to varying degrees of excitement, the camera crews stayed as close to the door, as far out of the way as possible. We'd done this enough to know almost exactly where to stand to still give them their shot while getting the kids on screen and have it appear natural.

After an hour of visiting the kids, some with minor injuries, some with life-changing injuries like Javier and some with debilitating diseases, the scum I'd made of my life was put back in its proper place. There were a lot of people who went through a lot more shit than what I'd created unnecessarily last night.

I'd hurt a woman I cared about for no reason, jumping to conclusions because I didn't give her—or us—time to get to know each other. And as soon as the day was done, I'd go to her house and do whatever I could to make it better.

It wasn't much of a plan, but it was all I had time for. Just knowing she was close and I couldn't get to her, that she didn't want me to be anywhere near her compressed my chest and made breathing difficult.

"Man, some of these kids are the total shit," Beaux said, coming up to me in the hallway. "I can't even imagine some of this crap they go through."

"Tell me about it," I said, and punched Beaux in the gut. The guys all knew about Harrison before the hospital stuff invaded my life and became a purpose. I had his jersey number from youth football, forty-five, stitched into every jersey I wore at games.

"Oh shit." He groaned. "Sorry man. I didn't mean to forget."

"I get it." Suddenly, a piercing sound blasted through the air.

"What the—"

But I knew that sound. And the words I expected quickly followed.

Code Blue room five fifteen.

Code Blue room five fifteen.

A dozen people rushed past us. Nurses in scrubs, tugging their stethoscopes to their chests.

It took a moment.

Five fifteen.

The bag of swag fell to my feet. "Oh fuck. Brandon."

I took off, following the crowd, slipping on my heels as I

hurried around the corner. I slammed my hand to the wall to stop from smashing into it.

It wasn't. It couldn't be. The alarm still sounded. A nurse ran by.

My feet pulled to a stop when I saw Elizabeth.

She was in the hallway, back braced against the opposite wall of Brandon's room, and in her arms?

Penny. Sobbing. Screaming. She wrestled away from Elizabeth and I trudged closer.

I didn't have to glance into his room to know what I'd find. A team of doctors and nurses. Machines. Hands on his chest. Airbag and mask pressed to his small mouth.

I reached them and for a moment, made eye contact with Elizabeth. Her eyes were soaked, cheeks showing off trails of tears. My hand went to her cheek as I said, "Penny."

Penny clung to me and I took her weight much more easily than Elizabeth had. "No! He can't!"

A sob clogged my throat. My own memories. My own horror. I'd been in the room when Harrison flat-lined.

It wasn't a memory anyone, much less a child or a mother should have. "You got this, Penny. Stay strong."

"I can't." She fell to her knees and I went with her, collapsing in the hallway, holding this woman I'd grown to know so well due to horrible circumstances all while the girl I wanted, was falling in love with, stood tall, brushing her own tears away. I reached up and grabbed her hand, thankful she squeezed back. And we sat there, the three of us, our bond the poor boy in the room. And waited.

TWENTY-SIX

Elizabeth

Three days. It'd been three days of waiting.

Three days of grieving. My heart so heavy in my chest it hurt to breathe more than the absolute required amount. It was a weight on my bones I couldn't shake, a weight I already knew would take years to vanquish. Even then, memories of the little boy I'd only known for such a short time but would remember forever, would cause a sharp ache in my gut.

Three days where the only contact I'd had with Gage was his hand squeezing mine.

But his hand reaching for me, the torment in his eyes, it unraveled me. The depth of his emotion for Penny and Brandon and even me in that torturous moment was so obvious, so bright and crystal clear I'd made a decision almost immediately.

As soon as he reached out to me, and I knew he would at some point, I'd listen to his reasons for being such a jerk, and I'd forgive him.

Life was too damn short to hold on to regrets. Brandon taught me that. And it would honor his life if I, and those of us who knew him, no matter how briefly, lived as vividly as we could, even if he couldn't be there to witness it.

I smoothed down my black dress. Cap sleeves with a cut straight across my chest beneath my collarbone, it was the most conservative dress I owned. Bought for a tea party last Spring, the last place I ever imagined wearing it was to a child's funeral.

A heavy exhale pushed from my chest and I took one last look at myself in the mirror. Black heels and sheer stockings clasped to a garter belt. It was dreary and chilly, the perfect miserable day that matched my mood. My hair was pulled back into a clip at my temple and hung straight, my energy not high enough to take the time to curl it. My makeup was minimal. No mascara, because despite it being waterproof, nothing could stop it from smudging all over my face.

"Oh." Which reminded me. Moving to my dresser, I opened the small, top center drawer I rarely used and pulled out one of my grandmother's handkerchiefs. Running my fingers around the silky lace edge she'd crocheted with frail, aging hands, tears sprung in my eyes and I forced them down. She had lived until ninety, alone until she was eighty-eight. At seventy, she learned computer programming and she took swing dance classes at seventy-five. She'd lived her life vibrantly and fervently. Exactly how a life should be lived. Not cut short by disease with no cure.

No crying. Not yet. There'll be plenty for that later.

I folded the handkerchief she'd always clutched in her hands on Sunday mornings at church. Memories when I was a little girl, curled up to her side. For some reason, when she passed, it was one of the few possessions I'd clung to and wanted.

"Take care of him, Mamma," I whispered and zipped the item into my small clutch. Lip gloss, keys, and my phone the only other items.

I took the day off work and immediately following the ceremony, my plan was to return home and sleep the rest of the day.

It took too long and not enough time to drive to the funeral home outside Raleigh. The parking lot was packed when I arrived, three limos already lined at the entrance behind a hearse with flags on top. I ended up parallel parking down the street two blocks and followed families and a few men I recognized from the football team into the funeral home.

My fingers clasped my clutch nervously as I entered, eyes scanning the anteroom. Clusters of young children in suits and ties stood with parents. At the sight of them, my knees buckled. These would have been Brandon's family. His classmates. His friends and teammates.

God. All of this sucked. I quickly removed my wool pea coat and hung it on a rack off to the side and smoothed down my dress again. It was a nervous habit, but it wasn't nerves making my fingers shake and my chin tremble. It was everything else. The sadness.

The unfairness of it all.

Even the uncertainty of what would happen if Gage saw me. For that very reason alone, I quietly moved toward the sign-in ledger and slipped into the surprisingly large chapel room where the service would be held.

I found an open spot in the back corner and picked up a copy of the program before I sat down.

At the front of the room, Penny stood next to who I assumed was her ex-husband. They stood together, avoiding each other and more pain pierced my heart at the sight of her.

Ravaged. Destroyed. Amidst all the pain and suffering her son endured, she'd always held out hope he'd pull through. She smiled a smile that didn't reach her eyes when a woman her age reached in and hugged her. Her eyes closed and next to her, her ex-husband placed his hand on the small of her back. He looked lost, as if he realized he'd lost everything that had once been so dear to him. And while she didn't look at the man whose name I didn't even know, my heart broke for him as well, even if I despised him for leaving Penny to deal with all of this alone.

Next to the two of them were two sets of couples, both older. His grandparents. God, I couldn't even deal with seeing them and the sadness lining their expressions.

I yanked my eyes off the family, quick to avoid the casket at the front, and noticed players from the Rough Riders standing off to the side in a corner. And among that gathered group was the man I hoped didn't see me. His head was dipped as he listened to Jones say something to him. He nodded once, accepted the pat to the shoulder and before he rose his head, I pulled my eyes off him. Today wasn't the day for drama. I was there for Brandon and Penny, and in part for Gage, my silent support for a man who had already been through this once.

I dipped my head, closed my eyes, and until the service began and through the rest of it, I struggled to choke down tears clawing at the back of my eyes.

When it was done, I exited quickly through a side door and hurried to my car. And once the procession pulled out, I followed the two-mile trek to the cemetery.

MY PLAN at the cemetery was the same as at the funeral home. Arrive right before it started, stand in the back, keep my head down and leave soon after paying my respects to Penny.

That plan faltered almost immediately as I cautiously stepped through the grass on heels. Near the back of the set up white chairs, a sweet brunette stood, eyes scanning the oncoming mourners. They landed on me and she smiled.

"Hey," Shannon said. She reached for my hand and squeezed. "What a horrible day, huh?"

"Yes." I squeezed her hand and tried to pull it from her, but she held on tight.

"Gage told me he wanted you with him." A worried expression momentarily hid her sadness. "Is that okay? He asked me."

I was stuck on that he wanted me. How he knew I was there. But he wanted me with him?

"Okay." I nodded and she finally let go of my hand.

She gestured for me to go first and as I stepped around her, she whispered, "And later, when it's a more appropriate time, you're going to tell me exactly why it is he was so adamant of wanting you nearby. And why you didn't mention anything going on between you before."

"It's—"

"Not nothing," she whispered. Her smile was faint but there and playful. "If that's what you were going to say. Even I can tell that."

Well. She could think whatever she wanted, but until Gage and I talked everything out which wouldn't happen today, it very well could be nothing.

I headed down the row of chairs and stopped when a large blockade stepped in front of me.

Gage. His hands were at his sides, tightly curled fists. And man, it was not the right time to drag my gaze up the length of his perfectly fitted black suit and shirt that fit him so damn perfectly he could have made the cover of GQ sizzle to ash he was so hot.

I met his eyes, took in his scowl, and the frown line etched deep between his eyes.

He had wrinkles around his eyes and his beautiful mouth was turned down.

My chin wobbled and all those tears I'd held back all morning rushed to my eyes, clouding my vision. "I'm so sorry." My voice shook and I could barely force out the words.

"Me too," he said. He sounded like he'd scrubbed his throat

with sandpaper. He lifted one of his hands, palm up toward me. "Sit with me. Please?"

Of course I would. Outside of saying goodbye to Brandon, supporting him was my purpose for being there. I placed my hand with his, stunned by the heat in his strong but gentle hold and followed him to where he'd set two seats aside.

We sat right behind Penny and before I could stop myself, I reached forward and squeezed her shoulder. She'd been talking to the older woman I saw at the funeral home and at my touch, her hand covered mine as she turned her head.

"Penny."

It was all I got out before she squeezed back. "Elizabeth. Thank you so much for coming."

I wouldn't have missed it. "I'm so—"

"Don't be sorry." God. The strength in her voice threatened to undo me. "Don't be sorry for him. Or for me. I had the honor of raising the strongest boy to walk the Earth and while he might have lost his war, he bravely won many battles. Honor him. But do not pity us."

I couldn't possibly pity her. The resolve in her words was so fiercely spoken, pieces of my own heartbreak stitched together while I marveled at her determined expression.

God. I couldn't stop the tears. At my side, Gage's hand still holding mine tightened. He placed it on his thigh, settled his other hand over our already entwined ones, like somehow, his job was to comfort me instead of the other way around.

"I will." It wasn't a promise. It was a vow I'd make to Penny and Brandon for the rest of my life. "I will, I swear it."

"Good." She grinned a heartbroken smile and squeezed my hand, patting it twice before nodding. "See that you do."

She turned back and my hand fell to my lap. I tugged my hand from Gage's strong grip and quickly gathered my handkerchief, patting my eyes and cheeks.

"Thank you," Gage said.

My chin lifted to meet him, and I knew he was thanking me for more than sitting next to him. "You're welcome."

He opened his mouth to speak, but I leaned in, pressed my hand to his cheek. "Don't. We'll talk but later. Okay?"

He turned, brushed his lips over my palm and then pulled my hand back into his lap. "Yes. We will."

The final service started then and through it, I sat straight ahead, wiped tears from my eyes, rested against Gage when his exhale turned shaky.

And when it was done, I stood in line, gathered the flowers we'd been handed and dropped one small daisy onto the small casket and hugged Penny one last time.

Gage was behind me the entire time, leading me, and once that was done, his hand guided me to where Shannon and Paige stood with Powell and Hale.

They hugged me immediately, and I returned it with all of my strength.

"It's good to see you again," Paige said. "Despite the reason. You doing okay? I've learned recently you spent some time with Brandon."

As she spoke, her eyes slid to Gage behind me and back to me. Jeez. Exactly how much had he said to people over the last few days? I'd figure that out later.

"I'm okay. Tired."

"Yeah. This was exhausting. So sad."

Beaux stepped to his wife and pulled her to his side, kissing her temple. "Hey Elizabeth." He flicked his eyes to Gage. "We're going to head to workouts. See you tomorrow, right?"

"Right," Gage responded. Like men did, they sealed their conversation with a fist bump.

Despite the sadness and how tired I was, I still smiled at the gesture.

"Take care," Shannon said, waving and grinning. "And we're talking soon. A whole bunch."

Her implication couldn't be ignored and as they walked away, I faced Gage. "You don't have practice today?"

"Coach Pomville gave me the day off and it's our bye week so practices are limited anyway." He pulled his eyes off me, looked to the sky. As he did, a heavy breath left him and he shoved his hands in his pocket. "I really need a nap. And I'd like you with me."

My expression must have got his attention because he lifted one hand, palm out. "Just sleep. We need to talk, I know, but fuck, Beth. I could use some company today."

What else could I say to the man I'd given my heart to despite the risks it meant? And who looked so shattered. Worse, he was also nervous and there was no reason to be. I took his hand and slid my fingers through his. "Of course. Whatever you need."

TWENTY-SEVEN

Gage

Letting go of Elizabeth's hand as we reached her car caused almost more pain than the idea she'd refused to sit by me. I'd had four long days to think of how I treated her. A long conversation with Shannon who stopped by after she heard about Brandon that ended with her reaming my ass for being such a gigantic fucktwit.

Her words. Not mine. Because I used real words when I was angry. But the meaning was clear. I'd royally screwed up in a thousand different ways.

And I didn't know if Elizabeth thought I wouldn't know she was at the funeral home this morning, but if she did, she truly didn't understand the depth of connection between us. For me, it singed my blood when I caught her ducking her head like she was avoiding me. It hadn't taken much to get Shannon to get her to me at the burial site.

But now with her hand in mine again, the last thing I wanted was to let go.

"You'll follow me?" I asked. My thumb ran against her inner wrist.

Sad, red-rimmed eyes blinked at me. And then offered me the best choice I'd had all week long. "I can leave my car here. You can bring me back later?"

There was no way in fuck I was returning to this cemetery later. Or tomorrow. Or ever. But I'd figure out a way to get the car to her.

"I'll take care of it." And because I couldn't resist, I leaned down, brushed my lips over her cheek. "I know I've been a dick, but thank you, for today, for that offer."

Her trembling hand pressed to the chest of my suit jacket. I covered it with mine and cringed at how cold she was. It was forty degrees and drizzling, miserable for this time of year, but not far outside the ordinary.

"Come on. I parked over here."

The guys had helped carpool me to the cemetery earlier and I'd hopped in Powell's Escalade where they drove me to the funeral home. Since I didn't have practice today, but they were still going in, it made it so I didn't have to figure out how to get home afterward too. Penny had asked me to ride in the limo with her family to the burial and while that had sucked, she appreciated my presence.

I'd been more of an uncle or friend to Brandon for the several years than his own dad had and not only was I honored to help take care of Penny, her parents had greatly appreciated it too.

Hell, my own mom had offered to fly in to be there for her even though they'd only met once in the last four years. But mom to mom, if anyone understood Penny's pain, it was mine.

God. What a fucking, miserable day. Week.

"You okay?" Elizabeth asked as we walked. She stumbled and I looked down at her shoes. Black, pencil thin heels sunk into the soppy grass. I didn't even hesitate.

"No. I'm not," I answered as I bent. She pulled back, surprise on her face, but before she could react, I swung her into my arms and hers flew around my neck.

"What are you doing?"

"Faster I get home, faster I can sleep. Faster we can talk. You were taking a year in those heels."

She huffed and I didn't think I'd be able to laugh that day, but as she buried her forehead into my shoulders and laughed, slapped me on the back, I let loose the first quiet laugh I'd had all week.

"That's not nice," she finally said.

"Yeah. But we're at the truck and now I can get you warm."

Her head rose, sparkling blue eyes still bloodshot from crying crinkled at the edges. "Thank you."

She had nothing to thank me for. I had a thousand things to beg forgiveness for. If anyone was going to be saying thank you, it should have been me. And I would after I heard that she forgave me for being such a world class asshole.

I opened the door and helped her climb into the Navigator. Then I hurried around the front, slid in, and while I started the ignition, I pressed the heat warmer buttons and cranked up the heat.

"Damn," I said, blowing into my own hands. "It's cold out there."

"I couldn't tell if it was the weather or my own sad heart."

I knew what she meant. I might have been ready to talk about us, but Brandon would take awhile. I rubbed my hands together again to warm them and threw the car into drive.

I lived north of downtown Raleigh, almost on the outskirts, and in good traffic, it took about forty minutes to get to.

That car ride was the longest lasting forty minutes I'd ever felt. We didn't say much, but we are both thinking a lot. Elizabeth pressed her head to the window almost as soon as we pulled out of the cemetery and more than once I caught her drawing little shapes with her fingertip on the glass.

She sighed a few times and closed her eyes.

Had I not been driving I would have done the same thing.

The whole thing sucked and there were no eloquent words to put into the life of a child ending in the way Brandon's had done. It wasn't fair. It wasn't right. Unfortunately, those of us left behind never got the answers that made sense.

Which meant the only way to move on was to keep putting one foot in front of the other.

I'd remember Brandon as often as I remembered Harrison. Which sucked, but more than once over the last few days I'd prayed and asked my brother to look after the new kid. I didn't know if God worked like that. If where the boys were worked like that, but it never hurt to ask, and if they were together, I could smile imagining them running routes and catching passes, happy and healthy and pain-free for the rest of their days.

"We're here," I said, slowing down at the private gates to my driveway. I didn't exactly like living like I had a stick up my ass, but my privacy and security was important.

"Wow." Elizabeth lifted her head off the window like it took effort and she blinked slowly, head swiveling to take in the land in front of her. You could see my house from the end of the driveway. It wasn't that far back and as she took it all in, her jaw went slack, her eyes wide. "You live in a palace."

I wished. But the house was huge. Ten thousand square feet of space that went empty most of the time and even if I ever did get married and have kids, it'd still be way too big.

"Yeah, but I liked the privacy and I didn't buy the house for the building, but the backyard." I punched in the code. "Code is four-five-four-five. Use it whenever you like."

"Do the numbers mean anything?"

"Harrison's youth jersey number." The gates opened and I punched the gas.

"I'm sorry. I can't imagine how difficult this day is for you. What kind of memories it brings back."

I drove up the driveway, not bothering to make the curve that would take me to the garage. It was closer to my room if we went in the front door anyway. Parking, I faced her. "Bad ones. Really bad ones. But mixed with those there's a lot of good ones and I try usually to focus on those."

Her lips twitched, slowly rose at the corners. "You're smart."

"Sometimes." I shrugged and pulled the keys out of the ignition, opening my door. "Sometimes I'm an idiot."

I hopped down and closed my door, but the glimpse I got through the windshield before she opened her door was her fighting a grin.

I met her at her side and reached for her hand. "All men are," she said.

"Comes with having a dick, I figure. Too much blood rushes to one part and cuts off the other."

"Can't always think when you want to?" Her words were teasing, the thinly veiled meaning behind them not. She yawned then, and while the teasing was good, rest would give us a clear mind.

I hit the buttons on the alarm, kicked the door closed, and reset the panel. "Come on. My room's upstairs. Let's sleep and then we'll pick up that conversation, okay?"

"Yeah," she said around another yawn. Her shoes clattered to the floor and she took my hand. "That'd be good."

We climbed the stairs together. Her hand slid on the banister. The exhaustion set in with each step as we trudged down the hallway, the air heavy, the mood somber, and yet through it all, she held my hand, leaned her weight against my arm and when we reached my room, she wore her dress, stockings, and a smile.

"What's the smile for?"

"Your house is really pretty. Huge but I like all the dark wood. Makes it feel cozy."

"I'll give you a tour later." I went to my closet and to the dresser-sized island that sat in the middle. Swear to God, my own closet was bigger than my dorm room in college, or any bedroom I'd had growing up.

At first, I felt guilty for buying such a large house, but the backyard with a basketball and tennis court, pool, and a fitness gym over the disconnected extra garage sold me. I'd lived my whole life in a minuscule three-bedroom home with a bedroom that barely fit a twin bed. I hadn't been built for a twin bed since I was fourteen.

So when I got traded here, I found the space I wanted. My only requirement was somewhere I felt free. Someplace quiet. Someplace that felt like home and the backyard was a killer. I could be active or relax, host parties or shoot a ball well after the sunset, which I did often. It was lonely sometimes in such a large house, but I wasn't often alone. A lot of the guys hung out at my place when we got together in the offseason.

Hopefully after today, Elizabeth would be spending a lot of time here.

I dug through my drawers and pulled out a gray T-shirt and a pair of pajama pants I rarely wore.

"I have a shirt for you," I said, walking out of the closet. She was sitting at the foot of my bed and the mere vision of her froze my feet to their spot on the carpet.

She had one leg lifted in the air as she rolled one of her thigh-highs down her leg. Which meant... she had on a garter belt. *Fuck me.*

Her other stocking was set nicely next to her, giving me a hundred ideas.

I willed my dick to settle, the blood to go to the correct brain for once, and tossed the shirt to her. "You can wear that to sleep in if you'd like."

Then I tore my eyes away from her body, so perfectly sexy at the edge of the bed like so many nights at Velvet and put my back to her. "I'm going to change in the restroom. You can use it when I'm done."

I left her there, looking enthralling and beautiful, a slightly stunned expression on her face at my sudden bluntness. But that couldn't be helped. Her anywhere on a bed looking so cute and sleepy could be the end of me.

I WOKE to a tiny body wrapped in my arms, the sunlight finally peeking through the clouds and shining in my bedroom. After Elizabeth used the restroom, she crawled into bed and without asking, without waiting, but assuming correctly, she curled her body into mine. I'd wrapped my arms around her and she covered my hand on her stomach with hers.

I'd kissed her temple, thanked her again for coming home with me, and on a yawn I'd been fighting for what felt like hours, I closed my eyes.

It was the exact ending I needed to a horribly shitty week.

Now, my phone was vibrating on my nightstand. Without wanting to wake Elizabeth, whose soft little sounds told me she was still sleeping, I slid my arms out from beneath her and reached for my phone.

"Hey Ma," I said, my voice was gravelly from sleep and stress. I put my feet on the floor and sat up, scrubbing a hand down my face. "What's going on?"

"How'd it go today, honey?"

Only my mom could call me honey and get away with it.

Then again, she'd changed my diapers and wiped my ass, a fact she reminded me of whenever I got sassy.

The question brought back an onslaught of emotion through the day. Seeing Penny. The damn small casket. Brandon's tiny face—now sporting a healthy hue thanks to the mortician. It seemed even more unnatural than his pale skin had when he was alive.

"It was...it sucked." I settled on the truth. "Really sucked, Ma."

A warm hand pressed to my back and the bed shifted. Without looking back, I held onto Elizabeth's hand as it slid over my shoulder. The bed shook as she moved closer and then her knees were at my hips, her cheek on my shoulder and both of her arms were wrapped around my chest.

Goddamn. I'd royally screwed up with this girl and she didn't hesitate for a single second to comfort me.

"I'd like to give Penny a call in a few days," she said on the other end. "Think that'd be okay?"

I had no idea. But my mom had the sweetness in her to heal the most angry and ugly wounds. "I know her parents are here for awhile, but I'm sure she'd like to talk to you."

"Good. Good." I could see her. Sitting in her living room, dragging a pearl across a simple gold chain, chewing her lip. Nervous and sad, so aching for someone in pain it went against her nature to not be here in person. "I'll do that then."

"It's all good, Ma. Penny would like to hear from you. And if anyone can help her, it's you."

"Well," she sniffed and I could tell she was crying. My mom's heart broke when people around her hurt. It's what made her such a good pastor's wife. My dad for years said he couldn't do his job without her and it didn't take a genius to figure out why. She knew what people needed whether in pain or joy and had the strength to give it to them regardless of the cost to her. "You don't need to make me cry by being so sweet."

"I'll try not to be sweet then." I laughed softly. At my shoulder, Elizabeth's curved into a smile. "I gotta go though, Ma, I've got things to take care of today."

Like finding the strength to mend something I'd broken.

"Oh. Okay. Your father and I will be there Saturday. Is that still okay?"

Shit. I'd completely forgotten about the center opening on Sunday. It was our bye week so we were doing the grand opening before the first game of the day so everyone could spend the day enjoying it while watching football even if the Rough Riders weren't playing on the screen.

"Yeah, Ma. I'll see you then. Tell Dad I said hi."

"Will do," she chuckled. "But you know your dad."

"I do." Work hard all the time. It killed him to miss giving the sermons on Sundays, but he'd learned long ago if he wanted to see any of my games, which he did, he had to loosen the reins and hire an Associate Pastor. I still knew he'd be watching the online streaming of it, ensuring Pastor Luke was doing a good job.

"See you soon."

"Okay dear. Take care and call me if you need me."

I promised her I would and hung up. Then I tossed my phone back to the nightstand. My head fell to my hands and behind me, Elizabeth's hands roamed my back, heels digging into the back of my shoulders.

A groan fell from my throat. "God. Damn. That feels good."

She worked my shoulders and back, her little hands not having the strength to get my deepest knots out, but it felt fantastic regardless. Mostly because it was her hands and she was kneading my bare flesh.

"Your mom is very sweet."

"Sweet as sugar. With a bite of a rattler if you crossed her."

"I could see that, too." Her soft laugh skated across my skin.

My shoulders slumped. This was too easy. So perfect. With too much to say. Clasping my hands in my lap, my gaze landed on the wall in front of me. "I owe you a very large apology and an explanation."

Her hands on my back stilled for a moment. "You do." She moved again, pressed the heel of her palms on both sides of my spine and God. Glorious. "Start talking."

I chuffed a laugh. "Demanding little thing."

"Impatient." She poked me in the ribs and I jerked. I had two ticklish spots on me and she was close to finding one.

"Easy," I growled, but damn. I was smiling and who would have thought I'd be smiling and laughing today of all days. "I was an ass. We've gone over that, and I should have handled it better. Powell said some things and took me by surprise. It's not right, and it's a shitty excuse, but with the opening of this center, all the work I've poured into it over the years, I've been more on edge than usual. The last thing I need right now is publicity harming my reputation in any way."

"I can understand that. It's why I go to Velvet, too you know."

I knew that. "Yeah, but then I learned Jaxon was your brother and you had that connection with Hale. And then Shannon. Plus Velvet. I had no idea you knew the girls and it didn't take long for my mind to spin and conjure a bunch of shit. It made me wonder if you were playing me, or if you and Connor were working together. It wasn't right, Elizabeth. I know that. It wasn't then, felt shitty even while I was thinking it."

I turned in the bed quickly and put my hands on her hips. "Oh!" she gasped in surprise, but I kept moving us until I was sitting, back to the headboard and she was in my lap. "I can't do this not looking at you."

Her hands went back to my shoulders. She trekked her own movement down my arm and back up, down the front of me.

My dick took notice and I gritted my teeth to will away the erection forming. "Keep doing that and it'll lead to a lot more than an apology, Elizabeth."

She didn't need the warning, I had no doubt she could feel my dick pressing against her backside. Somewhere I hadn't been in awhile but seemed like a really great fucking idea in the moment.

"You know how I met Shannon and I told you about my brother." Her eyes stayed on my chest and I hated she wouldn't look me in the eye. "And Connor, well, he's a jerk. I didn't know he had all that in him months ago. But I think what hurt more than your words, Gage, was that your instinct wasn't to trust me."

TWENTY-EIGHT

Elizabeth

Trust was something I freely gave. Perhaps too easily. Maybe I was naive. Growing up with such a great family and an easy life compared to many others, I gave that trust until you lost it or broke it. And often, I gave people several chances to lose it only because just like me, other people made mistakes, too.

I would have understood if Gage had come to me and asked me questions. Yet that's not what happened.

He'd flung verbal bombs at me and hadn't given me a moment to suit up in armor to defend myself against them.

It still hurt and while forgiveness came easy, being vulnerable to move forward with anything with him wasn't an easy decision.

"I know." His hands were at my hips, still holding me to him. Even through his soft Ohio State T-shirt, I felt the heat of his palms. The gentle brushes from his thumbs inside my hip bones.

His cock was hard against my ass, making concentration difficult.

A lot of this could have been avoided too if once he recognized me, he was upfront about it. Instead, he'd played his game, using me at Velvet while getting closer to me outside of it. Was I a game to him at the beginning?

That thought hurt even worse.

I dragged a finger down his chest, through his coarse hair there I loved so much. I loved he didn't shave everything. He was all man and muscle and heart and brain.

"Connor had a point though."

His hand gripped my finger and the speed of it made me gasp, meet him eye-to-eye. "Did he?" His jaw jutted and I almost smiled.

He hated Connor almost as much as I did, and I didn't hate anyone, but Connor was at the top of my strongly-dislike forever list.

"I'm up for a promotion. I can't have attention on me now, either. Not with that and if I embarrass the station...I've always wanted to be on the prime time news, sitting behind the desk, not out in the field. It's my dream and it's important to me. Connor made a point. NDA's or not at Velvet, you're too recognizable, at least now with the hospital. And if I get that promotion, if someone finds out..."

I trailed off. I didn't want to end things with him. I wanted Gage. I was falling in love with him and the mere idea of not having him in my life was unquestionable.

But was the timing right?

"I destroyed Connor's phone," Gage said, and the admission made me laugh.

"What?"

He nodded, brought my hand to his mouth, kissed my fingertips oh so sweetly and then pressed my hand back to his chest. His heart thumped beneath his skin, and he held me there, feeling the beat of his heart as for the first time all day, his eyes gleamed.

"Went back into Super Bowl, ripped the phone out of his hand and stomped it to shreds. Then I handed him a thousand bucks, told him to get a new phone, and warned him that if those pictures showed up, ever, on any outlet, I'd do worse to his balls." He grinned shamelessly. "Not one of my finer moments, but I don't really give a fuck either. I think he got my message."

I imagined Connor's face during that and my head fell forward. My shoulders shook with laughter and I collapsed against Gage's chest.

"We've done this all wrong, you know?"

He tensed beneath me and his hand went to my scalp, ran through my hair. Delicious tingles spiked down my neck and spine. "What's wrong?"

"It was supposed to be a night of sex. Maybe we shouldn't have continued that, not after you realized..."

"When I realized the woman I couldn't get out of my head was sitting in the front row of my first press conference? Yeah, I should have done something then, but I was worried you'd either done that knowing who I was or wouldn't again once you knew I was your story."

"It could cost me my job." I showed him my fear in my expression and the worry I had. "I can't lose it, Gage."

"I won't let you. I took care of Connor and the pictures. And as for Velvet, I don't need it if I have you. Besides," he ran his hand under my shirt. Pressed it up my back and I shivered. Lord, he felt good. Was so damn tempting. "The hospital stuff ends this weekend. After that, everyone will go back to not caring about us. If you're with me and you can get past how big of a dick I was, I'll call Tristan right now and end my membership. Give me the time to prove you can trust me."

I'd already made that call to Tristan's surprise. I had too much baggage there. One with Connor, and if things between Gage and I didn't work out, that was still the last place I'd want to return. I'd called the night I left the bowling alley. It could have been chalked up to a poor decision fueled by fury and wine, but in the morning when I woke up, I had no regrets.

I shoved my hand through his hair and grinned. "I don't know if you know what you're asking. We don't really know each other at all and this could get messy."

It was only a partial lie. I valued cleanliness and order to borderline obsessive tendencies.

He pulled me to him until our lips pressed together. "Then we'll be messy together and maybe through all our own messes, together, something beautiful could form."

I gasped at the beauty in his statement, the sincerity in his eyes, and the conviction in his tone. And then he kissed me.

I'd called him a thief for stealing my breath along with my heart, but you couldn't steal something freely given, so I melted into him, kissed him back, and when he yanked down his pants, pressed the tip of his cock against my center, I shoved my panties to the side and took everything he gave to me.

"Gage," I sighed his name as he filled me. My fingers clung to his shoulder.

"I know, Elizabeth. It's fucking heaven being inside of you."

"ROUGH MORNING?" Will asked as I arrived at my desk and plopped down my purse.

I sunk into my chair and groaned. "Shayla was leaving outside," I said. "Do you know why she was here?"

His brows arched above his glasses frames. "No. But she was only in Shane's office for a few minutes before leaving. She didn't really stop and say hello to anyone, either." He shrugged one shoulder. "Could be anything."

Great. I saw her outside when I was climbing out of my car that had somehow been delivered to my apartment building overnight. Gage meant it when he said he'd take care of it yesterday. I'd convinced him I couldn't stay at his place last night. I hadn't expected him to pack an overnight bag and insist on staying at my place with me, but I didn't bother arguing either. I wanted him with me.

"So, maybe she gave her notice?" I was trying to be hopeful, but I was exhausted. I could have easily blamed Gage for my lack of sleep last night, but it wasn't solely his fault. It wasn't solely him, either. I had an early morning and hours of work to do on the cutting room floor reviewing and editing footage for today's final clip of the pre-opening of the children's center. Considering everything that had happened in the last three days, I wasn't exactly looking forward to talking about Brandon, but I had to. And that alone kept me up last night. And Gage's sleep hadn't been much better.

"Elizabeth!"

I jumped at Shane's bellow and shot a glare at Will as he laughed. "Goddamn, woman. You have to stop doing that."

"I can't help it." I pushed away from my desk, still startled by the way Shane could make me jump like a rabbit every time. "He's so loud."

"Coming!" I called back to Shane and gathered my things.

I swiped my hand down my thigh, pointlessly smoothing out my gray wool pencil skirt and hurried to Shane's office.

"Good morning, Shane," I said, taking my seat at one of the chairs across from his desk.

"Elizabeth." He stroked his gray lined beard and clicked a button on his computer before turning to me. His abruptness slammed my shoulders straight back.

He was always friendly, and as his eyes landed on me, a trickle of unease settled low in my belly.

Oh, this wasn't good. Which meant Shayla's visit meant bad things for me. *Crap.*

"I saw Shayla this morning," I said. All my dreams and hopes were crumbling, but I could take this hit. My job promotion hadn't been guaranteed by any means. In all honesty, it'd probably been a long shot.

"We'll get to Shayla in a moment," Shane said and spun his computer monitor toward me.

As I caught the first glimpse of the photos on the screen, a curse fell from my lips. The images were grainy, and out of context, so...so very bad for me. But it couldn't be denied that it was Gage and me outside Velvet. His hand at my waist and his lips were on mine. I was plastered to the side of my Explorer.

This wasn't happening. My hands curled into fists with the sudden urge to strangle Connor.

"I can explain," I said. My mouth went dry and I squeezed my eyes closed. "It's not what it looks like."

"Really?" Two thick gray brows rose like bushy caterpillars on his forehead. "Because it appears you're making out with the object of your current story, Elizabeth."

Oh damn. I hadn't felt so scolded since I was thirteen years old and brought home a D in English Comp of all classes.

"I know, sir. But—"

"Outside of a fetish club?" He cringed at the word and bile rose in my throat.

So the picture was exactly what it looked like. "It's not... Okay. It is, but—" I shook my head. I had to know. "How did you get those?" The pictures on the screen weren't the ones Connor had shown me. They were worse in that Gage and I's faces were totally obvious. Fortunately, none of the pictures from inside Velvet were on the email. Thank God for small favors. But how many had he taken? And what else was coming?

Shane adjusted his reading glasses and leaned toward the

monitor, cringing again. "Came from an email lizzielikeskinkysex at gmail dot com."

Oh God. I was going to throw up. "What? Shane..."

He lifted a hand and faced me again. "What you do on your own business is your business, Elizabeth. You know that. And regardless of what you do, you also know you're always representing XTCP. And this not only puts you, and us, in a negative light, but it shows you kissing the source of your story." He shook his head and pressed his forearms to his desk.

Shit. Stupid. I was so stupid. I'd been so caught up in Gage and the crazy sex at Velvet with the stranger. Now it was too late. I should have walked away as soon as I realized they were one and the same. And there was no way I was explaining the ins and out of *that* part of all of this to Shane. Poor man might have a heart attack and I'd have that on my conscience.

"It's unprofessional at best, Elizabeth, and completely unethical at the worst of it."

His eyes were kind, blue eyes filled with so much disappointment, tears welled and threatened to spill. I'd screwed up. Stupidly. Hugely and there was no fixing it.

"I know. I'm sorry. Does anyone else know?" I asked, pointing to the pictures. A fake email? Someone, i.e., Connor, had gone through a lot of work to keep that anonymous...and slapping me in the face at the same time. It had to be Connor, but was he really so vindictive? Despite his creepy attitude lately, I still couldn't believe he'd sink this far.

"Email was blind carbon copied to me. I have no idea who else has received this, but it's the text that makes this even worse."

I didn't want to know. I still had to ask and when I did, Shane leaned toward the monitor again and read:

Elizabeth Hayes, reporter for XTCP gets up close and personal with the subject of her story for the last few weeks. Seen here, lip-locking with the Rough Riders very own wide receiver, Gage

Bryant, outside a sex club just a week before his new family center opens at the children's hospital."

Oh no. "I'm sorry," I said again, sniffing away more tears. "I know you're disappointed and this was such bad judgment. I know how bad this looks, and I should have told you when things changed. I know that now but I didn't think. But Gage and I are seeing each other. It's recent, but I can assure you that it in no way affects how I handled this story."

It couldn't have. I didn't even know the guy I was making out with was Gage until last weekend. It was such a lame excuse and yet honest at the same time. I should have gone to Shane as soon as I figured it out. I never should have gone to that private room at Velvet with him once I knew who he was.

There were a million things I should have, could have, would have done if I had the chance to rewind time.

In my lap, my phone vibrated and lit up. A text from Gage in all caps that sent my heart rate into overdrive. **CALL ME. STAT.**

Shane was as perceptive as ever. "Let me guess. I wasn't the only one to get the email."

I showed him the screen, shaking my head. "No. It appears not."

"This is disappointing. I had high hopes for you, Elizabeth, I really did. But you have to understand the position this puts me in."

Oh God. Did I? Wasn't I sitting in Gage's lap less than twenty-four hours ago worried about the same thing?

"Would you like me to clear out my desk today or come back later?" The gavel was dropping. My job was over. What in the hell would I do now?

"Let's wait," Shane said. And my brief moment of hope evaporated almost as quickly as it rose. "I have a meeting in an hour and if these photos go live and wide, I don't know what the fallout will be. For now, you're suspended and off the story. But let's give it the weekend, wait for the damage to settle and we'll see where you are."

It was better than getting fired. "I understand."

"I'm trying to be fair here, Elizabeth. But I can't promise you anything. And you've shown a severe lack of judgment that I don't know if my bosses will understand, and as far as Shayla—"

"She's coming back."

"No, actually. She stopped in early this morning and gave her notice. But I can most likely guarantee that if you are able to keep your job, you won't get her spot. I am sorry about that."

I closed my eyes and sniffed again, unable to keep the tears away any longer. In my lap, my phone buzzed again, and I gripped it harshly. It was Gage again. I knew it.

"I get it. And I really am sorry, Shane. I was caught up in everything and showed horrible judgment like you said. I take full responsibility for that. And I'm definitely more sorry for putting the station in the middle of this."

"You're a good girl, Elizabeth. I know that. But for now, go home and we'll touch base when I know more."

I nodded, swiped my tears and rose on trembling legs. The walk back to my desk took a lifetime and Amanda's presence at my desk, hip up against the side, phone in her hand made everything worse.

"They went public?" I asked at her expression. She didn't need the clarification.

Her lips twisted and her eyes held a heavy weight of pity. "Yeah. They're up on Twitter by some of the local blogs already."

"Shit." I dropped my head and grabbed my purse.

"If it's any consolation, he looks like a really good kisser."

"Jesus, Amanda," Will said, walking around our desks. He placed his hand on my shoulder. "You okay?"

"No. Suspended until we see the fallout. I need to go."

"We can do drinks tonight," Amanda offered, but drinking was the last thing I wanted to do. At least in public. I'd seen the way gossip blogs went viral and with Gage as the subject, it was bound to be bad. So bad.

Career ending, dream-crushing bad. I blew out a breath and reached for my purse. "Thanks, but I think I'll just head home and wallow."

"Okay. But if you need me, call me. I can always come to you." She wrapped her arms around me. I barely had the strength to lift mine and return it. "Love you, honey. It'll be okay."

I wished.

I said my goodbyes and left the station. Whispers and curious glances followed me. I kept my head down and ignored them all and it wasn't until I was safely tucked into my car in the parking lot where I dared to look at my phone again.

I wasn't surprised to have more messages. More from Gage.

PR JUST GOT EMAILS, **Elizabeth. Call me back.**
You okay? I'm sorry, damn it.
Call me.

BUT TWO WERE ALSO from Connor.

THIS WASN'T ME. **We need to talk.**
Fuck! I can explain. Call me ASAP.

I SENT GAGE A TEXT BACK. *We'll talk later.* And

dropped the phone into my purse. I had no strength to deal with this. Not now.

Not when I knew better and should have handled everything differently.

And as for Connor? He could take a long leap off a short pier because there was no way I was giving him the time of day.

TWENTY-NINE

Gage

I stabbed the decline button on my phone for the millionth time since our Public Relations rep rushed into the workout room, a printout of emails in her hand earlier. As soon as I saw the blood drain from her face, quickly followed by a hot pink on her cheeks, I clutched the papers in my hand without looking at them.

She didn't have to tell me.

Photos had been released. This was an epic fuck-up and it took me twenty seconds to debate who to go after first: Elizabeth or Connor.

Fucking shithead. He was worse than a pesky mosquito you couldn't kill.

Coach Pomville reamed my ass in the workout room in front of the whole team. Since then, my phone blew up. Karen from the hospital had called, almost screeching her fears into my phone. Which sounded much more shrill coming through my SUV's Bluetooth speakers when I was listening to voicemails. My agent Patrick wouldn't stop calling and I'd handle all of it. I'd already texted Patrick. We'd talk, but my career wasn't my priority.

Elizabeth was.

Lizzie likes kink. Because of course who did this would make it about her, and not me. My hands gripped my steering wheel tighter as I turned into her apartment building. If shit was bad for me, it was worse for her and we knew the risks of this. But how could I have been stupid enough to forget them? I was the one who'd approach her in the public room at Velvet. I was the one who revealed who I was. I was the one who kissed her like she was my next breath outside where any asshole could see.

I should have gone to the Rough Riders' PR team as soon as I knew Connor had those photos. They could have at least been prepared for this to happen. But I'd trusted him when he said he wouldn't do anything. The man must not like his balls as much I assumed he did.

Revenge was the only thing keeping me sane, which was fucked up in itself. But for the last three hours, I'd had plenty of time to plan on how to get even with that asshole while Elizabeth continued ignoring every one of my texts after she sent a reply of "we'll talk later," that told me nothing.

I called the station, smart enough to remember her friend Amanda's name and asked for her directly. She'd told me everything she knew. Elizabeth was sent home, suspended indefinitely. Which meant she had to be at home.

But her car wasn't anywhere in the parking lot as I yanked the Navigator into the visitor spot. I took the stairs to her place three at a time, breathless as I reached her door and pounded on it repeatedly. There was no answer so I yanked out my phone and called her.

"Hello, you've reached Elizabeth—"

I hit the End button on my phone and rested my head against the door. She wasn't home.

Where would she be?

If she was so damn embarrassed by the fallout from both of our mistakes and wanted to hide, where would that be?

Her family.

"Fuck," I groaned and slammed my fist to her door.

I ran back down to my car and folded myself inside. It took awhile for me to remember, but I replayed the night she talked about her brothers. Jaxon. Tanner. Blake. They'd all be Hayes. And her dad's name? My fingers rapidly tapped the center console as I tried to remember. By the time she talked about her parents, I'd been thinking of how sweet her mouth would be wrapped around my cock. Richard? Rob? No. It was Ron.

I scribbled down their names as I thought of them onto a scrap of paper and it took me one second to figure out whom to reach out to first.

Beaux.

I had to call Jaxon. The man was lethal enough if he got wind of this before I could warn him, he'd have my ass in a sling.

Before I called Beaux, I did something marginally insane. Pulling up an address site online, I found her other two brothers' and parents' home addresses, listed publicly and wrote them down.

I'd start with Jaxon. Then if I had to, I'd drive all over the tri-metro area until I found where she was hiding.

"Let's just hope this day doesn't end with Kinky Sex Fetish wide receiver turns stalker." Right. Because that was all I needed. "Shit, Elizabeth. Where in the fuck are you?"

It didn't matter. I'd find her. I threw my SUV into the parking spot and pulled up Beaux's name and as soon as he answered, I said, "Need some help. You got Jaxon's number?"

His laugh wasn't pretty. More scared for me. "Yeah but not sure he's going to want to talk to you."

"Yeah well, better from me than someone else."

"Your funeral, Gage, either way, really. Dude scares the shit out of me on a good day."

"Not what I need Beaux. Just the number."

"I'll text it to you. You okay? Coach is pissed the hell off."

"I know. I'll fix it. Somehow."

He made a choking sound and my pulse turned rabid. "Good luck. Call if you need me."

"Will do." I hung up and when he texted me the phone number, I was a dead man walking toward the electric chair as I gathered up my balls and called Jaxon.

AN HOUR AND A HALF LATER, I had survived a potentially deadly phone call with Jaxon, and finally found Elizabeth's Explorer. I was able to enlist his help and he said he'd get guys on hunting down the IP Address so we could at least figure out who sent the emails and he'd come home if he had to.

She was at Blake's house. Of course that's where she'd go. She'd told me he and Jaxon were her most overprotective brothers and there was no way she'd go to her parents' house and tell them how we met.

And she might not have told Blake, but she was close with his wife.

I parked at the curb in front of the house and checked my phone. I should have turned it off, but the sick part of me had to know what was being said.

Essentially, I'd be deleting my Twitter account immediately. People were crazy there.

Another call from Patrick came through and I sighed, staring out the window at Blake's house. I needed to get to Elizabeth, but I also had to talk to him. He'd been calling for hours and he wasn't the guy I wanted to piss off.

"Yeah, I know, I'm an idiot," I said by way of answering. "What's the damage?"

"To you or her?" Patrick said. This is why I liked him, he didn't mince words.

"Her. Although I already know she's suspended." I couldn't give a shit about me.

"Bad to be honest, but not as bad as it could be. It appears there are millions of women in the world with a kinky side and some of these comments are making me uncomfortable."

"Shit. That's not what I wanted to hear."

"Seriously, Gage. There are some fucking perverted women out there. You should hear—"

"No." God no. That was the last thing I needed to hear. "What's my damage? What's it looking like?"

"Been on the phone with the hospital. They're not pleased, obviously. But right now, it's a lot of speculation. So you're kissing a woman in public? Who cares you know? And fortunately on the photos, there's no sign you're really outside a sex club. So... you know, like I said, could be worse."

"Who's picked it up?"

"Every gossip blog on the planet but legitimate news stories seem to be steering clear for now." He sighed in the phone. "That could change, Gage. And if more photos are shown. Right now it's you kissing a reporter and no proof at the mention of the sex club. We can handle this. But the hospital is pissed and I don't know what that'll mean for the opening or your role. And for the woman? She's a reporter making out with the guy she's been following for weeks. That doesn't look good and that's where it's bad for her."

"Fuck." I scrubbed a hand down my face and blinked. There was movement at the window. A curtain fluttered. Moments later, another one moved. I had to get out of the SUV before I really did get picked up for stalking. "Keep me posted?"

"Obviously. But if I'm calling, it's important to answer your damn phone."

"I will. Later."

I ended the call and jumped out of my SUV. I was halfway to the front door when it opened. Expecting Elizabeth to step onto the porch of the small two-story home that looked like every home on the street, with pretty little lawns probably courtesy of strict HOA rules, I stopped when a man stepped out.

"You must be Blake," I said.

"You must be the asshole who's totally fucked over my sister and killed her dream."

I hadn't done shit to his sister except fuck her, but I wasn't arguing with the guy. He looked like he ate nails for breakfast and I might have been a big guy, but I kept my pounding to the football field. With pads. And rules.

Blake looked like bar brawls were his favorite pastime.

"I came to talk to her."

He crossed his massive biceps over his chest. I might have been intimidated by him, but honestly, I didn't give a shit. This was Elizabeth's and my's problem to deal with and we had to do it on our own. If she didn't want anything to do with me after I possibly ruined her chance at her dream like Blake implied, it was still her job to tell me.

"Who says she wants to talk to you?"

"Maybe she doesn't." I stepped toward him until I was a step below him. For a brief moment, his asshole glare dissipated. Like he just realized who he was in front of and I'd timed my visit on a day where he was wearing a blue shirt with the Rough Riders logo on his chest. The man was a fan. But still a big brother. "But I wouldn't be the guy I was if I didn't track her down to try to work this out face to face and see where she's at, what she's dealing with. I care about her, Blake. And I've already got people working on fixing it, including Jaxon."

"You got gonads of steel if you called him."

Gross description of my balls aside, I gave him that. "And I'd like to keep them, which is why I called. He's already called his office to figure out who sent the emails. But Elizabeth right now is my priority. So you can stand there and play her bodyguard, but I'll give you five seconds to decide if you want me to force my way in, or let me do what I need to do."

"You're tough," he replied. Still glaring. Then he grinned. "And if you don't take my team to the Super Bowl this year, I'll kick your ass."

Damn fans. I chuckled despite the tense and fucked up day. "I'll see what I can do. That I can promise."

"All right. She's in the living room, pissed I made her stay there while I told her I was coming out here to kick your ass. She'll be happy to see I didn't follow through." He stepped back and toward the door.

"If it'll make you feel better, I'll let you get one punch in."

He grinned. "Really?"

I shot him a look. "No."

"Bummer. Would like to be able to tell the guys at the garage I beat the shit out of Gage Bryant. They'd probably give me a medal. Or they'd kill me." He shrugged like either option was okay with him. "Come on in. Need a drink?"

A bottle of bourbon sounded fantastic. Too bad I didn't drink during the season. "I'm good."

THIRTY

Elizabeth

Gage walked into my brother's living room without a bruise in sight, which showed good things. When I showed up at Blake's, needing Haley and her world famous hugs, I hadn't expected Blake to be there. Bad timing on my part because it took him three seconds of looking at my tear-stained face before he went into a rampage.

Explaining everything to him was harder. Telling them the whole story of how I got involved with Gage, at his insistence, was harder.

Difficult to tell your brother about your sex kink and not want to vomit onto his carpet. Fortunately for me, I didn't need Haley cleaning up their house when she was already battling morning sickness.

"Ohh, he's even larger in person," Haley whispered next to me.

I rolled my eyes and grinned at her. "Everywhere." I wiggled my brows and stood from the couch.

"Lucky bitch," she muttered and stood next to me. "Hi Gage,

I'm Haley, Blake's wife and you can ignore all his threats. He's a big cuddly teddy bear in lion's clothing."

Gage walked toward her and held out his hand to shake it. "I'll take your word for it. Nice to meet you."

"You too." She held onto his hand a bit too long before letting go. "Blake and I will let you two talk." She glared at her husband. "Kitchen, Blake."

He stood like a guard behind Gage. "I'm good here."

My eyes rolled again. "It's fine, Blake."

"No, it's not. He's cost you your job and I want answers, especially about Jaxon."

What? I whipped my gaze to Gage. "What's he talking about?"

Gage slid his hands to his hips. He was wearing black athletic pants and one of those dri-fit athletic looking shirts. It was snug all over him and maintaining eye contact, especially as he rocked back on his heels, was difficult. "I got a hold of Jaxon. He's making some calls and might head back."

"But he's on a job."

"One I'm pretty sure he'd put on pause to help his sister," Gage said. "Also, he was fucking pissed, but I didn't want word to get out without me talking to him. Setting things straight."

My brain bounced. Setting things straight? "What'd you tell him?"

"Everything."

Oh God. I wobbled backward and settled my hand on the back of the couch. My brother's house wasn't big. A small two story with a simple kitchen and dining area. And considering it was all open concept, Haley's offer to head to the kitchen was pretty worthless.

"You told Jaxon about Velvet?"

"Jesus," Blake groaned. "I don't even want to know how my little sister learned about those kinds of places. Stop saying it."

"Don't mind him," I told Gage. "But talk."

"I had to." He stepped closer. My grip on the back of my brother's couch tightened. God, the man was delicious and I'd felt bad for ignoring all his frantic calls and texts earlier, I just needed a minute to get my head wrapped around everything happening. I needed quiet. And people who loved me. "He's going to find who sent the emails and we'll go from there. The good news is, I talked to my agent."

"There's good news?" The only good news I needed to hear was that I wasn't being fired. I'd handle stories at the zoo for the rest of my life if it meant I could keep doing what I loved.

"None of the pictures released show any proof of Velvet. So all it really is is speculation, and gossip about me finally having a girlfriend. According to thousands of fans of mine, the male ones are pissed I'm not actually gay."

He huffed a laugh, shaking his head. Who would have thought I'd be able to smile at anything. "Well, that's good for you."

His expression fell and he reached for me. I wasn't quite ready for contact with him. Even though this wasn't his fault. It was mine. All of it, really. "I'm sorry, Elizabeth. About your suspension. I called Amanda."

"Well, wow. You're just taking care of everything aren't you?" I said it with a bite I didn't fully mean, but he was invading everything. My family. My job.

"You wouldn't return my calls and I was worried. Please." He glanced at Blake and Haley. "Can we go somewhere and talk? Figure out what happens next?"

That was the part of my plan I had no clue what to do. If I stayed with Gage what would it mean for my job? If I walked away, what would it mean for my heart? There weren't easy answers for any of it.

"This isn't your fault, you know. Not really. I wasn't

suspended for kissing you outside a sex club. I was suspended for making out with the subject of one of my stories. It's unethical and shows poor judgment."

"I get that. And obviously there are things we should have done differently, even me once I knew who you were, but we can't go back."

"But can we go forward?" I asked. My throat burned at the question. The doubt. The fear. The wondering.

"I'm hoping we can figure out a way to get there, yes." Oh, my heart. My poor aching heart melted at his words. The sweetness in his dark, stressed eyes.

Next to me, Haley sighed and placed her hand to her chest. "Oh, you two are so sweet."

Only she would think any of this was sweet. I glared at her and she shrugged. "What? I mean, he's hot and he's taking care of you. I like it."

"He's also in the room," I told her.

"Yeah, I don't think he minds." She winked at Gage who didn't look amused.

"Actually I do." He held out his hand to me. "Come home with me. Let's figure it out."

Smart or not, being with him was the only place I knew I'd be able to think clearly.

I grabbed my purse and dug out my keys, tossing them to Blake. "I'll come get my car sometime, but in case you need to move it."

He grabbed them out of the air and skewered Gage with a poisonous glare that would have most men melting to ash. Fortunately for Gage, he wasn't most men. "Swear to God, you make this right for her. And expect I'll be calling Jaxon as soon as you leave."

"Wouldn't expect anything less," Gage said. He held out his

hand and Blake only hesitated for a split second before gripping it. "I've got this. Promise."

"Good." Blake let go and turned to me. "Take care, sis. And call me if you need anything."

"Um." I scratched the back of my neck and flinched. "Well, can you tell mom and dad?"

"You want *me* to tell mom and dad you met your guy at a sex club? You fucking insane?"

Haley slapped him on the chest. Fortunately she was closer or I would have. "You can leave that part out dumbass," she said.

"Crazy. You're all fucking crazy," I said. Gage was next to me, grinning down at my mutterings and when our eyes met, his lips lifted at the edges. "Ready?"

"Yeah." I gave Haley and Blake a quick hug and followed Gage out to his SUV. It wasn't until we were buckled in and out of his neighborhood that two thoughts came to mind.

"How'd you find Blake's house?" I asked.

"Public addresses online. Looked up all your family's and drove by. By the way, the house you grew up in is really cute."

"You did... you know what?" I waved a hand in the air. "It doesn't even surprise me."

"Went to your apartment and you weren't there so I tried to figure out where you'd go. I've been driving around for hours looking for you. I've been worried."

I hadn't meant to make him worry, but at hearing he did, my heart skipped a beat.

I slid my hand to his thigh and he covered it with his, squeezing tight. "Thank you. I didn't mean to make you worry, I just wanted some time before I called you back. Also, before you send Jaxon to rip off Connor's balls, you should probably know he texted me."

"The fucker did what?"

"Yeah." I unlocked my phone and pulled up his texts. I'd had dozens of notifications on my phone and it took awhile to find them. "Basically he said it wasn't him. He can explain and he was sorry. I was thinking of calling him right before you showed up."

Gage's hand on mine squeezed tight. "Do it once we get to my house. I want to hear what he has to say."

Funny. I figured he'd say that.

The rest of the drive to Gage's was quiet, and long since it was Friday afternoon and we were headed out of the city like so many others. But it gave me time to settle my thoughts too.

I loved being with Gage. The fact he'd driven all over Raleigh and Durham looking for me spoke volumes. So did the way he took over to try to fix everything.

But could I risk my job over him?

There were hundreds of jobs in the world. But only one man who made me feel the way Gage did.

Which meant, when it came down to it, the answer wasn't all that hard.

"HAVE YOU EATEN ANYTHING TODAY?"

"No," I answered Gage. We barely got into his house before he was pushing me down the front entryway straight to the kitchen. "I don't really feel like anything though."

"Tough." He took me to a stool and set me on it. I'd grumble if it wasn't sort of cute. "I'll make some sandwiches and I want to hear what your boss said. Then we're calling Connor."

"Bossy, bossy," I muttered and propped my chin into my hand, elbow on the counter. He was digging in his fridge and when I spoke, pulled out and slid his eyes to me. Narrowed and a bit wicked. I felt that look down to my toes. "I'm just sayin'."

"You like me bossy."

Yeah. I really did.

"So. Your boss." He changed the subject quickly and it took me a minute to get off the visions where his bossiness took me. "And do you like ham, turkey, or salami sandwiches?"

"Yes. All of it."

"Thought you weren't hungry."

"Well, I wasn't. But I'm hoping I'll need energy later."

He slid packages of meat and other sandwich fixins onto the counter. "Didn't bring you here expecting anything, Elizabeth. You need time to figure things out, I get it."

I opened the package of salami and took a bite. "So does that mean it's off the table later?"

"No." He leaned forward, palms pressed to the edge of his gray and white marble counter. Muscles popped on his arms and took my attention from the heat in his eye. Dang. He was so yummy. "You gotta know, I'm at the point where I'd give you anything and everything you want. All you have to do is ask."

There was a weight to his words. An implication I didn't dare read too much into. "Okay then. Food first."

"And your boss."

"Right." Somehow, knowing we were on the same page made things easier. "I have the excuse that I didn't know who you were, but honestly, I'm not defending myself if it comes down to it in front of a board of men with that answer. Plus, I eventually did. Professionally and ethically, once I even suspected I should have walked away. I was just...I was hypnotized by your dick and I didn't think straight."

He barked out a laugh and paused slicing a tomato. "My dick hypnotized you?"

"Well, I mean. Yeah."

"Jesus." He went back to cutting the tomato. "If you're ever asked for a comment by a reporter, please, for the love of God, keep your mouth shut."

"I'm the queen of no comments." I grinned and reached for a

piece of bread. Tearing off a chunk of the twelve-grain cardboard looking healthy crap, I chewed slowly. "So really it is all your fault."

"I'll shoulder the blame of hypnotizing you through my cock. Don't worry."

Had I guessed this morning I'd have anything to laugh at I wouldn have called myself nuts. But there I was. Eating Gage's food, watching him make me a meal, in his house and somehow, I knew—

Everything was going to work out just fine, even if it wasn't how I originally pictured.

"In all honesty, me getting suspended is on me. That's not your fault. We both could have done things differently and while at least for now I've totally blown my shot at getting the promotion to the prime time news desk, it'll be okay."

He was tossing our sandwiches together and looked up. "Yeah?"

"I mean it sucks, but if I can somehow keep my job, I'll be okay. Another promotion will come at some point."

"You're not just making light of this for my sake, are you? Because right now, you seem okay, but you didn't when I stepped into your brother's house." He sliced my sandwich in two and slid the plate in my direction. "Drink?"

"Water please." I took a bite, moaning over the taste of it. Apparently I was starving because as soon as food hit my mouth, I couldn't get enough of it. "This is good. Thank you."

"You're welcome. Now answer my question."

"It's life, Gage. I made a bad decision. One I knew was reckless and I can't fault you or my boss or the higher-ups at the station if that has consequences I don't like. From what Hayley said, the gossip isn't *that* bad—"

"Except for the fact thousands of fans thought I was gay."

"Well, okay, but still, that's not all that bad, either. And if I lose my job, it's my fault. I'm a big girl. That's life. Sometimes it sucks, sometimes you do stupid shit, and you have to fight through it."

I wasn't one hundred percent behind my pulling up my big girl panties and facing my consequences plan, but it was all true. Maybe after a weekend of wallowing, I'd get there. But I'd made my decision in the car ride there and that I wasn't going back on.

"You're impressively mature," Gage said and took a large chomp out of his sandwich. When he was done chewing, his eyes gleamed. "I love that about you."

I loved everything about him.

"Thanks," I said, blushing at the word love. It wasn't the time to talk or make declarations and I wasn't jumping the gun to admit I'd realized I'd totally fallen for him. Instead, I chewed my sandwich, we ate lunch, avoided all talk about work or the hospital and focused mostly on me telling him how crazy Blake was and about his parents coming in on Saturday.

"Speaking of," he said, dumping our plates into the sink. "I'd like them to meet you. Any chance we can see you Sunday?"

"Well, my day is free," I quipped. It wasn't funny and the reminder I wouldn't be at the opening stung. "But yeah. Sunday night. But oh...I might have to be at my family's."

Once my parents heard what happened, they'd insist. And Blake and Tanner would follow. They'd want to interrogate me to the high heavens and while I was an adult and didn't have to do what they said, being around family while I couldn't be doing my job would help.

Gage licked his lip over his top teeth. "We could come there later?"

"Meet my parents? My whole family?" Was he nuts? Combining the parents when we hadn't even finalized what we were to each other.

My breathing went erratic.

"I mean, I figure they'll have to meet and get to know each other sooner or later. Might as well be sooner."

Later? Families? Get to know each other?

My hand slid through my hair. Wow. I'd hoped...but this was fast. And weird. It was weird, right? I couldn't even think straight. I gulped down the rest of my water, pausing only when Gage started laughing.

"What?"

"You're freaking out. Am I off base here?" He walked around his island until he was in front of me. He cupped my cheek and tilted my head up. "Tell me I'm not off the mark in what's happening between us, Elizabeth."

"No. No. You're pretty spot on. At least with where I'm at."

"Good." He grinned and it was so beautiful he took my breath away. He leaned down, ran his nose over mine and pressed his lips to mine. His fingers pressed into the flesh at my neck, as he kissed me slowly, effortlessly....so damn sweetly my heart wanted to leap right out of my chest and into his hands. "Then I'll talk to my parents and we can come after the opening. Be there for dinner and watch the game with your brothers. Have them see I'm not the asshole Blake's most likely telling them I am right now."

My hand went to his wrist. "Blake loves me."

His lips were still brushing against mine as he replied, "He's not the only one." He gave me a quick kiss and pulled out, leaving me dizzy and spinning on my stool. "Now, let's call Connor and get this shit out of the way so I can report in to Jaxon."

Well, that was a bucket of ice on a suddenly good turn of events.

THIRTY-ONE

Gage

High on the top of my priority list was finding the right time to tell her I loved her in a much better, and clear way. Still, I think I got my point across, and that meant talking to Connor was the last thing I wanted to do.

But it was important and as she slid her phone out of her purse and sat on the couch, I sat next to her.

"Speakerphone. I want to hear what he has to say."

She knew better than to argue.

As she pulled up her contacts, I fought down a growl. It still came across in my tone when I said, "And after you're done, you're fucking deleting his number from your contact list."

"Jealous?" she asked, and it wasn't exactly a tease.

Things she'd learn about me. Other men who had been inside her weren't going to be her buddies. Not that Connor had that hope. "Would you like me to have numbers of women I've fucked in my phone?"

Her lips pushed to the side. "Point taken."

"Good." I kissed her because I didn't mean to be a dick, it just happened. I'd work on it like she'd learn to get used to it. "Thank you."

"Anything," she said and that promise went straight to my dick. "Okay. Here goes."

She hit the call button and her hand curled around my thigh while it rang. On the second ring, Connor picked up. "Thank God you called me, Lizzie. I swear to you, I didn't do this, and I'm so damn sorry. I fucked everything up."

Her brows jumped and if I wasn't mistaken, she was biting back a laugh at Connor's rambling.

Pussy. How did he ever think he'd be able to handle this woman next to me?

"Explain then," she said, and pride burned in my chest. She was a woman who knew what she wanted, took responsibility for her actions, fought for what she deserved. She impressed the hell out of me every day I'd known her and I knew with the glimpse of her I'd gotten, there were only more surprises to come.

"Okay. Listen. I deleted the pics of you and that fucker—"

"That fucker is listening," I said. "So fucking watch it. My threat still stands."

Silence hit the phone for a minute and if the timer wasn't running, I would have thought he hung up. "Okay. Right. Anyway. I deleted the pics from my camera roll, but I didn't get a chance to do it before you destroyed my phone. But after I got the new one, I had Mel set up."

Elizabeth leaned forward. "You told me you broke up."

Another beat of silence. This guy was wearing out my patience and quick. "Actually, I think I said I was going to break up with her, but since you made it clear you didn't want ..."

"Oh my God," she said. Her forehead dropped to her palm and she rubbed it. "You're a giant piece of scum, Connor. You know that right?"

He cleared his throat, ignored the name calling and attitude thickened his tone when he replied, "Anyway. She set up my phone. Saw the pictures. Threw a fit and left."

"You also said she was fine with you and me being together." Elizabeth laughed then and her forehead fell to my shoulder. Shoulders shaking, she couldn't help herself and damn I loved a woman who stood up for herself. "Good Lord you're a dick. I hope someone does come along and crushes your balls."

"She left me," Connor said. If I hadn't been on the phone, he'd have a slew of names to toss her way and I knew it was only knowing I was there keeping him in check. His tone was biting. He was a fool if he didn't think Elizabeth was smart enough to not be fooled by him any longer. "And she threw my phone at me when she left. I didn't think anything of it and I deleted them right after. She must have sent them to herself."

"That's it?" I asked. "You're just passing the fucking buck to an ex who also learned you're trash?"

"It's the truth."

Damn. The man didn't have the right to keep his balls. Pity for the next girl who fell for his decent All-American looks and public persona.

"I'll take care of it," I said. "But you come near what's mine again, anytime soon and we'll have problems and until then, stay the fuck away from me whenever you see me. Got it?"

If I was facing him, fire would dart from his eyes. I knew his type. All talk and bluster. No strength to back it up. Which was probably why he called Elizabeth so many times to explain.

"I got it," he finally said. "But I swear it wasn't me."

"We don't give a shit," I said. And before either Elizabeth or he could respond, I ended the call.

"Mel?" Elizabeth asked. Her voice was thin and she ran her hands down her thighs. "How fucking stupid. All of this because, what? She was pissed he still wanted to have sex with me? God!" She threw her hands to her hair and pulled them back, piling her hair in a messy pile on top of her head before letting it all fall. "I can't believe this. She'd risk ruining my career? What a selfish... stupid..." She stood and paced, hands flung wildly in the air.

I was the asshole enjoying her freak out. I leaned back in the couch, kicked my feet up on the coffee table and spread my arms wide on the couch. Tiny Elizabeth was sexy as sin pacing my living room, flipping her hand in the air, muttering more to herself than me.

"I mean, who does that?" she shouted and slapped her hands to her hips.

"Crazy people."

"Yes." She shoved a finger in my direction and nodded. "Yes. Crazy people. That's who." She turned and before she could take another step toward her goal of wearing out my wood floor, I grabbed her hips and yanked her into my lap.

"Gage!"

"Quiet," I muttered against her throat. She smelled like sweet flowers and had the attitude of a sassy little vixen. This woman was made for me. "I'm going to call Jaxon and fill him in. If we let him know where to start looking for the email origin, he can dig into servers and delete everything. At least then we'll know if there was more coming. And I have a feeling if Mel comes face to face with anyone Jaxon works with, she'll back down."

"Ugh. I want to kick her in the face with my heels."

And I'd like to see that. I had no idea who this Mel chick was, but I'd put my money down on Elizabeth winning any day of the week.

"Hold all that anger in, little one." At that, she shivered, my intent clear. "Because after I get off the phone with Jaxon, I'm taking you to my room and you can get all that anger out on me."

Her fingernails dug into my arm, but her legs stopped flailing. "Oh. That sounds like a better use of energy."

"Fuck yeah it is."

∼

I WAS on the couch at my parents' house. After I spent Friday night at Gage's, I spent the rest of the weekend stress-cleaning my apartment. His parents were coming and they had plans to go see Penny. I was invited to join them but begged off. Gage's mom and Penny deserved some time together and with my emotions going through the spin cycle over the week, I wasn't certain I could be a helpful addition. I hadn't seen Gage since he dropped me off at my car early Saturday morning and since he'd been busy all day, I'd only briefly texted him last night after he sent me one.

You sure your parents are okay with us coming by?

I think mine would be offended if you didn't.

Good. We'll be there around 5. You going to watch?

He meant the press conference. I hadn't been certain until he asked, but it was so important to him.

I wouldn't miss it.

Good. Sleep tonight and I'll see you tomorrow.

I'd hesitated. Typed out a text and deleted it. Repeated the same thing. It was too soon. And it shouldn't be said over text that I loved him.

You too.

I settled on that and hit send and it was the last time we spoke.

Sunday morning I'd gotten up and headed to my parents. Haley and Blake arrived late, Haley looking greener but after resting on the couch with ginger ale and crackers nearby, her color and energy level improved some.

Tanner and Heather showed up right before lunch, typical for Tanner, and Jaxon showed up shortly after. I'd looked at him expecting answers and he came to me. Kissed my cheek and whispered, "Later. It's all good."

And that was that. I trusted Jaxon. I loved Gage. They'd do whatever they could to salvage my job and make sure there weren't more pictures out in cyberland.

So really, there was nothing to do except grab a snack plate my mom had out on the kitchen table, a glass of wine, and sit down to watch the press conference.

As soon as Gage stepped up to the podium, my body tensed. Damn. He was so sexy. Dressed in a suit and tie, sporting a Rough Riders hat that didn't match the outfit, but fit him perfectly, he grinned into the cameras and leaned toward the microphones. "Good morning, and thank you for being here today to help me celebrate something close to my own family's heart. My own brother, Harrison, would have loved all of this..."

Gage didn't falter as he spoke. He made the small crowd chuckle at times, tear up at others, me especially when he mentioned Brandon and Penny, and so many other families I'd personally met. There were clips of the families entering the center for the first time, a red ribbon Gage cut with gigantic scissors looking more like hedge clippers. There were shots of him bending low, shaking hands with a boy in a wheelchair. Hugging a little girl with a casted leg as she leaned on her crutches.

Overall, as the opening and press conference continued, my heart grew twelve sizes and cemented the fact that I was totally head over heels in love with this man. It went splendidly until a question made all the women in my mom's living room gasp and my brothers stood at attention.

"You were in the news earlier this week, Gage. Care to comment?"

"Only to say who I love and how we show that love to each other is no one's business. Next question?"

The same reporter who I couldn't see didn't let up. He asked another question and while Gage had been pointing at someone else, the man asked, "Is it true it was outside a sex club?"

Gage's scowl went electric.

"Wow," Heather said. "Gage looks ready to rip that podium into pieces. That guy is dead meat."

"No kidding," Haley replied.

"I like him," my mom said.

I was too intent on watching every feature and muscle in his jaw and face harden and tick. "What it is, is none of your business like I already said, and it's shameful you call yourself a reporter while you're intent on throwing a fellow one under the bus. You're the only person in this room who has anything to be ashamed about. Now," he looked at another hand raised and pointed. "Next question."

"Wowzers," Haley said. "He's so totally hot."

"Your husband's right here, you know," Blake said, arms crossed over his chest, pouty expression.

"I know dear," she said, patting his thigh and not looking at him. "I know."

"Is anyone else going to comment on the fact that Gage Bryant just proclaimed his love for Elizabeth on live television?" That came from Heather, whose voice was close to squealing levels.

He'd done that. I'd heard it. He alluded to it, but he hadn't said it outright. Neither had I. But Gage had not only stood in front of cameras and live television and told everyone listening he loved me, he'd shamed that reporter, and side-stepped the question of Velvet perfectly.

God. I loved him so damn much.

Tanner pressed his finger to his ear and jiggled it. "Yeah, I feel like I need to bleach my ears now."

My dad pushed off the rocking chair. "I need a beer. Get me when the games start."

"Dad—" I called. He stopped walking and looked at me over his shoulder.

"What?"

I grinned at him. "I'll always be your little girl, you know."

"Damn straight. And if that guy didn't love you like I thought he should, he wouldn't be walking in this door later. He better make sure he deserves you or the first thing he'll be meetin' is the barrel of my shotgun."

He nodded once. Went to the kitchen. Next to me, my mom pulled me into a one-armed hug. "That means he likes him."

Haley, Heather, and I glanced at each other. Right before we burst into laughter.

IT WAS LATER, after lunch and after Gage's statement, "who I love..." looped in my mind on repeat a thousand times if not more, and in between games when excitement had turned to frazzled and crazed nerves.

Any minute from now, Gage was showing up at my parents' house. We were going to watch the second game together, eat dinner at halftime and when the game was over, I was going back to Gage's house. With his parents. For the entire night.

A lump the size of Texas had lodged itself in my throat and I was a pacing wild wreck.

"Calm down," my mom said. "The boy loves you. And you've already met his parents."

"Yeah, before I was caught canoodling with their son all over the internet."

"Canoodling," Jaxon snorted. "Is that what the kids are calling it these days?"

"Oh, they're here!" Heather shouted. She rushed out of my parents' formal living room waving her hands. "They're here. I saw them pull up. Seriously, girl. He is gorgeous with a capital G."

"I know," I laughed. But God, I was terrified.

"I'll get the door," my mom said, and there was no arguing with Marcia when it came to welcoming people into their home. Even knowing Gage's mom as little as I did, those two would be fast friends. *Hopefully.*

I was on her heels, my sisters-in-law hanging in the kitchen and my brothers near them, interested while pretending not to be, and when I reached my mom at the door, she was opening it before the bell had rung but with perfect timing.

Graham and Sue Bryant were stepping onto the porch, Gage stood behind them, a whole head taller than his dad, even taller than his mom.

Next to my mom, relief washed through me at the sight of them. Then something else. My love for him warmed, wrapped itself around my heart and spread through my veins until I shivered from the heat of my reaction to him.

God, I loved him. I was one lucky, lucky girl.

"Hello," my mom said. She clasped Sue's hand first, pulled her into a hug which Sue returned like they'd already been friends for a lifetime. "It's so lovely to meet you."

"Thank you for having us," Sue said. "Especially on such short notice."

"Yes. It's very kind of you," Graham said. He stepped up to my mom and held out his hand.

She shook it kindly before gesturing for them to enter. "Marcia Hayes and we're thrilled to have the whole family together."

Oh God. I was going to cry. She was laying it on a bit thick but it was Sue who grinned. "Seems like that's the way it's going to be anyway."

She pressed her kiss to my cheeks. "Lovely to see you, Elizabeth. You're just as pretty as I remember." Her hand curved around my shoulder as she passed and introduced me to Graham.

"It's a pleasure," I said to him, and then was dumbfounded when he forwent my hand and hugged me.

"Any girl of my son's is one of mine," he whispered in my ear. "And the pleasure is ours, I promise."

"Thank you." Oh dear. Tears were beckoning and it took all of me to step back so they could enter. My mom carried on with introductions, and as their voices faded, it was just me and Gage on the doorstep to my parents' house.

"Hey," I said. My hand ran through my hair and I shifted on bare feet. He seemed so much larger, in his suit, a bouquet of red roses in his hand, and a smile that made my heart leap and jump. I licked my lips, tingles spiking when his gaze dropped and watched the slide of my tongue. "You're here."

"I am. You're lovely as always."

I was in jeans and a sweater that wrapped and tied at my waist. I'd thought of dressing up, but that'd be weird at my own parents' house.

I was speechless. He'd said he loved me to reporters and cameras, but there we were, grinning at each other like fools.

"Are those for my mom?" I pointed to the flowers.

"No." He held them out to me. "Did you watch?"

He meant the press conference and not the game, but both had happy endings as far as I was concerned. The Rough Riders biggest rivals and team tied for first place in the division lost.

"I did. It was...interesting." I took the flowers from him and inhaled the sweet scent of roses. "You were wonderful."

He stepped closer, pressed his hand to my waist. The depth of his emotion for me shone in his eyes, making me thankful he was holding me up. Goodness. Would I ever stop reacting so powerfully to his presence? Hopefully not.

"I was honest. And I need you to hear it from me, here, at

your parents with our families inside so you have no doubts what I want from you. I love you, Elizabeth Hayes. I fell in love with you at the first sight of you and I hope like hell you feel the same for me."

"I do." I didn't hesitate. I couldn't. It felt like I'd been holding that back for years. And it'd been weeks. "I love you, too."

"Good." His other hand went to my neck and he yanked me toward him. His mouth slammed onto mine and he kissed me, harshly, pressing his mouth to mine and as I relaxed into him, he groaned and pulled back. "We'll continue this later. I should get in there and meet everyone."

I wanted nothing more. I curled my hand around the doorknob and glanced at him over my shoulder. Winking, I said, "Just watch out for dad's shotgun."

We opened the door to a cacophony of voices. Deep masculine ones, high-pitched feminine laughter.

Gage took my hand and led us into the living room where everyone was smiling, gathering, and fortunately for the both of us, no shotgun was in sight.

It was never needed. My dad fell in love with Gage Bryant the player years ago, and in a split second of seeing us enter the room together, knowing he was the man I loved, my dad fell in love with Gage Bryant, the man good enough for his only daughter.

EPILOGUE

Gage

Tristan stood as tall and proud as I'd ever seen him near the end of the hall. The lights on the wall cast an eerie glow, and the scent of something meant to seduce and relax slid over me.

I was focused on very little except the small, trembling hand clasping firmly in mine at my side as Elizabeth and I walked toward him and the small black box burning a hole in my suit pocket.

Beneath my ribs, my heart pounded with a steady but rapidly increasing thump. Tristan helped me plan the entire night down to the blindfold dangling from his hand. It was just like the first time I met Elizabeth, except this time we were entering the room together. And hopefully, by the time we left, she will have promised to be mine forever.

"Tristan." I greeted him with a small chin dip. I arrived hours ago to help set everything up and then went to get Elizabeth before bringing her here.

He returned the gesture and turned to Elizabeth. "*Ma chérie. Bonsoir.*"

She pressed a small piece of hair behind her ear, grinning up at the man like she'd expected to be here. In actuality, I'd promised her a surprise and when we pulled up at the back entrance, her face had paled. We hadn't been to Velvet in six months, since the photos of us broke. Media had surrounded the club for a week or two, causing Tristan myriad headaches with the members. Many had left, but many more had requested to join which had pissed him off even more. Elizabeth and I didn't come out of respect to the trouble we'd brought to his livelihood and also because we no longer needed it. She gave me everything I needed and craved in the privacy of our own homes.

"Hi Tristan," she said. Her hand trembled as it drifted down and curled around my forearm where I held her other hand. "How are you?"

"*Magnifique,*" he replied. "It is lovely to see you again. And I believe, it's been requested you wear this."

He raised his arm and from outstretched fingers dangled the blindfold.

Elizabeth let out a small gasp and looked up at me. "A blindfold?"

"Just for a bit."

A glimmer of excitement sparkled in her pretty blue eyes and she took it from Tristan. "Okay, then. Whatever you say, sir."

I choked down a laugh. She hadn't called me that since she found out who I was. This woman. I loved her more every day and she constantly impressed the hell out of me. After the press conference, she'd been suspended from work for thirty days. She was fortunate enough not to be fired, and even though it was upsetting feeling like everything she'd worked so hard for had been ruined, she was still grateful to have a job. She returned to the station after her suspension, dove in to behind the scenes reporting until all hints of attention on us disappeared and worked her ass off to regain any respect she may have lost among both her peers and viewers.

That was my girl. A fighter with the largest and strongest heart and mind of anyone I'd ever met.

A week after the press conference, all trace of photos of us disappeared courtesy of Jaxon's team. He'd found Mel in her apartment in Holly Springs. After a brief conversation he relayed to me with dozens of colorful curse words thrown in, calling her every wretched name I knew and a handful I didn't, she swore she wouldn't be a problem moving forward. He confiscated her laptop and cell phone, and the last update he gave me was that Mel Anderson was now living in Idaho, on her family's llama and alpaca farm.

Far away from us and hopefully she'd stay there. Once Jaxon and I reassured Elizabeth that Mel wouldn't be a problem, she never asked about her again. She trusted both of us to take care of her and from that day on, she put that blip in the road far in her rearview.

Her ability to move on and bounce back were only some of the many things I loved about her.

"Come on," I said, taking the blindfold from her and sliding it over her eyes. Once I assured she couldn't peek, I grinned at Tristan and clasped my hand to his shoulder. "Thanks for all your help."

"No problem. Enjoy your evening. And you too, *ma chérie*."

"Thanks, Tristan. Have a good night."

"I would say the same to you, but I'm sure yours will be much better."

She slid a questioning glance my way even though she couldn't see me and I rested my hand on her lower back. I already knew as soon as we went into that room that mine would end up being the best ever.

"I'm going to open the door and once it's closed, I want you to do everything I say. Understand?"

She brushed her hands together and nodded. "Of course. I always do."

Like hell she did. She had a mind of her own and only submitted when it came to getting my cock in her. "Sure you don't," I teased and reached around her to open the door. As I pushed it open, I turned back to Tristan.

He flashed me a wink, waved, and hustled down the hallway. He would hurry to get a front-row seat. When I called him earlier in the week to see if I could do this here, he'd emphatically declared there was no way he was missing it.

She inhaled heavily as we entered, her entire chest rising and lowering with her slow, intentional breaths. As the door shut behind us, I guided her to the center of the room. Curling my hands around her shoulders, I adjusted her so once she could see, she'd see everything.

"There are roses in here," she said. Her voice was quiet, a mere whisper of a breath I'd have a difficult time hearing if I wasn't standing so close. "Lots of them."

"There are."

God, she was fucking pretty. Earlier I'd told her to dress up for a nice dinner so she'd outdone herself and slid into a fitted black dress with shimmers of silver down the length of it. It stopped above her knees and she was several inches taller in her heels. I'd already removed her coat and even though the room was warm, goose bumps still traveled up and down the length of her bare arms.

I slid my hands to her shoulders and curled them around her neck. "Are you ready?"

"I'm always ready for you."

That, I knew well. Elizabeth could get turned on by a kiss to her throat, a fingertip trailing down her hand, or a few dirty texts

I'd send on the way home from a workout. The woman was always ready for me and I fucking loved her ravenous hunger to always be so close and connected to me.

"Good. You know I love you, right?" I lowered my mouth to hers and kissed her. My hands stayed where they were at her neck and I used my thumbs to tilt her chin up. "You know I love you, right?"

"Yes," she whispered against my lips.

Aware we were being watched, I kept the kiss chaste. For now.

"Okay. Close your eyes." I slid off the blindfold and ran my fingers through her hair. I was blocking her view to the gathering area, but the lights had been on this room for an hour and the crowd had gathered, waiting. I ignored them as much as possible, my focus solely on Elizabeth, but now that she was about to see them, I nibbled my lip.

Whatever. They wouldn't be open for long.

She stood in front of me, pulse wildly pumping at the base of her throat and I pressed my thumb over the stop. It was racing and at her sides, she had her hands fisted so harsh her knuckles were white.

"Why are you so nervous?" I asked, running my finger over her cheek. She hadn't been this nervous even the first night we met. Odd how a stranger could soothe her more than me.

She licked her lips. "I don't know. I'm not. Excited maybe? It's been so long since we've been here."

"And it'll be the last time you come unless you offer," I promised her. After tonight, we'd never need it again and I wouldn't have brought her here for this except she'd always said she wondered about how it would feel to be watched.

Like fuck I was letting anyone put their eyes on my woman's naked body though.

"It'll be a night to remember," I assured her, cupping her

cheek and kissing her. "I promise and you know I won't do anything you don't like."

"Oh, I'm sure I'll love everything you do to me."

If I couldn't feel dozens of eyes on us, she'd get a spanking for that. Mostly because she'd like it.

I left my hand on her cheek and stepped back. Running my fingertip over her closed lids, I put space between us, my arm outstretched.

"Slowly count to three and then you can open your eyes."

"One." I took my finger off her eyelid.

"Two." I grabbed the box from my pocket.

"Three." I dropped to one knee in front of her, adjusting my already hard dick.

She opened her eyes slowly, lips lifted into a smile until she registered everything going on in front of her. Around her. At her feet.

"Oh my God," she gasped. Her mouth gaped and her eyes popped wide. "What is this?"

Flowers were everywhere. So thick the floor could hardly be seen. On the bed, the gray coverings normally there could only be seen at the edges of the bed. The rest of it was littered with red and white rose petals.

Her head fell and her hands went to her mouth, eyes lifting to the crowd behind me and back to me. "The windows are open."

"They are."

Confusion mixed with something else swirled in her blue eyes and I gave her a moment. It'd been so long since we'd been in this room and I remembered every beautiful fucking second from the first time I saw her and my heart stalled, seeing her on the bed waiting for me to the moment now, as she returns her gaze to mine.

"What are you doing?"

A laugh bubbled from my chest and I shook my head.

Popping open the box, she gasped again as the light hit the diamond ring inside. "Our lives started here. The best part of mine did, anyway, and it was here we decided to be a couple. I figured it was fitting that it should be here you agree to forever with me and say yes to being my wife."

"Oh my God," she gushed. Tears welled in her eyes and her chin shook.

My heart raced and I swear the box wobbled in my shaking hands. "What do you say, Elizabeth Hayes? Will you do me the honor, make me the luckiest man in the world and marry me?"

"Yes," she cried. She reached for me, not the box, and soon she was at her knees, her hands at my shoulders and her mouth was fused to mine. She pulled back, wet streaks ran down her cheeks and I felt her tears on my own. "Yes, I'll marry you. Of course I will."

Best fucking words I'd ever heard. I took the ring out of the box, grabbed her hand, and slid the ring onto her finger. She was so petite, it was a smidge loose, but we'd get it properly fitted soon.

"Good," I said, and leaned in, cupping the back of her neck and slammed my mouth to hers.

I devoured her mouth, ravished her as I stood to my feet and took her with me. She was in my arms, exactly where she belonged forever. I carried her to the wall and hit the button.

At the whir of the blinds closing, she pulled back, looked out the window over my shoulder. "They're cheering!" she said and grinned up at me. "You're not going to let them watch?"

"Fuck no. The best parts are for my eyes only." I dropped her to the bed and climbed over her, pressed my knee in between her legs to spread her wide before shoving her dress up past her hips.

And fucking hell. She was naked beneath her dress and dripping.

"So wet for me," I murmured, sliding my finger through her slit.

"Always." Her fingers curled into my biceps. Even through my suit coat, I felt the bite of her nails digging into me. "I love you, Gage Bryant."

"And I love you, soon-to-be-Elizabeth Bryant." Then I lowered my mouth to her core and for the next two hours, I devoured my fiancée. I fucked her until she screamed and then I did it again.

When we returned to my place, I declared she was moving in immediately. She was too sated to argue, but she was awake enough to come again, riding my cock, her hands bound behind her, fisted in mine, screaming my name and telling me she loved me over and over. Only a few hours before the sun rose, I emptied inside of her, giving her the same back she gave to me.

Everything.

Forever.

***

DID YOU LOVE WICKED PLAYER? **The Rough Riders Series continues in September with Cocky Player! And I can guarantee, new-to-the-scene Connor Quinten is a man you do NOT want to miss. Click here to sign up for more information as soon as it releases.**

WANT to be the first to know about upcoming sales?

Follow me on BookBub!

Want to ensure you never miss a new release?

Follow me on Amazon.

Click here to sign up for my newsletter and receive information about all upcoming releases as well as sales and other exclusive content. Plus, as a thank you, you'll receive a FREE E-Book of mine.

Are you behind on the Rough Rider Series and want to get caught up? Start reading today!

Dirty Player: http://bit.ly/2FocQoY

Filthy Player: http://bit.ly/2x5ggpH

ABOUT THE AUTHOR

When Stacey Lynn isn't conquering mountains of laundry and fighting a war against dust bunnies and cracker crumbs, you can find her playing with her children, curled up on the couch with a good book, or behind closed doors, imagining the next adventures she'll soon write.

She lives off her daily pot of coffee, can only write with a bowlful of Skittles nearby, and has been in love with romance novels since before she could drive herself to the library.

Stacey Lynn lives with her husband and children in North Carolina.

If you would like to know more about Stacey Lynn, follow her here:

Website: www.staceylynnbooks.com

Facebook: www.facebook.com/staceylynnbooks

Twitter: www.twitter.com/staceylynnbooks

Instagram: www.instagram.com/staceylynn.author

If you enjoyed this book, please leave a review on the site where it was purchased.

Thank you

HUGE thank you to Hilary and all of Social Butterfly PR for throwing your full enthusiasm and support behind each and every book I write. I have loved working with all of you and can't wait to see what's ahead for 2019. Hilary, I miss you most of all. ;-)

To Dina and Tonya, thank you for reading an early copy of Wicked Player. You're both great friends!

Ellie and Virginia, as always, thanks for putting up with my mess and spit-shining each manuscript until it sparkles.

Shannon, you're the best. Always. Forever. Your talent is astounding and I'm thankful I can call you a friend.

To all the bloggers who devote their time and passion into reading books, book tours, release events, leaving reviews, promoting and pimping – you are all rockstars! Thank you for all the love over the years.

And last but definitely not least – to you the reader. I'm blown away with every release how much you adore my books. You have made my dream a reality and I hope I can cheer you on with yours.

OTHER BOOKS BY STACEY LYNN

Love In The Heartland

Captivated By You

This Time Around

Long Road Home

Before We Fell – April 2019

Crazy Love Series

Fake Wife

Knocked Up

Perfect Match Series - 2019

28 Dates

Weekend Fling

The Rough Riders Series

Dirty Player

Filthy Player

Wicked Player

The Luminous Series

Dominate Me

Crave Me

Long For Me

The Fireside Series

His to Love

His to Protect

His to Cherish

His to Seduce

Tangled Love Series

Entice

Embrace

Enflame

Just One Series

Just One Song

Just One Week

Just One Regret

Just One Moment

The Nordic Lords Series

Point of Return

Point of Redemption

Point of Freedom

Point of Surrender

Standalones

Remembering Us

Don't Lie To Me

Try Me – A Don't Lie To Me Novella